Autumn Dreams

by

Susan Edwards

Seasons Of Love
Book 2

Autumn Dreams

Contact Information: info@thewildrosepress.com

Cover Art by *Diana Carlile*

The Wild Rose Press, Inc.
PO Box 708
Adams Basin, NY 14410-0708

Visit us at www.thewildrosepress.com

Publishing History
First Fantasy Rose Edition, 2015
Print ISBN 978-1-5092-0459-5
Digital ISBN 978-1-5092-0460-1

Published in the United States of America

Evil lurks in the shadows, just a dream away...

With their hands locked together, Night Warrior closed his eyes with a long sigh. Everything he wanted was here, in her. All he wanted at that moment in life was to hold her tight and keep her close to his heart.

He wanted this woman. More than anything. Including regaining his status as a warrior.

The realization shocked him. With eyes open and wide, he tried to step away, but Kangee turned around, keeping his hands in hers.

Staring into her moon-shadowed eyes, emotion flowed through him and around them. The colors, normally sharp, clear, and distinct were swirls of silvery, glittering mist with the hint of a rainbow lurking deep. He felt as though he were falling deep inside her. All that mattered right now was Kangee and the aching need inside him.

"I cannot resist," he murmured, lowering his head slowly, giving her a chance to refuse and hoping she would not.

Faster, with more force than the rushing streams in spring, his insides churned, and his heart pounded so hard he could barely breathe. He slid a hand beneath her dark curtain of hair to cup the back of her neck.

Her hands slid over his chest, leaving a trail of liquid fire in their wake. Her fingers inched up his neck, her thumbs stroking up the center of his throat. He swallowed. Hard.

"What can you not resist?" she asked, her husky voice low, a mere whisper of sound.

Night Warrior tipped her chin up and brought his lips closer to hers. "This."

Dedication

My son Brandon who is the voice
of reason when it comes to my website.

My daughter Deanna who faced
and beat incredible odds to follow
her dream of becoming a veterinarian.
Congratulations Dr. Deanna Janelle

I am very proud of you both and love you
more than words can ever express.

Prologue

Death came fast, filled with fury, full of vengeance. It seized the young man in its heinous fist, ripped his spirit from his bloodied, broken body, then gleefully tossed, into a black pit, the warrior's soul.

The warrior cried out, a deep cry of anguish as death battered and pummeled him. Burning pain, like that of a fire devouring a forest, consumed him, heart, mind, and soul. He fought, but darkness surrounded him. Tired. Too tired to fight, he surrendered.

"No! Warrior of the night! You must live!"

The sharp command broke through the never-ending firestorm of poisoned arrows. "Who are you? Where are you?" Darkness left him blind.

"Live. For me."

The words came from nowhere yet everywhere, the voice young, desperate, and female. Her voice slid through him, warm and sweet as honey. It rose over the furious buzzing gnawing away at his insides. He whirled around in the darkness, blind and helpless.

"Help me. Show yourself." His cry came out a mere croak.

A spear of light shattered the black, smoky veil and revealed his limp, bloody, and lifeless body.

"Return and claim the life meant to be yours. Live! Warrior of the night, I need you. Come to me."

Compelled by something he could not name, the

young warrior fought his way out of Death's pit. One step, two steps, each through a sticky trail of his blood, leading his spirit and soul back to the shell of his body where life giving blood pumped out of a fist-sized hole in his chest.

In horror, he watched his body sink into the widening river of red gore. He reached for his lifeless form. Without warning, a thick, viscous fist rose up and slammed into him, sending him flying backward through the darkness. The sound of hissing grew louder, filled his mind as though he had a furious swarm of bees between his ears.

"Do not give in, warrior of the night. Fight evil. Choose to live. Choose me, not death!"

Focused on the woman's compelling voice, the warrior blindly obeyed. "Claim me not, Death," he shouted as he kicked his way through the blood back to his body.

Death responded. Each splash became a long, red monster that twisted and twinned together to form a wall between soul and body. They slithered and slipped around the young man's ankles and calves, and they pulled him deeper into the shadows.

"No!" Weak, tired, and in pain, he wasn't sure if he was speaking to Death or to the unknown woman. "Too tired," he whispered, his spirit fading. "You are too late."

"Free will. Chose to live. Chose to fight. Do not give in to Evil."

He heard fear in her voice. "Show yourself," he demanded.

The white light grew brighter, warmer. It blinded, beckoned, and promised both sanctuary and life.

You died in battle this day. The words were a hiss of fury in his mind. The writhing snakes pulled his spirit deeper into the dark shadows.

"No! I choose light over darkness."

Screams and shrieks filled his mind. Without warning, sickly yellow eyes popped open from the mass of snakes binding him. In agonizing slow motion, the creatures opened their mouths, revealing dagger sharp fangs. As one, they struck.

He screamed. Pain and fire consumed what was left of him. Defeated, he went limp.

"*Iche*! Please. Do not leave me alone." Her voice warmed, soothed, and offered hope.

"Who are you?" he whispered.

"Your future. Your fate. Your soul mate. You must fight for us."

A roar of fury drowned her sweet voice. Angry, needing answers, the young warrior shouted to the demons pulling him deeper into the black pit, "Release me."

A slice of blinding light stabbed him in the eyes and shattered both shadow and pain. Everything went still.

To his surprise, shock, and relief, the snakes dropped off his body as he floated away from the ugliness of death.

Where before it had been darkness and shadow, pain and fear, there now was light so bright it dazzled and even hurt his eyes. A swirling rainbow of color appeared above his head. Vibrant blues, greens, and violets swirled into a mass of soothing warmth. In that breathtaking moment, he understood. It was his time to leave Mother Earth and journey to the Spirit World.

Chanting his personal power song, the warrior lifted his arms and reached for the wondrous light and color, ready to accept his place in the land where warriors never feared attack, where food and game were as plentiful as laughter and joy. His battered spirit floated upward toward the rainbow world.

"No! It's a trick. Do not leave!"

The frightened cry of the woman interrupted his chant. The warrior glanced into the obscure, swirling darkness beneath his feet, to where his broken body lay in a sea of red. He shuddered. Death was ugly, messy. Yet, glancing up, he realized there was beauty in death. Once again, he lifted his hands. Suddenly, a tiny sphere of pure pulsating light flew at him.

"*Inihan!*" He ducked as he uttered the expression of shock and wonder and stared at the wavering ball of light that resembled a miniature glowing moon.

He lifted his hand to touch the dazzling ball, but it darted left and began circling him, faster and faster, spinning a web of translucent thread that cocooned him as neatly as a spider trapped its prey. Done, the sphere rose and sat above his head as though waiting.

For what? He frowned. The walls surrounding him seemed solid yet allowed him to view everything around him. Intrigued, he touched the soft, silky shimmering web that looked fragile but held with surprising strength.

Before he could break free, he began sinking, falling back into the darkness toward the writhing sea of snakes.

"No!" He shoved hard against the finely spun web of light. It melted into nothingness, leaving him chilled and filled with a stabbing pain that pierced his soul and drove him to his knees.

He lifted his hands toward the bright light of the after-world, welcomed the end of one journey and the beginning of another. He floated higher and higher until, once again, his ascent came to an abrupt halt, this time, by a brilliant and blinding flash of blue light that exploded around him and formed a bubble, trapping him in the center.

"Let me go," he shouted as he shoved at walls pulsing as though alive. They thinned but did not melt or fade.

"It is not your time."

Love and compassion poured over him, through him, into him. He whirled around and faced the approaching woman. An aura of golden light surrounded her, nearly blinding him. He knew her. She was *Blaze*, daughter of his tribe's medicine man and a woman his people feared. "You are *Tunkasila*. God!"

Her glittering blue and yellow eyes tracked his backward movement. The warmth of the bubble halted his retreat.

The healer smiled sadly. "No, I am the woman sent to help you find your way back to the life you were meant to live."

A splash of color near his feet startled him. Red, black, and yellow fingers cupped the walls of blue and crawled upward, like a grotesque claw clutching prey.

"Do not be afraid."

"I am not afraid." But he was. He feared this woman, feared her powers. He drew in a deep breath. "I died this day a warrior. My mother will be proud of her eldest son."

Blaze smiled gently, her long, shiny black hair

swung in time to the living, breathing aura she projected. "Your mother has reason to be proud," she agreed with a simple nod. "Her pride in her son will grow even greater over time."

Blaze closed her eyes and lifted her hands high, her fingers stretching out toward the rainbow world above their heads. The air shimmered with tiny pinpricks of golden light. Below their feet, a stardust trail of gold formed and forged a winding path through the darkness to the still body below. "The Gods offer the gift of life. Do you have the courage to fulfill your destiny?"

Around him, the bubble of protectiveness grew thinner, transparent, the pulsing heartbeat slower, fainter.

"*Kahnige. Choose*," she commanded softly.

A fist of darkness shattered the blue light. Blackness once again trapped him with the hideous creatures slithering against him.

Hundreds of gleaming yellow orbs with red eyes stared at him as they slid up and over his body, his chest, and around his throat, cutting off his cry. His choice. Waves of icy anguish pounded his body and mind.

No more pain. He craved the calming peace of the rainbow world. Thunder roared, and white-hot jagged bolts of light shot into the writhing mass. Shrieks of fury assaulted his ears, and the air sizzled as the creatures were burned off him.

Blaze stood before him, her eyes sparks of blue fire. "*Evil* wishes for you to die. *Evil* tempts you with promises of the Spirit World. You are a great warrior. Do you have the courage to return to life, to live and fight evil?" Blaze waved her hands. Stars formed a misty golden cloud around healer and warrior.

He stared at the glittering path that led the way back to his body. He glanced back at Blaze, then to the small shimmering ball of light hovering above the healer's head. "You would condemn me to pain?" He spoke to both women.

"More awaits you than pain. But you must choose. Now," Blaze said, her voice urgent. She stretched out her hands. The tips of her fingers glowed; the light that was in her, around her surrounded and warmed him.

He leaned forward to take her hand but something shoved him away from the healer. Once again, he floated upward. The tiny ball of light followed, pulsing fast, like the heartbeat of a man who'd run for hours.

"Warrior of the night. *Wiconi kahnige!* Choose life," came the voice of the first woman.

For a moment, it seemed as though an inner fog cleared, and he saw for the first time the woman who'd begged him to live. Her features were blurry except for her compelling gaze. Never had he seen eyes filled with the colors of the Earth Mother. "Who are you?"

Blaze lifted her hands and held them out. The light-ball drifted toward her and came to rest on her palm. From the world of rainbows, an owl flew. It landed on her other arm. She smiled. "The answers are there for you, but you must live in order to ask the questions. You are Night Warrior, warrior of the night. Return to life and fulfill your destiny."

Night Warrior stared first at the river of pulsating red, then returned his gaze to the sphere of misty light and the sad eyes of a woman who gave his soul hope.

"*Wiconi,*" he said, choosing life as he stepped onto the starry trail.

Chapter One

Thrust across the sullen sky, clouds writhed and formed a towering wall of shadow that loomed over the Indian village like a predator ready to pounce. The wind roared through the forest, tearing pine needles and cones from branches. The whirling debris became a tornado that circled and slapped against an ancient gnarled tree.

Owl! Awake!

Deep inside the hollow trunk, the old bird stirred. *Spirit of Wind. Why do you disturb me?*

It begins.

Instantly aware, the owl hopped to the entrance and took to the air. Beneath his wings, Wind cradled and guided him on a fast flight through the forest, then shot him out over a quiet village nestled between forest, mountain, and lake.

Wings stretched out, he soared, skimming over longhouses until spotting a lone warrior leaving the sheltering wall of trees that hid and protected the village. Owl circled, concerned, for the warrior limped and shuffled and walked with his shoulders hunched as though in great agony.

He is not ready, not strong enough. The owl shrieked his protest.

It matters not. It can be delayed no longer.

The large bird landed on the longhouse nearest the

warrior and watched as the warrior's mother and aunt rushed out. Though the man protested the help, the women ignored him and firmly led him back inside the longhouse.

Worried, the owl hopped across the thatched roof to one of the smoke holes so he could watch the warrior upon whom so much rested. Then he fluttered to another smoke hole, spotting a woman who sat with three young girls huddled close. They were SpiritWalkers, children of the Gods.

Much is at stake. Wind ruffled Owl's feathers. *The Gods cannot interfere.*

I taught my nephew well. He will accept his duty. He had to believe this was so.

I hope you are right, my friend. Wind left, scattering a flock of black birds. Another thrust of air sent them squawking deep into the forest.

The spirit of the old shaman spread his wings, and as he flew off, one lone spotted feather floated down the smoke hole.

****

Kangee, of the Earth Dweller clan had trouble breathing. She glared at the glowing embers that burned in the center of the aisle across from where she sat with her three young half-sisters. The day was already uncomfortably hot, and the fire made the air inside the longhouse thick and stifling. Outside, the temperatures weren't much better. Summer had yet to depart. A thick cover of clouds trapped the heat, turning the air sticky and humid.

She wiped the sweat from her brow and glanced into the sleeping quarters on the other side of the fire, which held two of the strange beds the Turtle clan favored. Instead of pallets of furs spread on the ground, these people slept on pallets fashioned of wood lashed with twine. Beneath the raised pallet, the space held storage for belongings, and stacked above the bottom bed, there was a second pallet, the same size as the one below.

Night Warrior and his brother each had one of these strange sleeping beds. Due to injuries in a battle before she'd arrived, he slept on a thick pile of fur on the floor. A quick glance showed him sitting propped by a backrest. Kangee resumed the mindless task of pounding pine nuts into a fine meal as she marveled over the warrior's good fortune.

Mortally injured in battle, he'd have died had it not been for her new sister-in-law and the woman's incredible ability to heal. Kangee had never known anyone who could bring a man back to life. Even the healer in her own village didn't have the skill Blaze had shown.

Blaze hadn't just healed the warrior; she'd given him the knowledge needed to finish what she'd begun. His wounds wouldn't fester, nor would heat and sickness prey on his mind, but the warrior's aunts and mother insisted on caring for him as though he might die any moment.

Movement drew her gaze, and she groaned when the warrior's mother once again stoked the embers of the dying fire to life. The warrior endured, but not alone. They all endured.

She glanced across at him and found his dark gaze focused on her. Pain glittered in his eyes and in his taut features, rigid jaw, and lips pressed together.

His mother returned. Kangee frowned when Night

Warrior closed his eyes, giving every appearance of being asleep. Turtle Moon set the bowl of savory broth on the floor beside him, then quietly left. Night Warrior's eye's opened and once more stared at her with the intensity of a man studying his prey.

Uneasy with the attention, Kangee turned back to pounding nuts, but surreptitiously, she watched the warrior, amused that every time Turtle Moon came to check on her son, he closed his eyes and feigned sleep.

A short while ago, she'd have been pleased to have gained the attention of a handsome warrior, but things had changed for her—changed her. Kangee lifted the weight of her hair from the back of her neck, wishing for even the slightest stirring of the air.

The hiss of fire licking and consuming yet another log made her moan. Enough was enough. About to get up and take her sisters outside where the air was not so stifling, she spotted a tiny feather drifting downward from the hole in the rooftop. She held out her hand and caught the feather. Her heart raced as she cupped the soft, downy feather between her palms and closed her eyes. Energy tingled and tickled, and like a seed sprouting, a ball of warmth grew.

Beside Kangee, eight-year-old Anika and Andre shifted. "It is from *mon père*?"

Kangee brought the tiny feather to her face and drew in a deep breath. "I sense great strength." She concentrated. Waves of pure love seeped into her, and with each inhale, she tasted...courage? Could you taste courage?

Puzzled, she mentally shrugged. "This gift from *Hinyin* is filled with great love." She glanced from one hopeful face to another, then shook her head sadly.

"But not from our father."

Her announcement dashed both hope and excitement for all of them. Kangee sighed and let the feather fall from her palm. Skye, her youngest sister at five summers, caught the feather and cradled it to her cheek. Kangee's shoulders slumped.

When she'd first spotted the feather, she'd thought—hoped—it was a message from her father as he often took on the form of an owl to travel. Her eyes blurred with tears of disappointment. She was tired. And afraid.

"*Mon père* has been gone long." Two voices, perfectly blended in tone, spoke.

Kangee glanced at the twins, noting the sheen of tears in each pair of earth-and-sky painted eyes. "*Mon père* will return soon," she comforted the girls, though she herself was worried sick. It didn't matter that Conrad "Bear-man" Cordell hadn't sired her. She'd called him father for more than half her life.

She rubbed the side of her nose, then her brows to ward off the growing ache. Her life had changed abruptly. Each summer, she, along with her mother and sisters, traveled with their trapper father as he set traps and collected furs. At eighteen, she'd daydreamed her days away, her only wish before now had been to find a man of her own to marry and start her own family.

But her dreams had been shattered the night she and her family came under attack. She and her siblings had been separated from their parents and forced to run for their lives. That night, she lost her sense of self, along with the innocence of a young woman without a care in the world.

Weeks had passed before she'd learned that her

father and brother were alive. Of her mother, there was still no sign. No one had seen Eagle Woman since the night of the ambush.

Eagle Woman was her father's spirit-mate, their bond strong, so she understood her father's need to search for his mate, but his children needed their father. Her heart broke when silent tears rolled down each twin's face. Kangee smiled, doing her best to be brave.

"We shall ask Luc to find our father and bring him back," she decided. Luc "Star Walker" Cordell had survived the ambush, and recently, he'd married Blaze. Another glance at the warrior across from her showed he still watched her. Kangee sighed. She had no time for handsome warriors.

"*Ina* lives," Skye said in a hushed whisper. The little girl got to her knees and stared into Kangee's eyes, then held out her arms.

Kangee shifted her weight, pulled Skye onto her lap, and cradled the child. Right now, she was both sister and mother to her much younger siblings. She tipped Skye's chin up, her thumb stroking the tiny dent, a feature inherited from her father.

"Our mother is alive? You feel her spirit?" Even with the mixed blood of a SpiritWalker and French trapper, the girl possessed more power than Kangee and the twins combined.

The solemn child nodded. Her eyes, a wild mix of blues, greens, and yellows slowly changed to wide pools of blue-slate in a face much paler in color than her sisters.

Kangee drew her brows together. She'd never seen Skye's eyes turn inward. Did Skye have the gift of sight? "Can you see our mother? Do you know where she is?"

Kangee's heart pounded and hope soared. She desperately wanted this nightmare to be over and her family back together. She needed life back to the way it had been before that horrible and terrifying night when her uncle had tried to kill them.

Skye's eyes swirled and misted, the dark centers growing larger, as though opening like a blooming flower. Instead of color, the little girl's eyes were black as a moonless night. Without warning, the child stiffened in her arms.

"Skye! Come back! Now!" She got no response. Kangee gripped her sister's face between her palms. "Obey me, my sister!" Her voice shook.

Nothing.

"Skye!"

Repeatedly, she called to the little girl. She lightly slapped Skye's cheeks, and when that brought no response, she shook her sister, raising her voice as she called her sister's name. Skye remained stiff, her eyes wide open, dark and unseeing.

"I can't reach her," she cried out, frightened when Skye's dark eyes took on a reddish sheen. Kangee's stomach clenched painfully as terror slid its icy fingers down her spine. Something terrible had happened to Skye, and it was her fault.

The twins scooted close. Within the lodge, all went eerily silent but for the hurried steps of Night Warrior's mother and aunts gathering around them.

Kangee kept her focus on Skye, concentrated on willing the child back from wherever she had gone. She begged, she commanded, and she shook her sister, but Skye remained unresponsive, her eyes wide and unseeing, her small body gone limp and lifeless.

Desperate, Kangee glanced around, but there wasn't anyone to help her. Her brother had gone hunting, and she had no idea where to find Blaze. Helpless tears fell from her eyes and rained over Skye's pale face.

"I don't know what to do," she cried. She touched a smooth talisman of stone that hung from a leather thong around her neck as she sought strength and prayed for answers.

"Bring her back!"

Kangee's head jerked up at the harsh command.

Night Warrior shoved his way past his mother and his aunts. "Get her out of there," he repeated urgently.

Kangee felt the pain radiating from the warrior. As he lurched closer, the wound that ran across one thigh tore open and oozed blood, as did the fist-sized hole on his chest. He held one helpless, bandaged arm across his body.

Beyond despair, beyond fear, beyond tears, Kangee stared at him with wide eyes. "How? I need Blaze."

Dark eyes bore holes into hers, and for a brief flash in time, she felt as though she knew this warrior. He seemed familiar, yet until a few weeks ago, he'd been a stranger to her. He staggered closer, then dropped to his knees with a hiss of pain. The twins scrambled out of his way.

Night Warrior gripped her shoulder with one hand, the other rested on Skye's chest. "Use your mind to find your sister." He took a deep breath. "I will be with you."

Kangee used the warrior's strength, his unyielding will, to calm herself. He held her gaze with his own intense stare.

"Go to her." Warmth flowed from Night Warrior's firm touch. It cocooned her and calmed her. With all his injuries, his strength surprised her, but not as much as the moment when she felt him enter her mind.

Go to her.

Kangee leaned over Skye, rested her forehead against the child's, and searched for a way into her mind. Skye had no trouble reading Kangee's mind, but Kangee had never been able to see into Skye's. This time, with Night Warrior's strength and her own desperations, Kangee broke the law of Free Will and forced herself into Skye's mind.

Darkness surrounded her. There was nothing and no one, just a vast sense of emptiness and despair. She called out to Skye.

As though that was all he was waiting for Night Warrior took control. He appeared beside her, grabbed her hand, and led the way through the darkness. She cried out when she spotted Skye huddled on the ground, and rushed forward, knelt, and grabbed hold of her baby sister.

Something dark and menacing rose from the shadows and towered over them.

Before she could scream, the warrior's arms went around her shoulders. "Hold the child!"

Pain tore through her mind, as though the monster had grabbed her and refused to let go. Then the darkness fled. She heard her own cry and the shocked gasps of the women and the near hysterical sobs of the twins as they gathered around her, Skye and the warrior.

Her head pounded, as though a dozen arrows had

pierced her head at once. She gasped and trembled, tried to open her eyes, but the pain stabbed and burned. She felt weak and tired, as though she'd just outrun an enemy. For a long moment, Kangee couldn't see past the agonizing darkness. She rocked side to side with Skye cradled in her arms and struggled with what had just happened. Had she really, for a brief moment, seen her mother? And a monster?

A soft touch to her forehead calmed the throbbing and chased away the darkness and the nausea rolling in her belly. Kangee opened her eyes and stared up into her sister-in-laws brilliant blue eyes.

"I came as soon as I felt your need, *Mithan*, my young sister." Blaze bent, picked up Skye, then knelt beside Kangee, drawing her close.

"I was so scared," Kangee sobbed. "I nearly lost her, couldn't get to her. It was my fault. I asked her if she could see our mother." Guilt closed her throat, made it difficult to breath, let alone talk.

She pushed herself up to check on Skye. To her immense relief, Skye's eyes had returned to normal, though the bleakness that had not been there before had swallowed the innocence of a child.

Next to her, Night Warrior lay on his back, each inhale somewhere between a gasp and grunt as he tried to draw in air. The warrior's mother hovered a short distance away. No one else spoke or moved.

"I'm so sorry," she said as she wiped the tears she couldn't stop. Blaze had dulled her pain, but the gasping of the warrior beside her told her that he was in even greater pain. She glanced at Blaze. "Help him."

Night Warrior waved his arm. "I am fine."

Blaze sighed. "You are stubborn." She turned to

Kangee. "He must be willing."

Kangee frowned at Night Warrior. "You saved my sister. I do not know how you did this or even how you knew what to do, but thank you."

Skye reached for Kangee and wrapped her tiny arms around Kangee's neck. "Dreams," she said then leaned over Kangee's arm and touched Night Warrior. "Dreams."

Night Warrior reared up with a grunt of pain, then shoved himself to his feet.

"Dreams," Skye repeated, her eyes darker than normal as she stared up at the tall warrior.

For a moment, Night Warrior stared at Skye. "No. Not even for you, Little One." He waved aside his mother and aunt and, without another word, fled the longhouse.

Kangee frowned and stroked her fingers through Skye's soft, silky hair. The child closed her eyes, a sign Kangee knew meant there would be nothing more from the girl. Skye rarely spoke and unlike most children at age, her sentences were usually only one or two words.

Blaze stood as well. "I will take the girls." She held out her arms. "We will talk tonight after Star Walker has returned."

"Thank you." Kangee needed time to figure out what she'd seen and how to describe her impressions. More than anything, she longed to be alone.

The twins, miniatures of their mother, hesitated, each child wearing a troubled expression as they stared at Kangee. Normally, they were mischievous as a pair of wolf cubs. The fact that they were silent revealed the extent of their fear and worry, for they normally talked non-stop. Her parents often joked they'd come into the world talking.

Her heart ached. "I'm fine. Stay with Skye."

Moments later, she was alone, except for Wise Owl, one of Night Warrior's aunts. Wise Owl's son was chief of the Turtle Clan, and the woman's sisters shared the longhouse along with their grown children. Each of the elderly women had lost their husbands, one in the same battle that had almost claimed Night Warrior's life.

"What can I do to help?" Wise Owl asked.

Kangee lifted her gaze to the kind woman with her wise and gentle eyes and shook her head. She pressed her fist into her stomach to calm the nervous quivering and moved to the doorway, needing the breath of fresh air on her skin and in her lungs. After a long moment, she said, "You have given us a place to stay. You share your food and offer protection. You and your family are kind and generous."

Wise Owl leaned down to pick up the owl feather drifting on the current of air at their feet. She held it to her face. "The man who killed `my husband is dead, thanks to Blaze and your people, but the events he set in motion echo still." Her voice trailed off as she stroked the feather over a cheek lined by time.

Kangee nodded. "Circles. He stole Blaze as a small child and brought her here to be raised among your people. She saved not just my brother's life, but my father's."

Wise Owl smiled and nodded. "Circles within circles. She, like you, is a child of the gods."

Kangee sighed, hating the fact that compared to most people in her tribe, she possessed so few gifts of her race. She could command the elements and play with the wind, none of which could help her mother who was in terrible trouble.

She stared at her feet. "Blaze is special, as is my mother and even Skye." Her shoulders drooped. "I am not."

Wise Owl moved close and touched Kangee's shoulders. "You underestimate yourself, child. Everything is connected." Her eyes sharpened. "Life and death. Past and future. It comes together. Here and now." The old woman's smile turned bittersweet as she stared at the feather cradled between her thin, wrinkled hands. "My husband watches over you." With tears tracing the lines time had stamped on her face, she left the lodge.

Kangee stepped outside, flicked her gaze toward the dark clouds piling over the village.

It comes together. Here and now.

In her gut, Kangee knew another storm brewed, and unlike the one menacing the skies overhead, this new storm threatened all she held dear—her family.

Chapter Two

Night Warrior shoved his way through the thick brush of the forest. Branches crisscrossed, forming walls that blocked his way, and the undergrowth hid large stones and deep animal holes. Each step, each twist of his chest, each swing of his arms sent flames of pain streaking throughout his body. His injured arm had no strength, and he couldn't feel his fingers. Every few steps, he stopped to let the ache in his thigh calm. Each inhale burned as though fire seared his lungs.

Though his body screamed for rest, he refused. Desperation to regain his status as a great warrior made him push himself brutally and had nothing to do with the young, sad-eyed woman living with his family. At least, that was what he kept telling himself.

The first time he'd seen Kangee, he'd thought he was dreaming for he recognized those sad eyes and her soft, sweet voice. A dream. He'd tried to convince himself that he'd dreamed of her, but he couldn't deny the truth. He had died, had seen her there, in that strange world that was neither life nor death. He'd heard her voice, and he had chosen to live.

Because of her.

For her.

Night Warrior pushed himself hard. He didn't want to think of Kangee or of what had happened to her young sister. He especially refused to remember his own role. Those thoughts only took him back into the past, back to dreams and death and to the vow he'd made long ago to never DreamWalk again.

Since Kangee's arrival to his village, he'd broken that vow. More than once.

Exhausted and near blind from the pain, he stumbled when his toe caught a root hidden beneath a flurry of leaves. Sucking in a deep breath, he flung out his arms and managed, barely, to grab the trunk of a tree and stop his fall.

At a price.

Pain seared and radiated across his chest, down his arm and dug deep into his thigh wound. For a moment, everything went fuzzy. Only sheer, stubborn will kept him from succumbing to the waves of darkness that seized his mind. He took slow, shallow breaths and waited for the pain to subside to an exhausting ache.

Night Warrior leaned against a pine tree that was wider than the breadth of his shoulders and sighed when life flowed into him from the tree. It seeped into his flesh, branched out like roots spreading beneath the earth. The healing energy, a gift from Mother Earth moved him greatly.

And terrified him completely.

He cradled his injured arm to his chest as he concentrated on the sounds of the forest—humming insects, the faint fluttering of a moth's wing near his head, the swish of wind against leaves, even the rustling of feathers somewhere high overhead.

He closed his eyes and drew in the earthy bouquet of composting leaves and plants blended with strong, aromatic pine and cedars. The air carried the story of each inhabitant, whether tree, plant, or animal, many with scents far too subtle for man to identify. Yet he could separate them out. Like a wolf or deer, he easily scented the essence of life.

Something rustled. He opened his eyes and at once spotted the drab, brown mouse concealed beneath thick clumps of rotting leaves, twigs, branches, and fallen trees that littered the forest floor. The tiny *itukala* darted in near silence, yet he both heard her and sensed her presence.

The thick treetop canopy along with the cover of clouds allowed the dark to prowl through the stands of trees. Shadows reached into each and every crevice and should have made spotting the mouse impossible. Yet, he saw the bright-eyed, nose-twitching rodent as she scurried across the forest floor.

Night Warrior wanted to deny the changes to his body and his senses. Since the day the healer brought him back to life, everything had changed. He was acutely aware of life around him. Keen sight allowed him to see in the dark, see farther away, and pick out the smallest of details and he heard sounds that should have been impossible for him to hear.

And those weren't the only changes he'd discovered. He rubbed his belly to ease the nervous, hollow feeling that had become a new companion and focused on the mouse.

There was a connection between him and this tiny animal. It went far deeper than just being aware of how *itukala* fit into the world they both shared. Moving carefully, he opened a small pouch tied to the waist of the breechclout. From inside, he drew out a pine nut. Using his thumb, he flicked the nut toward her—close enough to tempt the hungry mouse, far enough from him that she'd feel safe. He flicked another. Then another and yet another. Then, as though testing himself, he shut his eyes, focused, and blotted out all other sounds.

There it was. The faint sound of the mouse as she scurried over dried leaves followed by near silence as she shoved the nuts into her cheeks then, like a sigh on the wind, she darted back through the wall of ferns to the log. With his sharpened senses, he was able to follow her progress in his mind.

She stopped, waited, moved. Again and again until, finally, there was a much louder rustle, as though the rodent had made a run for safety. He opened his eyes and stared at a rotting log not far from where he stood. She was inside, the rasp of her teeny but sharp nails clawing over chunks of wood as she squeezed through a narrow tunnel in the center of the pine log. Then came the tiny squeals of babies, and he knew she'd just settled to care for her large litter of newborns.

His heart raced. Panic welled upward and threatened to choke him. He had no doubt if he took an axe and cut into the log, he'd find the nest right where he sensed. Seeking to calm himself, he concentrated on breathing. In. Out. In. Out. Yet, the questions continued.

How had this happened?

Why had he changed?

Once he felt calmer, he drew in one last breath, prepared to make his way back to the village and choked on the strong, pungent aroma of a male cougar.

His eyes flew open, and his senses zeroed in on the *igmu* crouched beneath a thick tangle of tree roots and dry brush. The feline's eyes were narrow slits that gleamed as he stalked closer to the rotting log where the mouse made her nest.

"*Igmu.*" His voice sounded loud though it was barely a whisper. "Go find your meal elsewhere."

The cat hissed but slunk away. Night Warrior could no longer see the wildcat and knew the animal was well out of normal hearing range. Yet, he could still hear the faint crunch of dried leaves beneath its paws.

The cat, the mouse, the sounds, the scents. The rush of sensation. He shook his head and blocked the assault to his senses, just too much coming at him at once. From childhood, he'd been taught that to survive to see the next summer, the next winter, he had, at all times, to be aware of what went on around him.

He believed that life—animals, people, plants, and even the tiniest insects were related. Everything was connected by the circle of life. But this, what he now experienced was more, so much more that it left him shaking with bone-melting fear.

And that fear infuriated him.

Before his injuries, he'd been a strong warrior, a leader, a protector, and provider for his family. That had changed the day he'd been injured in battle. No. Both the spear and war axe wielded by the enemy had each delivered a fatal blow. He had died that day.

His stomach clenched when he recalled how the axe had sliced into his arm and thigh, how he'd fallen, the gush of blood spraying outward, then the downward arc of the spear the enemy had plunged into his chest. Sweat beaded his brow and his knees shook. The pain had been unlike anything he'd ever known.

He stared unseeing into the brush. He had died in that battle, yet here he stood, alive. Life, death, life.

And like it or not, he felt more alive in that moment than before death had nearly claimed him. "No. Do not think about that day."

Or about what happened in that strange world that was neither life nor death or the fact that Blaze, the healer woman, had been there. It wasn't real. Couldn't have been real.

Yet, all he had to do was close his eyes to again see the golden stars, the blue bubble, and hear that sad, sweet voice begging him to live.

He shut his eyes and brought that small ball of light to mind, the shape of it, and the brightness of it. As though it were there, the hum of energy, the calming warmth washed through him. Once again, he saw that fragile, sad woman with eyes painted with the blue of sky and water, the greens of earth, and the yellow of the sun, moon, and stars.

He now knew that woman for she was a guest in his longhouse. "I lived. For you." He reached out for her. In his mind, the image of Kangee was so real that he was half-afraid if he opened his eyes, he'd find her standing in front of him.

She instilled a deep ache in his heart and mind. He longed to chase the sadness away and see love, warmth, and laughter in her fascinating eyes. Though his body trembled with the effort to remain standing, he concentrated on her image, recalling her scent and the calming, sweetness of her voice.

And for just a moment, he drifted into a dream world where he was strong, fit, and pain-free, where she waited for him with her smiles and laughter, where everything—

Went cold, dark and eerily silent. Something

noxious filled his nostrils, and a low buzz seeped into his mind. It grew in volume and pitch.

Murderer. Killer. Liar.

Over and over the words echoed. Then without warning, an image of the young girl he'd once loved shot into the darkness of his mind. Dead. At his hand.

Murdered her. Killed her.

"No," he moaned. "Accident."

The voice of evil held him prisoner in a dark cell filled with past mistakes that he'd made in ignorance and arrogance. Despair wound through him, pulled him deeper into a pit where something slithered and hissed.

Better to have died. Should have died.

"No!" Night Warrior blinked rapidly. "Past is past. I live." He gripped the tree behind him with his one good arm to keep from sliding down as his legs shook. "I lived. But why?"

That question haunted him as he stared up into the treetops at an unusually silent flock of crows. Twice, he'd overcome death. Others had not. Why?

So lost in his own world, the sudden snap of a twig from behind startled him. Long-honed reflexes had him reaching for his knife as he crouched low to face his intruder.

At once, pain flared, hot and furious. He instinctively went for the knife he wore strapped to one thigh, but his hand and fingers were numb as the damaged muscles refused to allow him to grip.

His breath wheezed in and out. Pain gathered like roiling storm clouds, then drove him to his knees. Vicious, thrusting waves of agony hurtled through his body, darkening the edges of his vision as he collapsed onto his side.

Someone dropped down beside him, and he recognized the woman from her scent. Kangee. The sad woman who haunted his mind, night and day.

"Are you all right? You are bleeding." Kangee's voice, her touch to his good shoulder, chased the chill and stench of evil from his mind and body.

Night Warrior rolled to his back. He kept his eyes closed and concentrated on her voice, snatched it to him as a drowning man grabbed a floating log.

"Do you not know better than to sneak up on an armed warrior, woman?" He spoke harsher than he'd intended. He could not bear to have this brave, beautiful, young woman see him as he saw himself—weak, helpless, and useless to his family and his people.

"I made no secret of my presence, Warrior. Next time, do not let dreams dull your senses."

Night Warrior ignored the censure in her voice as she moved away. Judging by her ragged breaths, he'd given her a fright, as much as she did him. He concentrated, then smiled grimly. It seemed like child's play to pick out the rapid beat of her heart.

Blinking past the pain, he stared up into the sky. Branches swayed and revealed patches of leaden sky. As humiliating as it was to have her witness his weakness, he couldn't have moved had his life depended on it. Watching her, he gave thanks that her features bore no sign of pity.

Above them came a loud cry. Together, they both glanced upward. Night Warrior spotted the round, deep yellow eyes of an owl watching them.

Kangee sat back on her heels. "I followed the owl. It led me here." With a loud screech, the bird flew away. "I'd hoped—" Kangee's shoulders slumped.

Night Warrior longed to see this sad-eyed woman smile and hear her laugh. "Finish," he said gently.

Kangee shrugged. "I'd hoped the owl carried a message from my father."

Night Warrior narrowed his eyes as his gaze traveled from one canopy of leaves to another until he found the bird who sat silent above them. More times than he cared to admit, he'd spotted the owl—that owl—watching him.

"My aunt believes the spirit of her husband lives on as an owl. She might be right. My uncle was a powerful shaman. He shared a special affinity with the owl" With all that was happening to him, he accepted that the old shaman's spirit had remained in this world to watch over his family.

Night Warrior watched Kangee's eyes fill with tears. His own eyes misted. While he could admit to himself that his physical injuries were serious, he grew stronger with each passing day.

But this woman from his dreams hurt from wounds of the mind and heart. Each night, he listened to her toss and turn, and sometimes cry out in her sleep. Those days when he'd been as helpless as a newborn babe, he'd somehow connected with her, and though he'd been unable to get up and go to her, he'd gone to her in his dreams, and then, at will, entered her dreams to calm and soothe her fears.

He closed his eyes. This woman tempted him. He knew better than to DreamWalk, but he couldn't help it. Just as before. Another time. Another woman. He moaned. If anything happened to Kangee, if she died because of him...

"I will go." Kangee scrambled to her feet.

Night Warrior snagged her arm, pulling her back beside him. "Stay." He needed her here, with him. He tried to sit but gasped against the pain slashing across his chest.

Kangee helped lower him back to the pine-needle covered ground. "I will remain here with you if you rest." The jut of her chin warned that if he didn't obey, she'd leave. She picked up his knife and stuck it in the ground between them. "I should fetch your mother and aunts, for you are not strong enough to be out here on your own." Unspoken between them was the knowledge that had she been the enemy sneaking up behind him, he'd have been dead.

"I will do whatever you ask."

"Then you will rest and let the pain ease."

Night Warrior knew she was right, but he hated knowing when she looked upon him, she saw a weak, sick warrior. To take her attention off his injuries and the sorry state of his body, he spoke. "I wish to learn from you what happened to your family." He put every ounce of command into his voice as he stared into her strangely colored eyes. And found himself drowning in her earth-sky eyes.

Blue, brown, green, and yellow swirled together. They were sharp and clear, revealing shades and shadows of all hues, but in his dreams, they were soft as the morning fog, dreamy, and full of sparkle as the two of them talked the night away.

Kangee's pull on him was strong. His fingers twitched with the need to touch her, draw her close, and breathe in her sweetness, the freshness of a new day that seemed to be her scent. He yearned to take her back into the dream world where he was a warrior, not a broken man.

Lifting his hands, just as she lifted hers, their palms touched, startling both of them. Something sparked between them, and his heart contracted as though a rope had wrapped around it, pulled it to hers, and bound them together. He shook off the odd sensation.

"Owl led me here because you are the one who can help me." Wonder filled her voice as she stared at her palm. "You saved my sister. You knew how to find her and bring her back. How?"

"Dreams," he confessed, looking anywhere but at the woman. He didn't want to admit to her, or anyone, the truth, for it meant revealing his gift—and curse. But she deserved to know. "As soon as you entered your sister's mind, I let myself dream of you." He shrugged, unable to tell her how easy it had been to enter her mind. "I took us to Skye."

"And brought us back."

He nodded. "When I dream, I am able to go wherever I wish." *Enter the dreams of anyone I choose.* Since Kangee's arrival and her presence in the same longhouse, he'd been drawn to her from the time he'd regained consciousness and found her there. And had lost control over his dreaming. It had been years since he'd DreamWalked. Now he dreamed nightly. Of Kangee. With Kangee.

Kangee shifted to her knees, her features intent as she held his gaze. "Skye told you to dream. You refused." A wave of her blue-black hair fell over her shoulder and brushed across his chest.

Night Warrior closed his eyes. Skye understood exactly what he'd done and recognized his ability. The little girl with the eyes of an old soul shook him to the core.

With effort he sat and accepted her help.

He rubbed his aching head. Darkness and monsters. Twice that day, he'd broken his vow to never DreamWalk. Twice he'd dreamed, and twice he'd been pulled into darkness where evil spirits lurked. His heart pounded, forcing him to calm himself as blood seeped from his wounds at a faster rate.

Kangee leaned forward and touched his arm. "I do not mean to 'cause you pain. It does not matter how you saved her. I am just grateful that you did so.

Night Warrior drew in her warmth and concentrated on stopping the flow of blood seeping from his wounds. "Ever since the healer brought me back to life, I have dreamed." His gaze sharpened on hers. "Of you. With you. Because of you."

Shame and guilt and anger drove him to his feet. He refused to repeat his past mistakes. He refused to travel again that destructive path. And he refused to return to Kangee where temptation lay in wait.

Ignoring Kangee's call, he shoved his way between two thick shrubs and moved as fast as his body allowed, but no matter how hard he tried to run, he couldn't outrun the past or run from his attraction to the sad-eyed woman.

****

Kangee frowned, wondering what she'd said or done to upset the warrior. Did he think she was going to criticize him after he'd saved Skye? "You saved my sister with your dream ability, brought us both back," she whispered, turning into the wind.

He was a DreamWalker, able to enter the dreams of others. And he'd entered her dreams. She found that unnerving. Until she recalled the comfort he offered and his willingness to talk to her about anything and everything during their dreams.

It was Night Warrior, and his gift that made it possible for her to get through not just the night but the long days as well. So she decided to be grateful. Another gust of wind tossed the long, black ribbons of her hair into her face. Impatiently, she shoved them away.

She wanted to follow him, learn more about the connection between them, yet she respected his need to be alone. Kangee made her way back to the village. Tonight, she'd talk to Blaze and her brother.

Another blast of air tore through her hair. Kangee loved the wind, the rush of air, the cleansing purity as she drew it into her lungs and the brush of it against her skin—the stronger the better for she had a special affinity for Air, Creator of Life. But today there was a taint, a bitterness in the air. Something was terribly wrong. She felt it, tasted it, and breathed it.

The air sizzled, snapped, and crackled, raising hairs on her arms and the back of her neck. High above, flares of light exploded and leapt from one storm cloud to another. Deep rumbles of thunder vibrated along her spine.

Anxious, worried, and more than a bit afraid, Kangee kept her gaze on the tangled weave of branches high above her as she headed back toward the village. Boughs, heavy with their fringe of long, thin needles swayed up and down, back and forth, moaning and groaning as though in pain. Pine needles rained upon her head.

A dark smear streaked across the sky. The flock of

ravens circled the forest, their raucous crowing echoing through the forest. One by one, the large, black birds dropped through the canopy of pines and settled on branches above her head.

Mouth dry, Kangee stepped back, one slow, cautious step at a time until the enormous trunk of an ancient tree halted her retreat. Kangee stared at the ravens, then reached behind herself and gripped the tree trunk with her hands, her gaze fixed on the birds. Normally, the hum of old life soothed and calmed, but the tree seemed as agitated as she herself felt.

"What is wrong?" she whispered. A sense of impending doom washed through her when the birds fluttered to the lowest branches. Wings outstretched, beaks open wide as though ready to attack, the birds turned their beady eyes on her. The raven was one of her totems. Her name tied her to the big, black bird, and she often called upon the spirit of Raven, but there was nothing friendly in any of these birds.

"Go away! Leave!" Kangee waved her arms, directed a stream of wind toward the crows. The flock took to the air then resettled, except for the two largest birds that dived through the air toward her, wings folded back, talons outstretched.

Kangee's eyes went wide when both birds blurred in flight as though her eyesight had gone out of focus. Blinking rapidly, she gasped. The two ravens had shifted into ugly, black buzzards with scraggly-feathered wings and a noxious odor that made her gag.

Shock and fear struck her numb. Many SpiritWalkers could shift at will, and some, like her uncles loved to play jokes, but no one would do this to her. She sucked in a breath.

"Shadowed Souls." Kangee had never encountered a Shadowed Soul. Any SpiritWalker who deliberately broke the laws of her race ran the risk of losing their souls. She watched, her mouth dry and her heart pounding. She knew of only one SpiritWalker who'd misused her gifts and abilities to the point where she'd been judged and found to be a Shadowed Soul and had been banished.

The birds flapped their wings and hopped up and down. The blast of air from their large wings pinned her to the trunk. Needles torn from branches whipped through the air like tiny arrows, striking her face, throat, and arms. Pinecones fell like rocks rolling down an unstable hillside. The noise made by the birds was obnoxious. And frightening, as she was alone.

She crossed her arms in front of her head for protection, then kicked out at the birds when they moved closer. The buzzards hopped back but eyed her hungrily. For a moment, a single, heart-stopping moment, Kangee thought she saw a glimmer of red in the black beady eyes.

Taking a deep breath, she jumped away from the tree, threw out her arms, then spun around and around in a tight circle. The air swirled in a narrow column, sucking leaves from the ground then sending them spinning around her faster and faster until they were a blur of greens, oranges, and browns.

Abruptly, Kangee stopped with her arms held high overhead, fingers stretched out toward the sky. In one sharp movement, she slashed her palms downward. The vortex of air she'd created snapped its jaws at the birds of prey.

Exhausted and frightened, Kangee watched the

birds take to the air, the two vultures once again blurring until they were once more ravens, surrounded by the rest of the flock of black birds. Her legs trembled and shook, but she didn't dare sit.

Shadowed Souls.

Her mouth opened but nothing came out. No one ever spoke of those SpiritWalkers who'd chosen to walk the forbidden path that led to the loss of one's soul. The shock of the encounter left her frozen with fear.

Once more, she sought the strength of the tree by leaning her head back against the bark. Weak at the knees, she slid to the ground, her gaze scanning the trees and skies. She peered into the darkness of the forest, afraid that the Shadowed Souls would come back, and if so, what shape would they take? She needed to get back to the village, to safety, but she couldn't move.

She felt trapped in one of her dark nightmares where dark creatures stalked her and no matter how fast she ran, she couldn't escape. Now, those dark dreams had followed her into the daytime. She remembered the image of something dark and menacing hovering over Skye when she and Night Warrior had found her. *Monsters.*

She hugged her arms to her up-drawn knees and shuddered. There was no doubt in her mind that the unnatural weather, her dreams, and the presence of Shadowed Souls were connected. To her, to Skye, and now to Night Warrior.

What did it mean? She needed her father. And her mother. "*Ina,*" she whispered, her voice hoarse and desperate. "Where are you, *Ina.*"

Deep in her gut, Kangee knew her mother stood at the center of everything going so wrong. Before today, she'd assumed her dreams were a reflection of her fear and worry over her mother. But after what happened with Skye, she was very afraid that there was something more happening.

Until this day, Kangee had been afraid her mother had died the night her uncle ambushed them. Why else had no one heard from her? Each of them, in their own way, had strong connections with Eagle Woman, and if she were alive, she would have found a way to connect with one of them.

Kangee leaned her chin on her knees. Tears slid from her eyes and splashed onto her arms. She believed that her mother had connected with her in her dreams. Like when she was a young girl. Often she and her mother would meet in her dreams and explore the dream world together.

She'd forgotten that, until talking about dreams with Night Warrior. She wiped the tears from her face, her eyes blurred as her gaze followed the spine-straight trunk of one tree as it speared so high into the sky that she could not see its top. The thick, nearly impenetrable forest backed up against the village. Her hearing, as that of all SpiritWalkers, was sharp, allowing her to hear the people in the village. She placed her palm on the ground and felt the vibrations of children running and the heavy steps of warriors moving about. This connection should have comforted her, but even surrounded by so many people, she'd felt lost and alone.

Waves of fatigue swamped her. She hadn't known a full night's sleep in weeks and didn't dare give in to it now, not with the presence of Shadowed Souls lurking in the forest. Fear drove her back to her feet. The wind had died down, but the gathering storm brewing high above warned that the worst was yet to come.

Arms wrapped tightly around herself, Kangee slid through the thick shrubs and branches until she reached the worn, narrow trail that separated village and forest. She had to find Blaze and tell her about the Shadowed Souls, and then, together, they could warn the chief.

Kangee stopped. Until very recently, Blaze hadn't known she was a SpiritWalker, and that meant her sister-in-law had no knowledge of those who'd lost their souls.

She ran her hands through her hair and thought of her brother, Luc. He was a powerful SpiritWalker, but only since his marriage to Blaze. Before, he'd just been the son of a French trapper and her adored big brother.

She could go to the chief on her own. And say what? That a flock of raven had threatened her, that two of them, at least two, were not just ravens but Shadowed Souls.

She laughed, low and harsh. These people barely understood—or accepted—that she and her family were SpiritWalkers, a race of humans descended from the gods. And while this tribe knew they were different, they had no true idea how different.

Kangee shuddered, afraid that, if these people learned the truth, she and her family would be forced to leave. That she could not risk, as her young siblings were far too vulnerable. So she'd wait and talk to Blaze and Luc tonight.

Worried, afraid, restless, and edgy, she paced. Lack of sleep left her mind clouded and her body weak. Part of her wanted to believe she'd imagined the Shadowed Souls, that she'd fallen asleep without realizing it, and the Shadowed Souls were nothing more than just another frightening nightmare. But she knew better. Lying to herself was not an option, not even to ease her own fear.

In the meantime, she needed to do something. But what? Wait for the gathering storm to break above her head? Wait helplessly for the return of the Shadowed Souls? Wait and wonder.

The words were a vicious circle in her mind. Frustrated, she called out, "*Ina*! Where are you, *Ina*?" Her voice was a horse, raw croak. Tears burned, demanding release, but she refused to let them fall. Crying would not bring her mother back. Standing there fretting and worrying was just as useless, but she was caught in a sticky web of fear.

Absently, Kangee fingered the long, dangling ends of her belt and stroked the silky, plush fur-strip of beaver. Her gaze traveled over the array of browns from light to dark shimmering in her hand. She held her hands up and in the light. The pelt gleamed with shades of pale blond to light browns.

With shaking hands, she brought the fur to her face. "*Ina.*" Her mother's scent surrounded her. Kangee drew in a deep breath. The fur belt accented the new tunic made by her mother. The supple elk hide flowed against her skin, soft as the down of a newborn chick.

She stroked the wide strip of matching fur her mother had lovingly stitched just above the fringed bottom. Her fingers bunched the material in her hand. She held the edges of the skirt to her face and clung to the comforting scent. "What happened to you, my mother?"

Letting the dress fall back into place, Kangee held out her hands, palms to the ground as she unconsciously guided the gentle breeze with hands and mind. Leaves at her feet stirred. She waved her hands and forest debris skittered around her feet as though being swept by an invisible hand.

She frowned when she realized what she was doing—living among outsiders, she wasn't allowed to reveal her abilities—but needing the comfort and even the sense of control this act provided, she gave in and let her mind flow free. Features taut with concentration, she pushed her palms down sharply, then yanked her arms up, her fingers moving in a rhythmic dance.

Focus! Keep your mind clear. She didn't want to think of everything that was happening. She wanted peace, safety, and security so she retreated into her mind and focused on her hands and fingers.

As though pulled upward by invisible strings, leaves and small twigs danced high off the ground and floated higher. Kangee turned her palms inward and flicked her fingers toward the sky. The leaves fluttered to the tune of her fingers. Another slight shift, a rolling motion as her hands faced one another, sent the leaves spinning in a circle.

Smiling, she rolled her palms back and forth as though she held a smooth round stone between them. Once, this bit of child's play with the wind would have calmed her, but questions the size of boulders continued to batter her thoughts and her imagination shot picture after picture of her mother alone, helpless, and afraid through her mind. Was her mother sick or injured? Or had the Chippewa Indians her uncle hired to kill them captured her.

Her hands jerked as though something struck her. She lost her focus and control, and the growing storm of debris spun outward, shooting off in all directions. She bent at the waist, her fist pressed into her abdomen, and thought of Skye. The child said their mother lived. She believed her.

Skye had connected with Eagle Woman, and for just a moment, Kangee had seen her mother, right before Night Warrior had jerked them from wherever Skye had gone. If her sister could connect with their mother, maybe she could as well.

Kangee concentrated on calming herself. First, she closed her eyes and focused her heart, mind, and soul on her mother, on the love-bond between them.

Standing tall as the pines, she flung her arms out to her sides, then lifted them higher as she called upon all that was available to her: Air and her sisters, Earth, Water, and Fire—the four who'd given her and everything around her life. She was Sister. She was one with all things that had a spirit. She sought the spirits of her world.

Her head fell back and she pulled life to her. The hum of it streaked into her very center. Turning in a slow circle, she commanded Air to form a protective shield. A burst of wind brushed over her and then spun in a circle around her, soft and warm as a mother's loving breath.

Eyes closed, Kangee called forth Fire, the dance of flames. Sun, Star, and Fire swirled into a wall of orange and red. She blocked out sound and fear, drawing on sister Earth, grounding herself to the Mother of Life. She drew nourishment, the connection that linked mother and daughter.

"*Ina*. My mother. Show yourself. Come to me." Her voice trembled, but she held both her intent and resolve. She pictured her mother, watched her mother's wavering image appear as a reddish-orange wraith-like image but complete with amazing detail, like reflections in a still-watered pond or lake at sunset.

"*Ina*," she whispered, her hands reaching out. Her heart raced with a combination of fear and exhilaration. Emotion clogged her throat. Her mother was alive. Kangee sensed her mother's spirit. It was faint, a mere shadow among shadows.

"Reach out to me, *Ina*. We need you." She thought of her greatest need, kept her intent focused on her mother. Eagle Woman always knew when Kangee was upset or worried and always reached out to brush Kangee's mind and heart with her comforting touch.

Kangee waited. Her heart pounded, and her chest tightened as she held her breath, held onto hope. "I am here. I am here. See me. Touch me. Show me where you are." She whispered the words, her throat tight, her eyes burning with unshed tears. She focused wholly on her mother's image, on the love, comfort, and reassurance she desperately needed.

Suddenly, there was a spark of connection and as though a dark veil lifted, and Kangee saw her mother. She didn't dare move though she longed to reach out and touch the image of her mother, but there was a fragile barrier between them, like a sheet of ice that would shatter if she touched it.

"Where are you, *Ina*? Tell me. Show me. I will come to you." Kangee willed the image to sharpen and show her mother's whereabouts. But the image began to fade into a black swirl of darkness.

Through sheer will and determination, Kangee held on to the image. "No! Stay!" Her heart pounded, cold chills skittered up and down her spine, and the bitter, acid taste of fear clogged her throat.

To her relief, the image of her mother sharpened, and she stared deep into her mother's gaze. "Talk to me, Mother. I am here. Let me help you."

Eagle Woman lifted a hand as though reaching out to her. Tears slipped from Kangee's eyes. "Yes, mother. I am here. Reach for me." She stretched out her arm, feeling so near that she expected her mother's hand to close over her own.

Without warning Eagle Woman let out a soul-chilling cry that shattered the image. Kangee's heart raced as darkness swirled.

"*Ina!* Where are you? What happened?" Keeping her eyes tightly closed, she struggled to bring her mother's image back. Her concentration so great, she barely noticed the wind had died as though it too held its breath.

Determined, Kangee fought the darkness until once again, her mother's spirit appeared. The form flickered in the red-orange light. Kangee's heart thundered, and sweat rolled down the sides of her face as she struggled to hold onto the image.

Then, to her horror, something large and dark slithered in front of her mother. An icy chill struck her mind.

"*Ina!* Come back," she cried, trying to pierce the darkness and bring her mother back.

Ina, come back. Ina, come back. Ina, come back. A low, cackling voice echoed her cry and tossed her words back at her like arrows shot into the enemy.

Shadows that reminded her of a fog drifting across a frozen pond swirled then formed into a grotesque shape. Two yellowish slits popped open. Red snake eyes gleamed at her.

Ina. Come back, the monster mocked repeatedly.

She sucked in her breath. Her chest hurt. Her lungs burned. The darkness shrank back, pulled away then coiled itself around her mother and squeezed.

Kangee screamed. "No! Let her go!" She tried to reach out and grab her mother, but the face of the snake suddenly distorted back into a dark blob with fire-red eyes.

Come to me, Child. Come to your mother. Find her. Find me.

The dark, evil form swelled. Writhing vine-like tendrils reached out for her. Evil laughter echoed in her head.

Kangee screamed and stumbled back, falling, landing hard on her palms. The pain of tiny stones digging into flesh combined with fright set the wind whirling. Sobbing hysterically, the air around her sizzled and crackled, heat gathered, and the wind howled.

She fought the frightening vision, tried to escape, but eyes opened or closed, she saw the darkness of evil reaching for her. Thrusting out her hands for protection, her fear totally out of control, Kangee screamed. Over and over and over.

Bright, blinding light grew from the storm building around her then a spear of light and fire shot straight up into the sky.

Chapter Three

"You are a shaman. What further proof do you need?" Chief Two Arrows sat on the floor of the lodge, a long bladed hunting knife in his hands. He tested the sharp edge, pleased when he drew a bead of blood along the tip of his thumb.

Night Warrior eyed the gleaming weapon—a gift from Kangee's father in return for the protection of his family. Holding out his injured arm, he opened and closed his hand, working arm muscles that screamed in protest. Would he ever be able to wield a knife? He lowered his arm to his lap.

The silence between cousins stretched and grew thick and heavy. His cousin would not repeat himself or ask for a response. The quiet swelled like waves in the lake during a storm.

Night Warrior sighed. "My feelings on this matter have not changed. I am no shaman." He put every bit of truth into the statement and dismissed the nagging doubts that hounded him daily.

Once, he'd been sure his refusal to become a shaman had been the right decision for him. Shaman's commanded power, and power often-bred arrogance and a thirst for more power—a fact he knew well—and the very reason he'd never accept that honor.

Yet, since the SpiritWalker had saved his life, he'd fallen back into the trap of dreaming, of taking others with him into the dream world to bring them a small measure of comfort. All because of one woman.

Kangee.

He thought of another woman, a much younger girl who'd died, because he'd kept her secret. Instead of alerting those in charge to what was happening, he'd wanted to be her hero. He wanted to save her and marry her. In his arrogance, his belief that he could save her, he'd failed to keep her safe—from herself.

He'd learned his lesson long ago: Power led to arrogance, and his arrogance had led to death. Now, he found himself in a similar situation. Across from him, Two Arrows waited patiently and silently.

Exhausted, Night Warrior wished he had the energy to just get up and end the conversation by removing himself. "You, better than most, know why I cannot be a shaman. Why I cannot command the power of the position."

His thoughts strayed to the memory of a young troubled girl whom he'd befriended. She'd died while with him in one of their favorite dream worlds. It had happened long ago, yet the despair and the horror was as fresh today as back then.

He shoved the memory aside and stared into his cousin's gaze. "The healer is much more powerful. The honor of Shaman should go to her."

Blaze was a SpiritWalker. She commanded power he'd never possess. He wished to regain his strength, the use of his arm and leg in order to once again protect and serve his people. He was a warrior and had no desire to be anything more.

Two Arrows lifted a brow. "Blaze is a healer. She's always been our healer. My father foresaw long ago that, one day, you would take his place. "

Chief Two Arrows set his weapons aside and leaned forward. "No man survives your injuries without purpose. Why did the healer choose to save you? There were many who died in that battle, including one of our uncles, yet she saved your life." He pounded his fist into his palm. "Why?"

Night Warrior glared at his cousin. "Ask the healer these questions," he shot back. He wanted to deny everything his chief said, but he feared he was being forced onto a path he dare not walk upon. Not ever again.

Two Arrows stood, his stance reflecting his frustration and an edge of anger. "Your path is clear to all but you. Why do you insist on turning your back on truth?"

"Because he is stubborn. As are all the men in this family." The voice of Wise Owl entered the conversation.

Night Warrior wanted to groan aloud. Instead, he schooled his features into an emotionless mask when she came and stood beside her son with hands resting on her hips. A tiny, thin woman, she didn't need size to intimidate or scare him or his male cousins.

"*Cinksi.*" Wise Owl used the term reserved for her sister's sons in a quiet voice deepened by time.

Cornered by his aunt and cousin, Night Warrior, swung his legs over the edge of his bed. His aunt moved closer, blocking his escape. "It is time you listen. If not to me, then to my son who is also *your* chief."

Night Warrior stood, forcing her to step back. He kept most of his weight on his uninjured leg and straightened to his full height, ignoring the pain caused by his chest muscles expanding. Though tempted to walk away, he knew his aunt would just hunt him down with the same dogged determination of a ferret after a rat.

"I am a warrior. Not a shaman." He crossed his arms across his chest. He'd always been a simple man who lived to serve his people. But now, he was more. Much more, but at the same time, far less. He swayed as his leg trembled beneath his weight. "I died that day. "My wounds were many, my blood poured into Mother Earth, and the pain was so great, I welcomed death, had only to take one last step from this world to the Spirit World." He ran a hand over his face. "I should have died," he whispered. "I chose death." Turning, he stared at his aunt.

Wise Owl shook her head. "No, *Thoska*, my nephew. You chose life. And in doing so, you accepted your true path."

For a moment, there was silence.

"I walked upon a golden path in the sky." His voice filled with the wonder of the memory. He knew with absolute certainty he'd never forget any part of what followed that brutal attack. It had been dreamlike yet it more real than life itself.

"You returned to life for a reason." Wise Owl moved closer, her gaze filled with love and understanding. "You know what you must do."

Night Warrior shook his head and avoided her eyes. "Even death does not make me into what my uncle wanted of me."

"You cannot fight what is meant to be," Wise Owl said, annoyance creeping into her voice. "Or your destiny. You lived. Does that not prove you are the shaman my husband forecast?"

Night Warrior eyed his aunt with frustrated love. Though her body was bent with the weight of time, her eyes were bright and as sharp as ever.

"No, my aunt." He kept the pain from his voice, though it twisted through him like a whirling wind. "My wounds are healing far quicker than normal, and I can stop the blood from flowing with my mind and feel—*feel*—my flesh mending. This I cannot deny." He ran his fingertips over the ugly chest wound. The heat in that area told him the edges were already attempting to repair themselves from his earlier movements. "Shamans cannot do what I can do. They can't see or hear what I see and hear. I do not understand what has happened to me or why, but I will not have another life on my conscience."

The entrance of his younger brother made Wise Owl sigh. "You travel a difficult path, *cinksi*, but in the end, you will accept your duty or I fear much will be lost." She nodded to Night Warrior's brother, then walked away.

Red Elk glanced from his brother to their Chief. "I informed the Chief of the Wolf clan of the attack on our warriors after we left the feast." He set his bundle of weapons and other belongings on the top of one bed frame. "Tatonga was most concerned upon hearing this."

Night Warrior winced. It had been on his way back from delivering his bride price that he and his band of warriors had been attacked by a volley of arrows and spears. The attack had been fast, furious, and vicious. He remembered how his brother had been teasing and jesting with him for a wedding meant days of feasting and celebration. That day had been one of his happiest, his greatest for in agreeing to marry Tatonga, he'd become their new chief.

Chief. He'd been honored that her tribe had wanted him to be their new leader. All he'd ever wanted was to become a great warrior and serve his people. Memory of the pain when the axe sliced through his flesh would forever follow him as would that instant slap of fear when the tip a spear ripped through his chest. He'd survived. Many had not. His dream of becoming chief had died that day as well.

"You told her I survived?" As soon as it was clear he'd live, but not as the man he'd been, he'd sent his brother back to her village to call off the wedding.

"Yes." Red Elk stowed his weapons, food, and water pouches on one of the top bunks, then sat on the bed beneath. "Be warned, she did not take the news well, or calmly." He tipped his head back and rolled his shoulders. "Insisted she needed to be here to care for you and got angry when we refused to bring her back with us."

Night Warrior groaned as he remembered how pleased and thrilled the woman had been when he'd agreed to both the marriage and the joining of their two tribes. Tatonga was much older than most marriageable girls were, and she'd been desperate for the union. His brother's report added to his guilt, but taking a wife was not an option unless he was able to provide for her. Right now, he couldn't hunt to feed himself, let alone a family.

An image of Kangee came to mind—not of her in the forest—but of her features trapped in that bubble of light. The look in her sad eyes, her sweet, compelling voice. He refused to admit that Kangee had anything to do with his decision to call off his wedding.

It didn't matter that she drew him to her or that there was an unexplained connection between them. Should he regain his strength and status as a warrior, he would honor his pledge to Tatonga. Unless she chose another.

And if his body never regained its strength, then he'd remain alone, a broken man of no use to his tribe. He buried thoughts of his future, for he feared being dependent on others to care for him above all else and right now he was as helpless as the eldest warrior in his village.

He turned his attention to his brother, studied the fatigue lining his face. Red Elk had been injured in the attack. "You should not have gone. You should have sent others."

"It was my duty to deliver news of your injuries. And when we learn who attacked us, I will lead our warriors in revenge for you and my uncle and the other warriors who died that day."

Night Warrior nodded. He wanted to lead his warriors in that attack. The fact that he couldn't burned like an angry wasp in his gut.

Silence fell between the men, broken by Night Warrior's shuffling steps as he paced. Questions that he'd rather not ask pummeled his mind. The biggest was *why?*

Why him? Why had the healer chosen to save his life that day? He tried to stop the flow of questions, for questions needed answers.

Limping to the back doorway, he stood there in the

cool breeze and allowed it to soothe his aching body. Unbidden, came the thought that it had been his thirst for knowledge that had made him choose life. All his life, he'd been full of questions that begged answers. Until the death of the woman he'd loved. That day, he'd stopped asking. Stopped searching. Stopped seeking.

Was this not a mark of a shaman, the need to search out knowledge and share knowledge with others? He'd spent most of his boyhood with his uncle, the shaman, talking and exploring their world.

At the time, he'd wanted to become a shaman, had embraced his thirst for knowledge like lovers refusing to part. He'd been determined to find answers to questions and answers that needed someone to ask the right questions. His head had been filled—no—consumed—with the need to seek truth.

His head ached and dark images slid through his mind. That innocent thirst for knowledge had turned into an obsession, then later, into arrogance. No one knew better than he that knowledge led to power and power to greed. Power seeking more power seeking more power. A never-ending vicious circle.

Somewhere near the edge of the forest, Night Warrior heard tiny feet scampering from branch to branch. A quick glance upward to a thick branch that shaded the path between lodge and forest was all it took for him to locate the silent squirrel watching him.

Everywhere he looked, Night Warrior found reminders of the changes in his body. The healer had made him so much more than just a warrior. Why? How? The woman had healed many of their people and none of them was so different.

So why him?

Why had her act of saving his life changed him so drastically? He wanted to ask her but was afraid of the answer. For the first time since his thirteenth summer, Night Warrior wondered if he'd made the right choice when he'd rejected everything to do with becoming a shaman, something that had hurt his uncle. Had his status as warrior been taken from him to force him back on the path he'd once walked?

A sudden blast of wind slammed into him with the force of a fist to the gut, followed by a bright flash of light that lit up the sky. A storm brewed, both within him and out. Thunder rumbled, and the wind howled and shook the lodge.

Just as he turned to go back inside the lodge, a scream tore through his heart, mind, and soul.

Fear coated his skin with a sheen of sweat. "Kangee!" He bellowed her name and ran out into the storm, tasting her fear on the battering wall of wind.

Without thought, he stumbled down the alley between trees and lodges, forcing his injured leg to move and bear his weight. Around him, he heard the frightened voices and cries of his people, but he had but one thought. Find Kangee.

He followed her screams, which seemed part of the storm itself, then came to an abrupt halt when he saw Kangee writhing on the ground as though in great pain. Her hysterical screams slashed through the air.

She flung out her hands, as if struggling against an unseen attacker. Around her, a darkening whirlwind spiraled downward, pulling dark clouds into the wall of wind.

People came running from all directions, and like him, came to an abrupt, disbelieving halt when a flash of light from Kangee's hands shot straight into the sky. The wind howled and spun debris in a wide circle, keeping him from reaching her.

Before he could comprehend what he was seeing, another jagged arrow of light followed by a loud crack split the air. Night Warrior's jaw dropped when a giant tree exploded. Horrified, he watched the top third topple over in slow motion.

"Move," he shouted as he flung himself into the wall of wind.

Kangee didn't respond. Her screams continued. Caught in the midst of her storm of emotion, Night Warrior threw himself over her and braced himself for the pain of the tree crushing him. He'd survived a battle that should have taken his life and would willingly surrender that same life to save this woman.

Time froze as he waited for death to once again find and claim him. But nothing happened. Thinking the gods had been watching over them and that the tree had somehow missed them, he glanced up then blinked at the sight of the young child standing over him.

Skye's eyes glittered in an array of translucent blues, greens, and browns with shining golden stars adding an unearthly sheen to her eyes. The world around him went silent and still. Warmth seeped into him, calming his seizing, screaming muscles.

Beneath him, Kangee, shocked out of her hysteria, gasped. She yanked her arms up and held them up over his back. "Do not move, Warrior," she said, her voice low and trembling and frightened.

The hum of energy traveling along his body where he and Kangee touched was almost painful. He opened his mouth, but the look in her wide, scared eyes stopped him from speaking. He twisted his head around and looked behind and above them.

A sharp exclamation exploded from his lips, and he couldn't have moved if his life had depended on it. The sight of the pine tree suspended over them as though held by invisible string froze him in place. Only then did he become aware of the prick of pine needles along his back for the tree just hung there in midair, branches draped over him, Kangee, and the child like a pine-green cloak.

Aware that Skye stood near her head, Kangee didn't dare take her eyes off the chunk of tree that stood taller than the lodge and was three times the width of her and Night Warrior. Taking a deep breath, she tried to use her own command over air to shift the tree away from them, but her mind was too fractured to focus, her emotions raw, and her heart pounding frantically.

Fear trapped her breath as the tree wavered. "Skye?" She croaked her sister's name. Her sister was using everything she had to hold the tree motionless in mid-air. If she and Night Warrior rolled out of the way, they'd leave Skye in danger alone. The branches were wide and heavy.

"Warrior. Help me." She sought from him that familiar and comforting hum of energy she'd sensed from the first time she'd been in his presence. He was a powerful man. He'd proved it when he'd brought Skye out of the darkness.

"We roll," he gasped, his dark eyes wide.

"No. Skye cannot move. She needs us to help her." She framed his face between her palms and gazed deep into his eyes, seeking the connection that, in the space of one heartbeat, had bound their spirits as tight as bark to a tree.

"Share with me your mind. Your energy. Your power." Above them, the tree began to shudder. Night Warrior's dark hair blew around his head, the strands a wild, dark cloud and his shoulders tightened as though he had braced himself to take the brunt of the tree trunk, but his gaze never left hers.

"Skye." A soothing wave of warmth from her sister seeped into her mind. "Find Skye within me." She had no idea if it would work, but then she felt him in her mind. No, not in her mind. It was like before, like a dreamscape. Then Skye was there, sharing an image of the tree shifting to the right, rolling on a sea of air, lifting the tip of the tree upward so that it stood on the sheered trunk.

For Kangee, there was only this warrior, her sister, and the tree that threatened their lives. She didn't break eye contact with Night Warrior until Skye retreated from her mind.

"Take us back," she ordered as she gathered her will and raised her arms over Night Warrior's back. "Let go, sweetheart. Let go of the tree. Now!"

Kangee used everything she had to create a blast of air to shove the tree against the forest wall. It crashed through the shrubs and branches at the edge of the forest, out of harm's way.

Night Warrior dropped his forehead onto hers. His arms rested and framed the sides of her face, surrounding her with his heat and scent. For a long time, no one moved or spoke.

Kangee let her arms fall onto his sweat-slicked back. Unconsciously, she soothed him and herself. At her head, Skye sank down to rest her head on Kangee's shoulder.

"That was close. So close. I am so sorry, warrior of the night."

Night Warrior lifted his head, his gaze intense. "What did you call me?"

Kangee grimaced. "I know your people call you Night Warrior, but you come to me whenever I need you. You take me from the dark. At night in my dreams. And twice today. You are my warrior of the night."

Night Warrior's eyes softened. He cupped her face and stared into her eyes. "You have called me by that name many times. It is wrong for me to come to you in your dreams, but you are sad, scared, and alone. When you cry out at night, I can do nothing but offer to ease your sadness.

For a long moment, neither said a word.

"What happened?" he asked. "Why were you screaming? Are you hurt?"

Sick and ashamed, Kangee let her arms fall away. "I lost control of my emotions."

Her people were not just connected with the earth. They were bonded with their world so completely, that the elements often mirrored the emotions of a SpiritWalker. She turned her head, saw the gathered crowd, and wanted to sink into the earth.

Night Warrior stared at her in disbelief. "I would not wish to be around you if you were angry."

He rolled off her and lay on his back beside her. Around them, his people gathered, talking all at once. The women's voices were high, the men's low, fierce. Children wailed and cried.

Without the warrior's comforting weight and

warmth, the cold hand of dread squeezed her chest. She had scared these people, had put them in danger. Before she could move, or even think what to do or what she'd say, Chief Two Arrows hunkered down beside her, his deep brown eyes filled with concern.

"What happened, child?" His commanding voice silenced the fear-filled voices of his people.

Kangee stared into his eyes, searching for signs of condemnation or hate or fear. The chief and his family had been kind enough to offer her and her family lodging while her father searched for her mother, but after this, she and her sisters would have no choice but to leave. Not even the chief could ignore the anger and edge of fear from the crowd, for he answered to those he led.

Though weak and ill to her stomach, she struggled to sit. The chief reached out and lent his strength. She glanced at her hands. Her palms tingled painfully with unspent energy so she placed them flat on the ground, sending heat from her body back to the earth. The action calmed her, and she once more became as one with her Earth Mother.

Night Warrior had yet to move. His ragged breaths told her that he was in great pain. Had she asked too much of him? Beside her, Skye moved close, leaning against her.

Kangee wrapped an arm around her sister. Later, she would think about what Skye had managed and the extent of her sister's abilities. Right now, the Chief waited. He deserved an answer.

"I…" She lifted her shoulders helplessly. "I don't know how to explain what happened.

Chief Two Arrows reached out and tipped her chin

up, forcing her to meet his gaze. He gave her a rueful smile. "This is not the first storm created by one of your people that I have seen. Our healer, in the past, has done this many times." His brows drew together. "I will admit the storms Blaze produced as a child were not so powerful," he said, humor softening his voice as he smiled reassuringly at her.

Kangee had expected fear and contempt not this bit of humor. Still, she'd put them in danger and knew what she had to do. "I know I must leave, but I ask that you honor the promise you made to my father. Do not ask me to take my sisters from here. They need your protection."

"Why do you think you must leave?" His voice was gentle.

Kangee thought of the Shadowed Souls lurking out in the forest and the vision of her mother, the evil that had seemed so real it had caused her to lose complete control of herself. Her heart raced and sweat slicked her skin just thinking about what she'd seen and faced in that strange vision. "There is something bad out there. I saw it. Felt it. I cannot bring danger to your people."

Beside her, Skye reached up and touched the side of her face. Her panic calmed. She hugged her sister, silently thanking her. Her fingers shook as she rubbed Skye's silky hair between her fingers and searched the crowd for Blaze. She needed to tell her what she'd seen and ask her to look after the girls. "My brother will take me to a place where I will be safe until he finds our father."

Chief Two Arrows sat back on his heels, his piercing gaze holding hers. "You are not leaving." He spoke firmly, glancing around to meet and hold the gaze of every man, woman, and child.

"But—"

His voice gentled. "Child, I know what you are. What your family is. I promised protection. There is nothing more to discuss." He stood, then motioned to Blaze who'd come running.

"She stays," he repeated. "Take care of her." When he walked away, the rest of the tribe followed.

Blaze knelt and drew Kangee into her arms. "I'm sorry I wasn't here sooner. I was up in my cave."

Kangee couldn't stop crying. "I did not mean to lose control," she whispered. She slid a quick glance over at Night Warrior, but he refused to meet her gaze. He stared up into the sky. He hurt and she knew he was working to smooth it out.

Blaze stroked Kangee's cheek with one hand. "Little Sister, do not apologize. We are what we are. Your brother can tell you about my last storm. It was so strong that my own brother, far away, spotted it and knew I was alive and where to find me."

Kangee frowned. She'd forgotten that Blaze had just been reunited with her brothers and sister. "I put everyone in danger." She stared at the debris of pine needles, cones, and broken branches littering the path around them. "We are taught never to lose control."

Blaze chuckled. "We are children of the gods, not gods. We are not perfect." Her smile grew rueful. "I, too, have created storms. Ask your brother."

Kangee stared into Blaze's eyes, a melting pot of blues with rings of yellow webbing that marked her as a SpiritWalker. Blaze spoke the truth, but it didn't take away her shame. Blaze hadn't known she was a SpiritWalker, hadn't been taught and trained from a child, as had she. Still, what was done was done.

"No more blame," Blaze ordered. She motioned the twins forward.

Kangee gathered Anika and Andrie close and kissed each girl on the top of their head, then did the same to Skye. The power the little girl held at her young age promised a greatness that humbled Kangee. Skye pulled back and moved to Night Warrior. She put a hand on his chest.

"Bad." Skye said.

"Yes, his injuries are great." Kangee stared into Night Warrior's pale face. She had drained energy he didn't have to spare. He seemed unable to move, and his eyes remained closed, his lips clamped shut, but his nostrils flared with each and every ragged breath. Pain etched lines around his mouth, his nose, and eyes.

"I am sorry," she whispered, her voice raw and hoarse. "Once more, you came to my rescue and I have caused you pain."

Skye glanced from Night Warrior to Kangee. Her eyes darkened as though the light within had dimmed. "Shadows." She leaned her head in the hollow of Kangee's shoulders. "*Ina.*"

"I know." Kangee had stood in those frightening shadows with her mother until Night Warrior had yanked their minds free. And again, he'd come to her and broken the dark spell that had held her prisoner.

A warm breath of air brushed her mind and calmed her. Kangee wanted to cry. As the eldest, she should be comforting her baby sister.

Blaze joined Skye and placed her hand on Night Warrior's chest. "You will accept this gift from me. Your body had been through much today, and I fear time grows short for all of us." No one spoke until Blaze removed her hand. "The day you chose life, I told you it was not your time to die. *This*, Warrior, is your time. You seek answers to many questions. Start now. Today. Ask what you will and seek your answers."

She stood. "You lived for a reason. Seek out that reason." She turned to Kangee. "There is much to be said between you and this warrior." She gathered Skye in her arms, then motioned to the twins. They walked away, leaving Kangee and Night Warrior alone.

Kangee got to her feet and held out her hand. "Take it."

Reluctantly, Night Warrior took her hand. Tremors of pain coiled like snakes beneath his skin. The warrior had been so sick when she'd arrived and had she not known he'd been healed, brought back from death to life by Blaze and her amazing ability to heal, she'd have feared his death imminent.

Kangee swept her gaze over the multiple wounds. Angry, raw wounds, along with purple, black, and blue bruises starting to turn a sickly yellow-green covered most of one side of his chest.

"You are in pain because of me." She put her arm around his shoulders and helped steady the warrior until he stood beside her. A sheen of sweat dripped down the sides of his face just from the effort it took to stand. Where they touched, warmth flowed, and once again, the hum of something strong and powerful zipped between them.

Stepping back to give Night Warrior the distance and respect that was his due, Kangee met his gaze and nearly gasped aloud. A tiny golden flame flickered like firelight in his eyes. She blinked. Looked again, but it was gone.

Tired. She was so tired, she was seeing what was not there.

****

The silence stretched. Night Warrior was drowning in Kangee's gaze of blues, browns, and greens with bits of sunlight shining within their depths. He fisted his hands to keep from reaching out. Her pull on him was strong, and he wanted to touch her and have her touch him. He yearned to draw her close and breathe in her sweetness, the freshness of sun, rain, and mist up close.

When she turned away, he felt as though something had been snatched from him. His growing dependence on her, his need to see her, hear her voice, and be close to her made his knees tremble so he shoved it aside, telling himself he was vulnerable because of his second brush with death.

So he let his mind whirl with the speed and frenzy of the storm they'd both survived. What he'd done in the lodge with Kangee and Skye had shaken him, but what had just happened out here made him feel as though he was being drowned in a storm-churned lake by some unseen force.

He wasn't sure what it was about this woman that had changed his world, but he was sure of one thing. He could not walk away from her.

Kangee scuffed her toe in the dirt. "You need to rest. We can talk later."

"No," Night Warrior said. "We talk now." She looked so tired and worn as she glanced up at him. In her eyes, he saw worry, shame, and fear.

"You are exhausted and in pain." When he remained silent, she sighed. "At least let us go into your lodge so you can sit."

"I do not need to lie in my bed like an old man." He'd had enough of the stifling heat of the lodge and his female relatives fussing over him. "I remember how our healer once created a storm and destroyed much of our crop. From that day on, she lived in a cave outside the village, for everyone, including myself, feared her. And not long ago, I heard she did this again, but this storm was so powerful it was not only seen, but also felt by her family a long distance away. How is it your people can do this?"

Kangee sighed. She grabbed a handful of leaves and let them fall from her hand. "We are one with the gods, created by them. We command Air and her sisters, Earth, Fire, and Water. We have the ability to create storms, fires, and more—"

Following her gaze, Night Warrior saw several older boys peering at them from around a lodge. "Come."

Kangee followed, keeping her pace even with his slow, uneven gait. "You are stubborn. You need to rest. A breath of wind could knock you down."

Night Warrior turned his head. "There is no wind."

With humor in her eyes, Kangee lifted her hands. "That can change, Warrior."

His tension eased, and as they walked, he watched her fingers and hands. Her movements seemed to scatter leaves out of their path.

A puff of air rose to caress his face. Wary, he eyed her. Leaves skittered over the ground, then fluttered as though being swept upward by an invisible hand. Mesmerized, he watched. Another slight shift of her fingers followed by a gentle rolling motion of her hands sent the leaves spinning, forming a tiny whirling column that rose over their heads. He stopped, his mouth dropping open.

It was one thing to be told she'd created a storm from her emotions, but seeing her calmly and almost without thought doing this? Her obvious command of air left him speechless.

For a moment, their gazes met and held. Hers filled with mischief as she flicked her fingers and scattered the leaves between them. Then she began spinning in a circle, and the leaves drifted around her like snow in winter.

Transfixed, he watched her graceful movements. Her hair formed a dark cloud, the long silken strands brushing against him as she spun in a dance that held him captivated. Abruptly, she stopped and flicked her fingers toward him.

The gentle gust of air fluttered through his hair and rained pine needles over him. Night Warrior shook his head and realized this woman came from a different world.

Kangee dropped her hands, and her features turned serious. "Your pride is misplaced. If you do not listen to the needs of your own body, you harm yourself."

He gave in and admitted she was right as he led the way toward a felled tree a short distance from the shoreline. "I will sit."

In truth, he was a bit shaken. This small deliberate display of her abilities to get him to rest shocked him more than the wild storm that had consumed her earlier, the one that nearly claimed not just her life but also his. This, more than anything, was proof of just how different she was…and how powerful.

He waited, respecting her need to gather her thoughts. At last, she turned to him. "What do you want to know first?"

So many questions popped into his mind, but he told himself they'd have to wait. He would have his answers. In time. "You were screaming. What happened?"

Kangee's shoulders slumped as she joined him, sitting on the ground in front of him. "I saw my mother."

Frowning, Night Warrior narrowed his eyes. "A vision?"

Kangee plucked a blade of grass from the ground beside the log. "I don't know. I've never before had a vision." She glanced at the lake, the water lapping against the shore, then back at him. "Like Skye did earlier, I sought her out. I called to her, thought of her, and then, I *saw* her in my mind. Then, somehow, I was there, with her, in that dark place like before."

Night Warrior stared at her in disbelief. "After what happened with your sister, you put yourself at risk?" Anger at her foolish actions made his voice harsher than he intended.

Kangee nodded, then tossed the shredded blade of grass aside. "I've never done this before. I needed my mother and wanted to find her and see what Skye saw. You took us out so fast when we were there together, I wasn't sure if I had really seen her or not." She reached out, her trembling hand on his knee stopping him from saying more. "I saw her, Warrior. And I saw the monster. Evil." Tears trailed over her cheeks. She covered her face with her hands and rocked.

Night Warrior didn't blame her for wanting

answers. After all, was that not what he was doing? Hadn't he lived not just for her but also to find answers? He tried to still the fear in his gut when he thought about what had almost happened to her. Better than most, he understood the power of visions and dreams.

He slid down from the log, stretched out his injured leg before him, then with his good arm, he drew her close, offering comfort as he did in their dreams. "I, too, saw the evil spirit when I found your sister."

He kept to himself his own nightmares of demons and monsters and the hideous voice that came to him when he'd deliberately tried to create a dream around Kangee. Something had happened when he'd taken Kangee with him to find Skye. An opening to the Spirit World had been breached, leaving them vulnerable.

More than any other time since his uncle had died, he wished for the shaman's counsel. He drew in a deep breath and shoved from his mind the darkness that hovered at the edges. "Tell me what you saw."

Kangee closed her eyes. "I saw my mother. She is alive, but something is wrong. I wanted to go to her, but there was something else there. Something bad. A monster. It kept calling me and tried to pull me into the darkness. I don't know what it was. I—"

Night Warrior stopped her with a hand to her shoulder. "Shh. It's evil. I saw it, and it spoke to me, too."

He shook his head clear of the hate-filled hissing voice that had tried to instill guilt and fear of his gift of dreaming. The voice had reminded him why he no longer dreamed, something he seemed unable to prevent around the woman huddled in his arms. For now, he put it from his mind and concentrated on Kangee who shook like the leaves she'd spun.

"The storm? Did it create that storm?" he asked.

Kangee pulled away and wiped her face with her skirt, then stared out at the lake. "I was so scared that I lost control of myself and let fear consume me. That is what created the storm." She glanced at him. "I created that storm." She tipped her chin, as if daring him to take her to task. Or maybe she was bracing herself from whatever reaction he might have.

He kept his silence as though taking in her statement, and in a way, he was, for it was inconceivable to him that any one person had the power to make a storm of that strength.

He finally spoke. "Your storm blew apart a tree and…" He shook his head.

Surprised that awe, not reproach filled his voice, Kangee leaned back in his arms. "For that I am sorry. And we have my sister to thank for our lives. She stopped the tree from falling onto us."

"Your sister couldn't have done it on her own. You helped."

Kangee sighed and glanced up at him, ashamed and proud. "No. I was unable."

"Skye?"

Nodding, Kangee added, "My sister is powerful. One day she will take her place as the leader of my tribe. Even I cannot tell you how she did this."

Night Warrior leaned back. The lapping of water and the buzz of insects filled his ears as well as other noise from the forest behind him. He tuned them out and tried to understand Kangee and her people, what they were and what they were able to do.

He just shook his head and stared blankly out over the water. "Woman, you scare me. What you and your people do is frightening. I think I do not want to know more right now." He didn't think he could handle any more shocks or surprises.

She sighed and rested her head on his shoulder as though it were the most natural thing to do. Their hearts beat together, and their breaths mingled. "That is why we hide what we are. But you are powerful, Warrior. Without your strength and help, Skye could not have held onto that tree and moved it away from us. It took all three of us."

"I did not do anything," Night Warrior protested. "You or your sister projected that image in my mind. I just—just allowed you to do so."

Kangee got to her feet. "You gave to us what is within you. We connected. The three of us. I cannot explain it more than that."

He watched the young woman pace and rub her fingers back and forth on her fur belt. Instinctively, he knew this woman was far more dangerous to him than the spear the enemy had buried deep into his chest. In her presence, he felt vulnerable, mind and heart. And safe, warm, and whole.

He'd been bed-bound for days after the battle and in so much pain, he'd wished himself dead. Then Kangee and her family arrived. Her voice in that dark, pain-filled time had given him light and peace that helped dispel the terrifying blackness.

She'd called to him, brought him out of the darkness and into the light. In his dreams, he walked with her as a whole man, a proud warrior in his ceremonial headdress, holding his coup stick, every feather speaking of his courage and bravery. Even looking at her now eased the ache that was his constant companion.

Seeking to comfort her, he spoke. "We will share what happened with your brother and the healer. They will know what to do."

She shook her head. "No. They won't be able to help us, and even if they can find my father and bring him back, this is beyond him. We need my family, my grandmother." She paced before him. "I need my grandmother," she repeated as she stared up into the forest.

Frowning, Night Warrior sat up. "You are not leaving the safety of this village to go to them."

The loud screech of an eagle drew his attention. One of the nesting pair of birds skimmed the water for fish. It rose with a flash of silver in its talons and flew to a dead tree where it landed in a huge nest on the other side of the lake.

To distract her from thoughts of leaving on her own, he ask, "Tell me of your people." He wanted to know about her, and in her answer, maybe he'd find his own answers as to what the changes within him meant.

Kangee glanced over her shoulder. "We are of an ancient race put here to protect Mother Earth and all who depend upon her. We command the elements and share the minds of her children."

"Explain." Nothing at this point could surprise Night Warrior.

Walking to the edge of the lake, Kangee stared at the appearance of a second adult eagle soaring overhead. "If the spirit of an animal or bird gives its permission, we can share their mind and see what they see and feel as they do." She turned briefly. "Our people can travel great distances in this manner. It is hard to explain so I will show you."

Night Warrior rose and limped to the water's edge. "No," he said but she'd already turned away from him and lifted her hands high.

Chapter Four

A chill wind blew off the lake. Kangee scanned the entire lake. One side was flanked by forest. Across from her, there were trees and a large meadow. The eagle nest sat in an old, long dead tree near the edge of the water. To her right, a ridge of rock sprang from the earth and stood tall and proud, like royalty surveying its kingdom of lake, stream, forest, and meadow. The village lay behind her, beyond a wall of protective trees.

Each evening since her arrival, she'd climbed up the path to the top of that ridge, craving the peace that came from watching the lake transform from a deep, calming blue to a pool of molten gold as the sun dipped below the horizon and spilled into the lake like a golden waterfall.

Today, there was no sunlight to add color and sparkle to lake. The water mirrored the sky, a sulky pit reflecting the darkness crawling over the horizon.

Standing on the shore with gentle waves lapping over her feet and around her ankles, Kangee thought of what she was about to do. She'd never tried this alone. Always before, she'd been in the company of her parents, for mind merging carried its own share of danger. But remembering her vision—her mother, the monster, and hearing once again her mother's cry—convinced her that she needed her grandmother and with Night Warrior with her, the risk was low.

Still, a shaft of cold fear settled in her center. Her legs shook, and her breath caught in the back of her throat. Instinct warned that time was short, that her mother's life was at risk. She spoke to the warrior standing slightly behind her. "I trust you to watch over me, warrior of the night."

Ignoring his protest, she turned her attention to the single, lone tree that speared up out of the meadow like a palm held up to the sky. In its center sat the large, empty, eagle's nest.

She scanned the sky and waited. When the eagles flew close, she drew in a deep breath and lifted her hands high, her fingers pointing stiffly upward. She emptied her mind, called forth her intent, and visualized her needs and her desire. What she so desperately wanted rose from her heart, her very center. She opened her eyes and sent out her request to merge her spirit with the spirit of the eagle.

The eagles swooped down toward her with shrill cries that echoed along the tops of the trees and across the lake. Keeping her mind focused, she fed the birds her need to fly with them, to join her mind, her spirit to theirs. The feeling, the need swelled and burst free like a stream unable to contain its contents.

She needed them, their help. Not just for herself, her mother, or her family but for every innocent man, woman, and child who lived in the village. A storm brewed unlike anything she'd ever seen or felt. Darkness and the taint of something evil lurked, something that paced and waited.

Just thinking about that dark, evil spirit with its hideous eyes sent her heart racing for it was wholly dark and evil, and even now, it skirted the edge of her mind, waiting. Just waiting.

But for what? She was afraid, for herself, and for the lives of all those around her. Before she could force the fear from her mind, something dark slid behind her eyes, blotting out the stormy sky and lake.

Look at me, it whispered.

"No." Kangee willed her mind clear, focused her gaze on the turbid sky and the birds. She called upon everything stubborn, willful, and determined from within. She would not give in to the dark spirit or her fear. She would not lose control again. Dare not.

The eagles swooped toward her with shrill cries that continued to bounce and echo across the lake and forest. As soon as they were overhead, Kangee swayed side to side, her long hair rippling like a dark waterfall in the stiff wind.

Please, she begged. Desperate need swelled, then burst free like a breached dam. *Honor me with the gift of joining our minds. Our spirits.*

The female, the larger of the two birds, dipped her wings, then pulled them back as she dropped lower and lower. Kangee kept her gaze on the bird flying straight at her.

In times of need, her people drew on the strengths, traits, and spirits of their world. Anything with a shadow had a spirit, and any spirit could be called upon.

"Help me," she begged, breathing the words repeatedly. She'd never before managed a mind-merge on her own and could not shift shape as many SpiritWalkers could. Neither Luc nor Blaze knew where to find her family and her father was gone. This was the only way she had of quickly getting word to her grandmother.

Hope rose inside as she felt a swelling of power, a gathering of energy rise from her very center. She needed to merge her mind with the eagle, see with the majestic bird's sharp eyesight. As soon as the eagle was directly overhead, she called out, "Spirit of *wambli*. Your vision I need to find my grandmother."

Kangee put all her need, all her love into the request and repeated it over and over as the bird soared lower in ever tightening circles. Holding her breath, Kangee had an urge to reach out and take what she wanted. She was desperate. What harm was it? Was her need not real? The needs of the many over the one? Could she not justify taking what her family and these people needed?

Respect and honor all things. Respect free will.

Her mother's words echoed in her mind. One of the first rules a child learned was to guard her spirit, control her thoughts and emotions so that later, if so chosen, she might be given gifts and privileges including the ability to merge their spirits with their cousins who shared their world—the winged ones, two and four-leggeds, swimmers, the creepy-crawlies, and even the rocks and trees.

Kangee focused on her prayer, her need, her call for help, and her heartfelt and selfless intent. Her voice rose. The wind swirled around her as energy poured both into her, then shot out of her from her fingers.

Above her head, the shrill cry of the eagle continued to echo, closer and closer. Hope soared. Her heart pounded with anticipation when the majestic bird flared her wings slightly and seemed to stop in mid-flight. The bird's head dipped, and Kangee found herself staring into the eyes of the great, majestic eagle.

"Now," she whispered as she eagerly waited for her spirit to leave her body and merge with the eagle. The bird had given its permission. She sent waves of pure love to the bird, followed all the steps she'd been taught. Then it happened.

Threads of wickedness slithered into her mind, then sprang upward as though it, too, sought the mind of the bird. The eagle let out a shrill, piercing cry, then tumbled across the sky, as though blasted backward through the air.

"No!" Kangee screamed and gripped her head. Pain pounded relentlessly behind her eyes. Stunned, shocked, and devastated, she fell to her knees, then rolled to her side as she fought waves of dark, cold hopelessness. She moaned, battled the shadows seeking to take over her mind. Sharp stones dug into her ribs, her arm, and the side of her face and head.

The eagle had agreed. The power to merge her mind with the bird had filled her along with the joy and love of acceptance. But something dark and evil in her mind had swallowed and destroyed it.

She felt Night Warrior's hands on her shoulders. "What is happening?" This failure, the presence of evil, it was just too much. "What does all this mean?" She closed her eyes, curled into a ball to ease the gut-wrenching pain in her stomach. "I failed her. I failed you, my mother."

Kangee sobbed. Tentatively, she reached for her mother, needing the contact, the reassurance that her mother was still alive. Immediately, a fist of hatred slammed against her mind.

Yeesss. Come to her. Save her. Only you can save

her. Come to me, child. Together we will save your mother.

"Save her, yes. I want to save her." She needed to save her mother, but something wasn't right. The voice should have reassured her, given her hope for the words were precisely what she needed to hear, but it was off. Something buzzed angrily beneath the surface and made her stomach heave.

Moaning, her fingers gripped handfuls of hair as she covered her ears and tried to block the insidious voice.

"Stop!" Night Warrior shouted. His fingers dug painfully into her shoulder. "Now!"

His harsh command lashed into her mind and shattered the dark voice as her bolt of lightning had shattered the tree trunk. He shook her, forcing her from the shadows of her mind as he hauled her up.

She wept, tears rolling down her cheeks and dripping off her chin. "How can I save her?" She shouted the words. She felt weak and helpless. In that instant, she knew that, in many ways, she and Night Warrior shared much. He was weak physically, she spiritually.

He stood and drew her up with his good arm. He cradled her close.

She felt cold. "What is happening? First, the Shadowed Souls, now, this Evil Spirit. Something terrible has happened to my mother."

He tipped her chin up. "What Shadowed Soul? What is this?"

"Earlier, I saw two Shadowed Souls. They are enemies of our people." She turned and staggered to the log and sat.

Following her, Night Warrior paced in front of her, his limp worse in the sandy soil. "Explain. If there are enemies near, I need to warn my chief."

Kangee let out a humorless laugh. "Your chief and warriors cannot battle or guard against Shadowed Souls."

"Are they spirits, like the evil spirit with your mother?"

Sighing, she ran her hands through her hair. "They are real as you or I, yet they are different." How much should she tell him? He didn't know the secrets of her people, like their ability to shift shapes.

"SpiritWalkers are given many special abilities and gifts. With those abilities, comes great responsibility. We are held to a higher standard because the gods created us and gave to us the task of protecting the Earth and all who live within her." She paused when Night Warrior sat beside her.

He rubbed his thigh. "Continue."

"This is what my grandmother once told me. 'SpiritWalkers live in the light of life, seek to honor life, but beware the shadowed souls that walk in the darkness for they honor none. Once you step onto the path of darkness, the light that is your soul will begin to fade. Evil awaits those who turn to the darkness.'" The words of the elderly wise woman resonated deep in Kangee's heart and soul. "My people live in the light. We honor all life and respect freewill. If someone is hurt, he or she has to want our help and accept it freely. Even an injured animal has to accept the gift of healing. Free will is the one rule that we cannot break without consequences. Anyone who does not respect the choices of others or who seeks to gain at the cost of others risks the loss of their soul."

She turned on the log so she could see how the warrior was taking what she said. "To lose our soul is worse than death, for we can't travel the Spirit World without our soul."

Restless, needing to move and think, she paced in front of him. She honored life, walked in the light of life, and had been taught to use her abilities not just for the good of their people but also for non-SpiritWalkers with honorable needs.

"You said you saw two of these Shadowed Souls."

Kangee nodded but kept to herself the fact that they had only done so in the form of birds. "Yes, they revealed themselves to me." She paused. "I once knew a girl who was banished from our village. She was a Shadowed Soul." That day still haunted Kangee.

"A girl? A child?" Night Warrior sounded shocked.

Kangee nodded. She hadn't thought of Red Flower in a very long time. She stared out into the lake without really seeing the calm, mirror-like surface.

"Tell me about her." Night Warrior got to his feet and joined her. "Let's walk."

Reaching the lake, she bent and picked up a smooth rock. She held it, felt the hum of energy. "Red Flower liked to listen in on private conversations, then spread what she'd learned to others. She used her ill-gotten information to bully or tease the other children. She caused pain and suffering and enjoyed doing so. Her fingers rubbed the stone as she talked. "No amount of chastising stopped her. As she grew older, she got worse. Then she started stealing. Whatever she wanted."

Stopping, Kangee tossed the stone, watched it skip

across the smooth surface. She closed her eyes and let her mind follow the threads of memory. She sensed that there was something there she needed to know or remember so she focused in on that time.

Fortunately, she had not been of interest to the mean-spirited girl, but she had studied exactly how the girl had used her gifts to torment others and how she'd actively used her mind on those weaker or younger to steal from them whatever she selfishly wanted.

"She stole," Night Warrior prompted.

"Yes. It always looked as though others gave to her freely, but I knew the truth. I watched her, saw how she controlled others to get her way.

Again, she kept their shape shifting ability to herself. She'd been envious when the other girl had learned to shift shape. All her life, Kangee had looked forward to shifting shape and merging with the spirits of her world so completely. Though she'd known it was wrong, she'd been jealous of the girl who'd defied the elders to do as she pleased.

"Red Flower's stealing grew worse, but there was no proof. Only suspicion. One day, I saw her steal a power stone from my grandmother." The girl had shifted into a raven to enter her grandmother's lodge. "I couldn't believe my eyes. Stealing was bad enough, but from grandmother?" She shook her head.

Night Warrior used his arm to steer her around a fallen tree.

"Red Flower tried to blame another."

He stopped and stared into her eyes. "You told the truth."

Kangee nodded. "She was banished after that."

"And you felt guilty."

"She was young, a bit older than I am now, and she was sent into the forest to live or die on her own. I cried. I was six and didn't understand." She often wondered what happened to the girl but had never asked, for in the minds of her people, once banished, you were no more.

Sighing, they turned and made their way back toward the village. She wished she knew more of the dark side of her race, but the mere thought of becoming a Shadowed Soul was just too frightening a thought. Suddenly, it seemed important for her to know more of these Shadowed Souls.

But how? No one talked of those who crossed from light to shadow except during lessons to children to make them understand the responsibility they, as The Chosen, carried and the consequences of breaking the laws of their people.

Where did a Shadowed Soul go? Were they killed? Or were they left to wander on their own, to live or die by their own wit and strength?

"What does all this mean? Shadowed Souls, an evil spirit, my mother. Nothing makes sense." She hugged her arms to her chest as images of her mother began circling around in her head.

No. She didn't dare think of her mother. She couldn't handle another encounter with that evil spirit.

Story, Kangee. Story.

Skye's loving voice pierced the darkness consuming all thought, all ability to think and reason. The voice of her sister sent light and warmth into her aching head. Kangee grabbed hold of Skye's love, desperate to escape the evil whispers.

There were only two people Kangee could connect

with in this manner. Her mother and Skye. It had been Skye's gift, Skye's connection that had allowed Kangee to touch Night Warrior's mind and draw upon his willingness to help save them.

Feeling his body stiffen, she pulled out of his arms and glanced toward the forest. He slid smoothly in front of her when two figures emerged from the line of trees.

Kangee sighed when she saw her cousins walking toward her and Night Warrior. Skye skipped between them. Kangee hurried forward and knelt down when her sister ran to her.

"Yes, Sweetheart. I will come tell a story." Each evening she gathered the children and told stories, assuming the role of storyteller. Though she was tired, body, mind, and soul, she wouldn't disappoint Skye or the others, and maybe, she could just lose herself in the wonders of her stories for just a little while.

"You okay, Kang?" Travers moved closer to her, his stance protective as he stared hard at Night Warrior.

Kangee hid her smile when Alex rolled her eyes. Alexis and Travers were her Uncle Albert's children. She sighed but sent her cousin a gentle smile. "I am fine, cousin." She switched to French as Travers spoke very little Lakota. She also deliberately used the family connection in her address to him, as he fancied himself in love with her.

"Skye was worried," Alex added. "She insisted we come find you."

"I'm glad you are here, Skye," Kangee said, taking her young sister by the hand. She glanced at Night Warrior. He was pale, and judging from the deep lines around his mouth, he was also in pain and exhausted. "We should return to the village," she suggested, feeling guilty for putting him through so much in one day.

He motioned them toward the forest. "Go."

She didn't press, knowing not to refer to his weakness in front of the others. She simply nodded, then turned and walked between her cousins who took great pleasure in their bickering.

Kangee vowed that, for at least a little while, she'd try to put everything that had happened that day aside.

****

Imprisoned within a rock of granite, the Shattered Soul, Ardong, danced victoriously. Freedom! After eons in his prison, he had a way out. He laughed, a wheezing, harsh cackle that bounced off the walls of his cell. The curse of the gods who'd imprisoned him would soon be broken.

He calmed, his demeanor fierce as he plotted and planned. Once he regained his freedom, he'd find and reclaim each and every shattered piece of his soul. He swirled in anticipation. And when he was once more whole, he, Ardong, son of Dragon, would rule the world.

He turned toward the woman who shared his cell. He needed her to leave. Very simple. All she had to do was leave, the same way she'd arrived. Yet, she refused to leave his prison and set him free. Ardong concentrated, waiting for the daughter to try again to find her mother. He'd touched the mind of a small girl-child. Then another, much older, had come seeking.

He'd drawn her voice into him as mortals drew air into their lungs. He'd filled himself with hope and satisfaction as he focused on her, and then followed that thin, narrow connection between daughter and mother.

Come to me, child. Come find your mother. Find her. Find me! Repeatedly he'd called to the sad, young voice seeking her mother, but she'd gone away. When she returned, he'd be ready.

Mother to daughter, prison to freedom, and the curse would soon be broken. Anticipation and triumph swirled through him as he probed and searched for the daughter, for that connection he'd use brutally.

Slowly, he sniffed it out. "Yes. Yes." She fought him and instinctively closed her mind to his, but her fear fed him and gave him strength.

"Leave her be. You will not touch her." The shout came from the woman, and the tenuous connection between him and Kangee broke.

Anger spewed from him in a wall of flame. He hurtled himself against the walls, then whirled around to the SpiritWalker called Eagle Woman. The woman had, while seeking sanctuary, burst into his rocky prison. Her body was one with his, merged with him and the rock, yet they were as separate as night and day. She stood proud in one corner of his cell. A thin aura of blue surrounded her, shielding her from the evil that oozed from him like pus from a wound.

"You will not use my children." Her voice was strong and determined.

"Foolish woman. Free me. I give you this last chance. Free me, and I will spare your daughter." His shrill command echoed and ricocheted off the cool stone walls. The woman drew herself, her heart, her soul, her essence of life into a tightly protected ball as he whirled and flung himself at her like a windstorm. He probed and searched for chinks in her protective shield.

"My daughter cannot free you. Only I have the power to do so," she said even as he pounded her with his fury.

The fact that she was right infuriated him. How dare this mortal defy and deny him. He was immortal, son of Dragon. He was cunning. He was smart. The woman was merely human, even with the gifts the god's had bestowed upon her race.

Ardong swelled in an attempt to smother the SpiritWalker. "You cannot stop what you began," he said, the glee back in his voice. "Leave. Set me free and be done with it."

The woman remained silent as though conserving strength. Ardong flung his huge, monstrous fist of darkness into the wall of rock and screamed. The ground beneath him shook and trembled. A tiny fracture shot up one side of the rock and branched out into hundreds of web-thin cracks.

As it had done for eons of time, the cracks immediately knit back together, keeping him imprisoned. He shrieked again and again. More cracks, more mending, but the woman's presence had weakened the curse, and where before he could not touch or affect anything outside his prison, the evil of his nature leeched outward.

His freedom was so close. He tasted it, he felt it, he caught brief flashes of it each time the surrounding stone cracked. Agitated, angry, he stretched his spirit, pushed against the walls, but the woman was right. He might have glimpses of the world, could touch that world, connect with it in a way long denied to him, but he still needed the woman to break the curse completely. He needed her to willingly leave. Only then could he follow her out and reclaim the life taken from him so long ago.

Merged with his mind, the woman laughed softly. "I willingly sacrifice myself to keep you from going free, Ardong, Son of Dragon.

"No!" Gathering his resolve, his shattered hope, and the fury raging in him, he launched another attack, prepared to pit the strength of his will against that of the woman until he wore her down and she gave him his freedom.

He was immortal. The woman was human. Humans valued life, feared death. So he threatened, struck out at her. He called up the image of the girl-child who'd tried to find her mother, he echoed the voice of the other daughter searching for her mother.

He dug into the woman's mind, found image after image of her children, and turned them into bloodied images of death. The ground shook, and high above the battle in the boulder, flashes of light lit the heavens and thunder roared across the sky.

Eagle Woman cried out. "No! You cannot touch them."

"They will seek you out, and when they do, I will be ready. I tasted her fear, but she will return. How can she not? You are her mother." He laughed, the sound wild and manic.

"Leave if you do not wish me to seek her out and torment her with images of her mother." He hurled at the woman pictures of her torn and broken just to prove he could send to her children any image he liked.

Eagle woman screamed when a bloodied image of Kangee flashed across her mind, then abruptly fell silent when she understood it was a trick. "I will not leave."

She braced herself for another attack. The dark soul oozed evil, but she stood her ground.

"Woman! Break the curse of the ancients. You cannot win." His voice became a low, vibrating hiss. Swelling in size, his spirit filled each corner, every hollow and crevice of the prison. Striking out, he shot slimy, spears of dark daggers that shifted into writhing snakes that slithered, wormed, and crawled over her.

Braced for the vicious attack, Eagle Woman felt the snake-like creatures sliding over her aura. Thousands of tiny red eyes broke through the darkness, washing her in blood red slime as the dark soul oozed evil.

Instinct told her to flee. Instinct said she needed to leave and warn her people of the presence of the Shattered Soul. Instinct made her yearn to go to her children and hold them close.

Eagle Woman fought to keep her emotions tightly reined as Ardong slammed her with hatred-filled punches. How could she have been so foolish? One moment, she'd been fleeing the enemies attacking her family. She remembered taking on the form of an owl to save her son from a fatal gunshot wound, and then everything went hazy. She'd been hit, injured. She recalled flying through the air from the blow and hitting her head. And to save herself, she'd shifted and merged her body, mind, and soul into the boulder.

And broken the first rule of her race—free will.

To merge with another spirit, another life, without asking, without ascertaining free will, carried grave consequences. It mattered not that she'd had no way of knowing the boulder held within its walls a monster most believed to be just another legend. A myth.

"No myth, foolish woman." Fingers of darkness raked over her. "Real. And soon, I will be free." The voice of Ardong snaked into her mind, seeing and feeling all that was in her. He coiled tightly around her like a snake squeezing the life from his prey. "You are no match for me."

Eagle Woman blocked out the insidious voice, tamed the fear crawling through her mind and body. "I carry the blood of the ancients in my veins, the wisdom and teachings in my mind, and the love of the gods lives in my heart," she whispered the words. Her soul was light and pure whereas the evil entity hammering away at her knew nothing but hate and greed.

He was the dark to her light, the bad to her good. Legend said her people had been created to protect the earth from Ardong when he'd shattered his soul to escape judgment yet in her lifetime, she'd never encountered anything so purely evil.

Life beckoned and tempted, but she resisted. One thought. That was all it would take for her to be free from the stench of evil that choked her very soul.

Ardong laughed. The earth below her shook. "You grow weak. Return to your daughter. To your family. To your mate who searches for you. He calls. Go to him and free me. Let me taste the air, see the earth I once ruled."

"No," Eagle Woman shouted. "You will not go free."

Ardong's monstrous form surged into one long, writhing mass. Yellow oozed from large, round eyes with red gleaming from slit-like centers. "You will never again see your children.

Eagle Woman couldn't suppress the cry of pain at the thought of never seeing her children or her husband ever again.

"Yes," the evil voice of Ardong hissed. "Return to your grieving family. Does your mate not come to this very place searching for you? He calls to you. He is here now. See him. Hear how he suffers. Go to him." The voice of evil coated her mind like honey seeping from a hive.

Her husband. Her SpiritMate. Pain stabbed deep into her soul, and she held onto her soul stone worn on a thong around her neck so it rested against her heart. Eagle Woman pulled the love and light from it and used it to strengthen the protective light guarding her own soul, drawing on the strength of her love-bond to block her mind from her husband and keep him from finding her.

If he knew where to find her, he'd come. He'd sacrifice himself to be with her but they had children who needed him. Her actions had deprived her children of their mother, and she would not take away their father.

"Go to him. End this. Now."

"No," Eagle Woman said. "I will not set you free." The pain stabbing holes in her heart only strengthened her resolve. She drew herself tightly into a ball to protect herself for she knew the threat of evil to her own life was real. To remain within the rock with the trapped evil spirit meant eventual death—physically and spiritually—and it was one she had no choice but to accept.

The taunts, laughter, and threats continued to pierce her mind. She tried to separate herself from the evil spirit, but it did no good. Her spirit and his were firmly twined, twisted, and merged like sap trapped in the veins of a tree.

The cold, slimy breath of evil made her shudder. She could leave, flow right out of the rock, take back her human form, and return to her husband who was once again calling her name, his voice filling with pain. Her will wavered.

"Yes," the sly, desperate immortal soul of Ardong whispered. "He hurts. Ease his pain. Return to him. Return to your grieving children."

Pulling her heart and soul into a tighter ball, Eagle Woman withdrew into her light and grieved for the family she'd never see or touch again. And worse was the knowledge that her husband and children would never know what happened to her.

"Spare them," he whispered. Without warning, he struck out at her, his darkness thrusting into the wavering light of her soul.

Eagle Woman cried silent tears of regret. "I will not betray my people. I will not set you free." She repeated the words over and over. Not for her husband. Not her children. Not even for the unborn lives she carried in her womb and condemned to death.

Ardong roared, and his malevolent chill filled her as he leisurely fed off fear and guilt. He whirled, a storm of frustrated fury as he threw dark daggers of hate and rage into the bluish-white wall that protected her soul. Menace and hatred vibrated inside the stone prison.

Chapter Five

Conrad Cordell turned in a slow circle as he scanned the forest, his gaze sharp as he searched. *Where was she? Where was his wife?* She was here. He felt her presence, yet there was a barrier between them, one that had never been present before.

He fisted his hand around a green and black stone the size of a newborn baby's fist that hung from his neck. Warmth and the hum of life—her life—traveled from his palm, up his arm, and into his heart. He held the stone up to the weak afternoon light. Threads of gold glittered, like blood pulsing through veins.

Eagle Woman had given him the stone the day they'd merged their souls. He was as connected to her as his arm to his body. Always in the past, no matter how far away they were, he was able to reach her. But not today. Not since the attack that had taken her from him.

All he knew was that she was still alive. Eagle Woman, his beloved wife and the mother of his children, was alive, and that gave him hope. As long as she lived, he would not stop searching.

Dropping his heavy pack, he fell onto his knees. His leather breeches were filthy, his hair unkempt, and he couldn't remember the last time he'd bathed. For weeks, his sole focus had been on finding his wife.

"*Cœur de mon cœur*. Heart of my heart. Where are

you? Why do you not reach out to me?" His cries echoed across the treetops and ended on a sob that crawled from the deepest reaches of heart and soul. Without his beloved at his side, he wasn't sure he could survive.

He thought of their children. His son from his first marriage, Kangee, daughter of his heart, and the three sweet girls Eagle Woman had gifted him. Guilt for leaving his children ate at him. He'd left them in the care of his son and the boy's new wife. They were safe. Protected. Yet he felt as though he'd abandoned them. He glanced up into the thick cover of clouds. Would the sun ever shine again in his heart?

"Where are you, *cheri*?" His voice sounded dry as the leaves that crunched beneath his knees. He studied the area where, not long ago, death had stained the earth. It seemed like yesterday that he'd fought for his life in this very spot and saved his son from death. This place, that night, had also been the last time he'd seen his wife.

They'd been attacked, were battling for their lives when he'd shifted into the form of a wolf to save his son. Both he and his son had been shot. His wife had shifted into an owl to flee the ambush. He'd seen her, had been so sure she'd flown to safety.

He rubbed his aching forehead, then his hollow stomach. His body cried out for food and sleep. He couldn't remember when he taken care of either. The days and nights were a blur.

Once again, his sharp gaze pierced his surroundings, but no matter how many times he returned to this spot, he found nothing new. There just was no sign or clue as to what had happened to his wife.

Anger warred with despair. The enemy that had attacked his family, sent them fleeing into the forest had been paid to do so by his brother. The hurt, still raw, festered and rotted deep in his heart. He hadn't had time to take in the betrayal or to deal with the grief, anger or bitterness. William was dead, everyone else safe. Except Eagle Woman.

With his soul stone flat against his heart, he closed his eyes and sent his mind searching but was unable to find his beloved. He turned in a slow circle. This spot was the last place he'd seen her. It had to hold the key to her whereabouts.

The breeze, brisk and cool, carried a foul taint that had nothing to do with the residue of death that lingered. What it was or where it came from, he had no idea, but it was as though the entire area felt it. The ground was hard and cracked, and several shrubs were dead.

Conrad's gaze lingered on every tree, shrub, and boulder, some as tall and wide as a man. At the back of his mind was the fear that in her bird form, a predator had attacked her. Whenever they shifted shape, they were just as vulnerable as the being they became but he'd searched every branch, high to low, looking for an injured bird in case she'd been injured and was caught in the leaves or branches. But it had been weeks since the attack, and if she were still in the form of a bird, she would not be alive.

But he knew she wasn't dead. Staring into the treetops, unsure what to do or where to search, he noted that daylight was quickly fading. As soon as it was dark, he'd shift back into the form of an owl and search every campsite, every village he could find in case the Chippewa his brother had hired had captured her.

The swish of wings drew his attention. Two spotted vultures landed high in the tree, then hopped from branch to branch, moving downward and ever closer. At once, Conrad knew something was wrong for the behavior of the birds was not right.

He reached out, seeking information from them and hit a wall. Shocked and caught off guard, he realized that for the first time since becoming a SpiritWalker, he faced not one but two Shadowed Souls. His wife had been very clear and firm about their code of honor, of the responsibility that came with the power they commanded, so he knew what corruption did to one's soul.

"Show yourselves," he ordered when the birds continued to stalk him by jumping and flying from one branch, from one tree, to another. He drew his knife and widened his stance as the birds fell from their branches. They blurred and shimmered, and by the time they hit the ground, two warriors stood where two birds should have landed.

Conrad judged them both to be around his own age though time had not been kind to either man. The men were pale and gaunt in the face, their lips twisted, yet their bodies looked warrior-strong. But it was their colorless eyes that spoke of their choices in life. Eyes as colorless as their souls, he recalled his wife saying.

"What do you want?" Conrad shifted his weight to the balls of his feet in case they attacked.

"You." The Shadowed Soul's voice was a low rasp.

Conrad lifted a bushy brow. "Well, now, shall we

see about that?"

The two warriors circled him. The one who'd spoken began taunting him. "Where is your mate? Why is she not here with you? Call her."

Alert, prepared to defend or attack, he asked, "Why is my wife of interest to the condemned?" He recalled that Kangee's father was a Shadowed Soul. Could this be him? If so, what did the man want with him or Eagle Woman?

The smaller of the two warriors leapt forward. Conrad avoided the point of the man's knife and slashed the man's arm with his own knife, then danced out of the way.

"Call her. Or die." Both men charged.

He spun, catching one man with his foot and sending him sprawling. The other managed to nick his arm, ripping through the buckskin shirt he wore. The fight turned vicious.

"She doesn't love him."

"She watches him bleed. She can watch him die."

Their words made no sense, but Conrad was too busy defending himself. A low growl from his right startled him. He nearly dropped his weapon.

Another growl flanked his left. He glanced down to see two black wolves, hackles raised. Their growling turned to snarls with lips curled, fangs bared as each wolf lowered its head and crouched.

The Shadowed Souls backed away. "The fight is not over. If your woman loves you, she will return or you will die. Next time, we attack your children. None of you will be safe until she returns."

In the blink of an eye, each warrior shifted, this time taking wing as large ravens. The wolves sprung forward with jaws snapping, but the birds managed to escape unharmed.

The animals turned and stared up at Conrad as he sheathed his knife. Since becoming a SpiritWalker, his affinity with the creatures that roamed the earth had deepened, helped by his years trapping. He folded his arms and waited for he knew both animals well.

"I thank you for coming to my aid." He shifted to keep watch on the birds crowing high above. "Why are you here?"

Before him, the two wolves blurred, becoming black clouds that shimmered with colors of the earth before forming into a man and woman. "Your timing was perfect." He spoke the language of his wife's people.

"Good thing we arrived when we did." Bright Star walked over and stood shoulder to shoulder with her brother-in-law, her gaze focused on the birds high in the tree. "Shadowed Souls."

Nodding, Conrad folded his arms across his massive chest. "I've never encountered one." He noticed that the birds had once again dropped to the lower branches and were watching them.

Bright Star lifted her hands high, then made a sharp downward movement. The branch the birds perched upon broke. The ravens fluttered to a higher branch. Again and again, Bright Star went after the birds.

Sighing, Dark Star addressed his twin. "Enough games." Without moving his hands, he sent a strong blast of air into the tree that hurled the ravens out of the treetops and carried them away in the turbulent wind he created.

Conrad was impressed.

Bright Star rolled her eyes. "Show off."

"Time is short," Dark Star said then turned to Conrad. Like his sister, his eyes were shades of browns and golds with a hint of a deep, orange sunset. "You are to come with us."

"Not until I find my wife." Especially after his encounter with the Shadowed Souls. Wherever Eagle Woman was, she couldn't free herself. That had to be the only explanation.

Bright Star touched his arm. She wore a dark deerskin dress, and her long, blue-black hair cloaked her body. She was a younger version of his wife. "Grandmother sent us."

Grimacing, Conrad rested his hands on his hips. "Tell her I cannot."

"Your children need you," she said.

"My children need their mother." He turned away, brought his soul stone to his lips and drew in the reassuring warmth and hum of life.

Bright Star went after him and grabbed his arm. "They are in danger," she said firmly.

Conrad froze, then whipped around "The Shadowed Souls?" They had threatened to harm his children. Their taunts hadn't made sense, but if Bright Star said his children were in danger, he believed her. If grandmother sent them, then the threat was real.

"I will return at once." The guilt in his stomach sat like a lump of lard in his belly. How could he face them with his failure to bring their mother back to them?

"It is to Grandmother we go," Dark Star said.

Bright Star reached out and gripped Conrad's hands. "Trust Grandmother, brother-of-mine. She travels toward us even as we speak. We will join the rest of our family, then go to your children."

Conrad trusted the elder who was a powerful woman and SpiritWalker. Decision made, he grabbed his pack. "Let's go."

****

Night Warrior returned to the village exhausted, his limp more pronounced. The air carried the mixed aroma of wood smoke, pine, and remnants of meals cooked earlier.

Near the entrance, he caught scent of two guards hidden in the trees. He shook his head and entered. A quick scan revealed his mother sitting with her sisters and two other women in front of a fire several lodges away from where he stood.

Relieved to avoid his mother's overprotective fussing, he pulled aside the painted deerskin flap at the entrance to the lodge. The sound of laughter, light as air and sweet as a new spring day, caressed him and soothed his soul like a gentle morning mist.

Kangee.

He turned his head and found her, sitting on a tree stump across from his lodge.

Though three giant trees and broadleaf greenery shadowed her, he clearly saw the curve of her face, the long, slender nose, the firm mouth, and even the gleam in her eyes.

She sat in the storyteller's place of honor, the group of children sitting before her in hushed silence. Leaning against the doorframe of the lodge, he soaked in the sight of her and let her beauty and the sweetness of her voice ease the pain wracking his body. He shoved from his mind her face in a sphere of light, her sweet voice begging him to live. For the moment, he just wanted to enjoy, even accept, so he silenced the questions that plagued him.

He concentrated on the here and now. How could he not find a measure of peace in the intense animation of the woman or the innocent awe and wonder shining in each child's face? The laughter, the giggles, and the quick surprised gasps were contagious.

Without taking his eyes off the woman who'd suddenly become important to him, Night Warrior knew he was not the only adult drawn to the scene. Mothers and grandmothers stood or sat on woven mats in small clusters, forming an outer ring behind the children. Some talked as they divided their attention between their children and each other.

When one small toddler grew restless and started turning in circles on his bottom, his grandmother sat behind him and pulled the youngster into her lap, and without a word, the boy stilled, his attention once again on the storyteller.

The men hung farther back, gathered in lodge doorways or around fires that burned low.

It wasn't just the children who loved stories, especially scary ones told in the darkness. Night Warrior had to admit that Kangee had no trouble enthralling her audience, young and old alike. She was a gifted storyteller, possibly better even than his uncle, the old shaman, had been while alive.

Kangee stood and as she moved, her long, blue-black hair swung and swayed, a molten sheen of liquid beneath the round moon. She mesmerized him as she told the story of how the rainbow path was destroyed and pulled him into her vibrant world. Her voice cut off, and she reared back with one hand raised high.

A hush fell over not just the children but the adults as well.

Night Warrior found himself holding his breath, anticipation humming through him. Without warning, Kangee spun around in a complete circle, then brought her hand down, a hard slash through the air.

The youngsters nearest her gasped. Several children jumped to their feet, then tripped over those who'd remained seated. Good-natured giggling followed. Even he couldn't help but grin.

His gaze continued to follow the silky flow of her hair, the swing of fringe edging her deerskin tunic and skirt, the graceful movement of her arms as she acted out many parts of the story. Her sparkle held him enthralled. She wasn't just recounting a story passed on from grandfathers to fathers to children. She *was* the story, the emotion of it, the life it carried.

He was so in tune to her and focused on her that he saw beneath the image she projected to her audience. Shadows lurked deep in her eyes, and in her voice, he heard weariness. Though she laughed and appeared involved in her story, he sensed within her a desperate edge that had not been present before tonight.

Kangee's gaze swept her audience, lifted, and then found his. For one long moment, it seemed as though it was just the two of them, that she was telling him and him alone her story. She sent him a small knowing smile before lifting both hands high overhead, then dropping her head back and sending the ends of her hair sweeping across the back of her thighs.

Night Warrior's fingers itched to stroke her hair, feel the soft, glossy strands slide across his chest. He longed to hold her against him and breathe in her scent.

In one afternoon, her touch had forever been imprinted on his skin.

Her voice dropped to an alluring whisper as she resumed her seat and leaned forward, drawing all who listened deeper into her story.

He let her voice calm his heart and ease his pain. He relaxed, and the worst of the throbbing faded to a dull ache. As he did each evening, he allowed her voice to take him where he wasn't a wounded warrior any longer, but the man he'd been before. It amazed him that he didn't just see what she spoke of or hear what she wanted him to hear. He came alive in her story as though he shared the world her words created.

As a DreamWalker, he'd first believed it was his own gift that allowed him to experience her stories as though they were real. But he was beginning to believe it was something more. Much, much more. Today was proof that there was a deeper connection between him and his sad-faced woman.

When her voice faded, his eyes snapped open. The story was over. The children stood, and everyone moved toward their longhouses. A crowd of older children remained, begging for another story.

With the magic of her voice gone, the exhaustion that lived in him returned. His legs trembled and when he straightened, the vicious arrows of pain returned to shoot through thigh and chest. In his mind, he echoed the children's pleas not so much for the story but for her soothing voice and the time she gave him without energy-sapping pain.

As though she heard his thoughts, she snapped her head up and stared right at him. Despite the darkness, he had no trouble seeing the swirl of colors in her eyes.

For once, he didn't care that he should not have been able to see her this clearly, for her eyes, that strange blending of Mother Earth, fascinated him. Would his eyes change as well? He couldn't help but wonder whether he was a SpiritWalker?

He didn't see how it was possible, yet he couldn't ignore the facts. He'd survived multiple mortal wounds with the help of a SpiritWalker, and that had somehow changed him in such a way he suspected he might be one of them. But how? More important, why?

The answers will come. Be patient.

Night Warrior turned his head and saw a small, dainty woman walking toward him. "You know my thoughts?" he asked the healer when she joined him. Nothing surprised him anymore.

Blaze shrugged and flipped her long black braid over her shoulder. "We are connected."

As he met her gaze, Night Warrior saw the truth in the blazing blues with their strange yellow webbing. He once again heard the words she'd spoken to him— words that were burned into his mind.

You choose to live. You walked the path one takes when death is upon him. You stood at the brink of the Spirit World and beheld the power of all that is Wakan Tanka. All that is Great and Mysterious. Your life will never be the same. You've gone full circle, from life to death and now back to life. Live your life in the honor of our people and hold close to your heart the spirits who give life to your heart and soul.

Those words were never far from his thoughts and neither was the truth he tried hard to ignore. He had changed, and he wanted to know how and why.

"You've healed many others in this village. Why is

it that no one else has become whatever I am becoming?"

Blaze shrugged but held his gaze. "Perhaps they were not powerful shamans, or perhaps they did not walk through death to find life." She paused, as though deep in thought. "Death is powerful, as powerful as life."

She sighed. "Who is to know the truth?" She stepped closer, her hand reaching out to grip his good arm.

"You have been given what you need to walk upon your rightful path, yet you fight what you cannot hope to win."

Knowing she referred to his becoming a shaman, Night Warrior stared over her head. "I made my choice long ago." He kept his gaze trained on the darkness of the forest.

Blaze sighed again. "You travel a rocky path by your own choice." She turned to go, then stopped and once more commanded his attention with no more than a thought. "Listen to the voice that lives in your soul, your heart. Listen to it. Let it guide you and light the path of life that you are meant to live."

When he stepped back, she reached out and grabbed hold of his hands. Her eyes blazed with a hot, blue intensity. "Listen, Warrior. Listen and learn. Fulfill your destiny, walk the path that was always yours to take." With that, Blaze turned and walked away.

Night Warrior drew in a deep, harsh breath and fisted his hands as he forced his body to straighten to his full height. "I will not become a shaman," he said, his voice a low rasp. As soon as the words left his mouth, he realized he hadn't said that *he was not a shaman* as he normally said.

Shaken, he also realized that no matter how hard he fought, he was being forced into accepting the role of shaman.

Power created a thirst for more power.

Once, he'd been full of greed, seeking more, needing more. His past haunted him and dictated his future. Yet now, he was no longer a sturdy, strong warrior able to provide and protect his people.

So what did that make him?

The soft hoot of an owl above drew his attention. He found himself staring into the intense golden eyes of the bird sitting on the edge of the lodge. The bird flapped its wings, and a feather floated to him.

Night Warrior caught the twirling feather. *Shaman* echoed in his mind as soon as he touched the owl's gift.

The owl flew away, leaving Night Warrior stunned and speechless.

Chapter Six

Kangee battled to keep her fear and worry from edging into her voice as she narrated one last story to the older children left in the storytelling circle. Her movements felt stiff and forced, and to her own ears, she sounded flat and even shaky. But as she eyed her audience, she saw only rapt attention.

Tipping her head back, she glanced up into the branches above her head, then gasped and nearly stumbled when she spotted two silent vultures staring down at her. Light reflected from the fire pit between her and the first row of children made their eyes gleam red. One of them flapped its wings and let out a screech. She backed up, caught her heel on a root, and fell.

She had no doubt they were *Shadowed Souls.*

Above her, they hopped and flapped their wings. The children, thinking her fall was part of the story laughed. She stood and tried to hide her fear by adding the birds into her story. As she had done earlier that day, she used her abilities to aim a blast of wind at the vultures and, to the delight of the children, sent them head over tail through the trees.

Silence fell, and the children stared up at her expecting her to continue. Her legs shook so she sat on the stump with her hands clasped tightly together to hide her trembling. She tried to gather her thoughts but couldn't even remember what story she'd been telling.

A deep voice came to her rescue. "Caw. Caw." The children gasped, then giggled when Star Walker jumped out of the shadows behind Kangee. "What story should I tell?"

One young boy jumped to his feet. "How the Crow Turned Black?"

Grateful that her brother had come to her rescue, Kangee stood. "Star Walker has joined us. Who would like Star Walker to tell this story?"

Immediately, the twins jumped up and down. "Luc! Tell the story. Please." Their voices rang in unison. Kangee smiled in relief for no one told this particular story as well as their brother.

Two girls in the front row giggled and whispered, "*Monstre*."

Though sick with fear and worry, Kangee couldn't help choking on a small laugh as several other children repeated the French word for monster. A warm glow in her heart chased some of the shadows from her mind. The children in her brother's new home were getting to know him well. She indicated the seat of honor.

Luc Cordell, son of Conrad, took two giant strides, and without warning, he swooped low and grabbed a toddler sitting beside his elder siblings. The boy squealed. Star Walker growled. "Ze rug rats. Many rug rats. This *monstre* is hungry!" He spoke in a combination of Lakota and French.

Around him, the children laughed. Star Walker released the giggling boy and approached Kangee. Reaching out, he pulled her close with one hand. "Go. I'll finish. "

Her throat seized, so she nodded and with a wary

glance upward, she left the storytelling ring. Behind her, Star Walker jumped up onto the stump and spread his arms wide.

"Caw, caw, caw," he shouted as he flapped his arms up and down. Most of the children now knew Star Walker's exuberant style of telling a story. They stood and flapped their arms in the manner of the great black bird whose story was a favorite among children. The air filled with the call of the *wahpa tanka,* the large bird honored in tonight's tale.

When Luc lowered his arms and sat, the children settled quickly. Kangee rested her back against one of the trees. Exhaustion swept through her as she used her sharp eyesight to scan the branches. She didn't see the vultures, but if those birds had been the return of the Shadowed Souls, and she was positive they had been, then they could be anywhere, as anything—bird, insect, rodent. Shadowed Souls, like SpiritWalkers were free to shift into any shape and assume any form, the difference being that SpiritWalkers asked, Shadowed Souls took.

She returned her attention to her brother. Her gaze roamed the scene. There was nothing so sweet, so innocent as a child immersed in a world created especially for them. Not only did they follow the tale and learn the lessons in each story, but they experienced the story as though they were part of it.

Bodies tensed, then leaned forward with anticipation. Some squirmed, other shifted or held their arms folded tight to their chests or twisted their hands together. Even the small twitch of their fingers portrayed simple reactions and emotions.

"He is almost as good as you, *Mithan.*"

Kangee smiled faintly at Blaze. "Yes, he is good. Soon, he will have his own child begging him for stories."

Blaze cupped her still flat belly where new life grew. "Yes, I will enjoy that."

Kangee loved her new sister and admired her strength and abilities and wished she too had more to offer in the way of talents and gifts. She might have the eyes that marked her as a SpiritWalker but, so far, little else. Grandmother, and her own mother, had both told her that, in time, her special gifts would be revealed. She sighed. She didn't have time. Her mother didn't have time. She needed help now.

"Kangee?" Blaze's voice drew Kangee back to the present. She met her sister's concerned gaze. "What is wrong? What happened when you were telling your story?"

Kangee shook her head. "I'll explain later." Blaze knew nothing about Shadowed Souls as, up until a few weeks ago, she hadn't even known that she was a SpiritWalker. To fill the awkward silence, she said, "I feel as though I'm trapped in a nightmare." She hugged her arms to her chest. "Did you talk to Star Walker? Will he go find father tonight?"

Blaze nodded. "We leave after everyone is in bed." She reached out and drew Kangee to her. "We will find your father and bring him back."

Kangee watched the children and her brother without really seeing them. "We need Grandmother. Tell him this." Whatever she had faced was beyond what any of them could handle, including her father. He was a SpiritWalker by marriage, but he didn't have the knowledge or skills to deal with something that evil.

"Do not worry, *Mithan*."

"What's wrong, Kang?" Travers asked as he and Alex joined the two women.

Kangee shook her head, unwilling, even unable to voice the events of the day. She only wanted to tell everyone what happened once so she forced herself to smile.

Before she could change the subject, Travers grinned. "Heard what you did today—" A sharp jab from Alex stopped him. "Ow—" He subsided when the three women glared at him. "Sorry," he muttered.

Alex rolled her eyes. "My brother doesn't know when to keep his mouth shut."

Kangee sighed. Travers looked miserable. He was sweet, but at times, his mouth ran ahead of his mind. "It's okay, Trav. Let's not talk about it."

Blaze patted her shoulder. "Star Walker and I are going to go find her father when he is finished with his story."

Alex frowned. "My father and brother should be back soon." She lifted worried eyes. "Neither of them have heard about William yet. Everything has changed."

Each turned pensive, for Albert, the head of the Cordell family had left, along with his eldest son, to take the furs to the trading post and to purchase new supplies. He'd been gone when William had tried to kill Conrad and his family. It was because of William's greed, hate, and resentment toward her father that her mother was missing and her father gone. Williams's betrayal had hurt all of them.

"You're right, Alex. Everything has changed." And she didn't like it.

Travers cleared his throat and stabbed his toe into the dirt. "Nice story back there." Though he grinned, she saw the uncertainty in his eyes.

"It is one of the favorites of the children in our village. The twins and Skye love it." She sent him a look of gratitude.

Leaning forward, Travers whispered, "You can tell me a story anytime."

Kangee snorted, then rolled her eyes, but before she came up with one of her pithy comments, Alex jabbed him in the ribs. Again.

"You *are* a pitiful story, Trav." Her eyes gleamed wickedly in the firelight. "Did you hear what happened on the hunt today?" Alex, dressed as a trapper in her buckskin shirt and pants, addressed Kangee.

"Shut it." Travers shoved his sister.

Kangee lifted a brow as her cousin shifted from one foot to the other, a sure sign he was embarrassed, which meant that he had done something worthy of being teased and tormented over, in a loving, familiar way. "What happened?"

Grinning widely, Alex bent her knees to examine a small tear in Traver's breeches. "He tripped over a log and fell," she murmured. "Heard it was wider than a man's shoulders." She straightened. "Made enough noise to scare every living creature and wake the moon."

Travers scowled. "Thanks for telling everyone, sis."

Kangee raised her eyebrows, and her jaw dropped. "Travers. A log? How can you trip over a log?"

"Just did," he muttered as he dug his toe into the dirt.

Alex shook her head with dismay. "Travers, you have to pay attention. You can't stroll through the woods with your mind filled with cotton." Her gaze cut to Kangee. "Or silly dreams—"

Eyes narrowed, Travers put his hand over his sister's mouth. "Shut it, A-lex-see-us," he said, drawing out Alex's given name.

Alex, who despised being called Alexis, punched him in the arm.

"Hey!" he yelped.

Nearly a head taller than her younger brother, she leaned in close. "Say it again, and I will knock you onto your ass," she promised sweetly.

Travers jumped back, then jammed his hands into the pockets of his breeches. "Geez, sis. Just jesting." He spun around to leave.

The dark look in Alex's eyes told her that the woman not only could but would flatten her brother on the ground. Taking pity on the man, Kangee reached out and pulled him back. "We're just teasing you, Trav."

Kangee shook her head at her cousins. They shared the same father yet were as different as night from day. She loved them both, but it was Alex she admired and looked up to as a big sister.

Thinking back to the day when the woman first joined their family, Kangee was amazed at the changes. Alex had been pale, thin, and distrustful of everyone. And filled with hate and resentment. But she'd learned fast, toughened faster, and in two years, embraced a life far different from the brothel she'd been raised in before running away.

Travers on the other hand hadn't grown into

himself yet. Though he was often a considerable pain in her side, he was a sweet boy. Just awkward and unsure of himself.

Someday, he'd make someone a good husband. But not her. She knew he thought himself in love with her, but Travers wasn't her SpiritMate. His soul did not complete and complement her own.

He would love her more than life itself and he'd cherish her and any family they created, but Kangee wanted a marriage like her mother had found with Conrad.

She frowned as she thought of her birth father. It had been a long time since he'd come to mind. He'd left their village just after she'd turned six and had never returned so she barely remembered him.

He'd been a distant father, too busy being an important warrior to bother with a small girl. No one in her village talked of him, and no one missed him. Including her. She thought it was sad to not miss her father, but how can one miss what one never had? The day her mother had introduced her to Conrad Cordell, the man had become her father in every way that was important.

Kangee tuned out the conversation between her cousins and Blaze. She tried to focus on her brother's story, but she was just too unsettled. The events of the day consumed her mind and threatened to swallow her whole.

Her gaze shifted and roamed across the peaceful village and, once again, latched onto Night Warrior. Here was the one warrior who not only drew her attention but also held it. She frowned. After several weeks in the village, why had they suddenly become so aware of each other?

Up until today, they'd never really spoken to one another. She shared the lodge belonging to his family, but other than a nod here or there, they'd had no contact, except in her dreams. Yet, she'd been very aware of him, especially once he'd been able to leave his sick bed.

Now, she sensed his presence no matter whether he stood in plain sight or was somewhere in the immediate vicinity, shielded by the forest. The air carried more than his scent. It carried the feel of him, the hum of life, of energy that he radiated.

He watched her. As she now watched him. Physically, he stood a good head taller than most of the men in the village. He wore his hair long, loose, and flowing. The wind pulled and tugged at the fine strands, drawing her attention to shoulders that were as broad as the trunk of the ancient trees.

Kangee studied his features—the piercing dark eyes that saw far too much, strong, straight nose with no hawk-hook like so many of the men in the village. His cheeks were bronzed by the sun and smooth but for the lines of pain that cupped his mouth. Stoic. The face of a proud man, yet earlier, he'd been gentle and caring.

Her gaze shifted to his taut jaw, then down his chest, over the healing wounds, and scanned his rock-hard belly. She held her breath as her gaze traveled over the flap of his breechclout.

As though aware of her perusal, he shifted and planted his feet farther apart, which revealed strong, muscular calves and thick thighs. The gash on his injured thigh seeped with fresh blood. She wanted to go to him and bathe his wound. And make the stubborn man rest. But mostly, she wanted just to be close to him, like earlier when he cradled her close and surrounded her in his scent. She'd felt safe.

This, she thought, as she lifted her gaze back to his face, was a man who drew her like a moth to the moon.

Especially at night.

Each evening, during the darkest part of the night, she dreamed of him and he came to her as a strong, healthy warrior. He was confident and he was whole, a proud warrior in his finest garments and a feathered headdress that proclaimed his status to all. During her dreams, he held her close against his solid, unblemished chest. His arms were strong yet gentle, and his voice soothed and comforted. And sometimes, he kissed her tenderly. Just thinking about her dreams sent heat flooding into her face.

As though she'd called his name, Night Warrior's head whipped around and their gazes met and held once more.

Kangee sucked in her breath, tried to turn away, but couldn't. This warrior, with his eyes, had drawn her down into a long, deep tunnel. She tried to break contact, but something flashed between them, a light that sparked like a star in the night sky exploding into tiny fragments.

His brows rose, as though he too had seen that flash and knew her thoughts. The air between them vibrated as strong wills clashed and neither broke contact. What did this mean, her attraction to him, her gut-deep awareness? Was it his troubled and tormented soul that drew hers, or was it something deeper? Stronger.

She rubbed the chill off her arms, refusing to break

off what had turned into a silent staring contest, a challenge.

Why do I want you, Warrior? She asked the question in her mind and fought the urge to go to him, offer words of comfort, touch him as he touched her in her dreams. She wanted to ease his pain and reassure him that he was not a helpless warrior to be pitied.

Why do you see me as a whole man when I am not?

Kangee gasped, and her eyes widened. *You cannot know my thoughts. You are not SpiritWalker. We are not related.*

Normally, blood ties allowed people of her race to communicate with one another silently. Most often, it was a sensing of the other's emotion more than actual conversation, with exception of SpiritMates who were bound—heart, soul, and mind.

For just a moment, he looked as stunned as she felt, as though he hadn't realized that she'd *heard* his response. Then he sighed so deep, it vibrated throughout her heart and soul. *We share dreams. Perhaps our dreams created this path.*

Horribly embarrassed, Kangee tore her gaze from that of the wounded warrior. How could he know of her dreams and how she often found herself weaving a romantic setting around the two of them?

He couldn't know whenever he wasn't looking in her direction that she watched him, fully appreciating the width of his shoulders painted a warm bronze by the sun, the narrowness of his waist and hips, and his strong buttocks that peeked out when his breechclout swung side to side. And how many times had her fingers twitched with the need to touch him, to dig into his firm, bronzed flesh? He couldn't know what she dreamed.

Low laughter rolled through her mind. *I know more than you think, skuya, sweet one, for I am a DreamWalker. I come to you each night. You comfort me as much as I comfort you. I did not realize you were aware of our dreamtime.*

"Stop it," Kangee said. Realizing she'd spoken aloud, she subsided into embarrassed silence as her family stopped all conversation around her and were looking at her.

A small group of children ran up to her. "Brother Dragon! Tomorrow, will you tell the story of Brother Dragon?" Andre and Anika spoke together.

"We have no Brother Dragon story." This came from a tall, gangly boy who stood a bit back from the other children.

"Our tribe has Brother Dragon." The twins turned to glare at the older boy.

Kangee held up a hand to stop the twins from protesting. She addressed the frowning boy. "Our people have many Brother Dragon stories. Tomorrow, I will tell how he came to be."

It amazed her that these children could so easily accept that, while she and her sisters were Lakota, same as they, they were also SpiritWalkers and very different.

The boy nodded respectfully. "I will come to listen to this story." He walked off, his shoulders held stiff with pride.

Kangee hid her smile. Five nights ago, he'd sat among the rest of the children. Last night and tonight, he'd chosen to stand on the perimeter of the circle. Soon he'd leave childhood behind for the warrior's world, but right now, he was both boy and man.

With everyone heading for their lodges, Kangee went to her brother. "You will leave and find *mon père*? I need to talk to him. It is important." Her throat closed up, and her stomach seized. She didn't want to speak of the evil, of the frightening visions or the Shadowed Souls. Not until her father was here, with her.

Star Walker reached out and pulled her close. "I heard about the storm and the tree—and Skye."

"There's more." Kangee pulled back. Tears threatened and the words tumbled out. "I saw Shadowed Souls and a monster. With our mother. She is trapped—"

A tug on her skirts stopped the flow of words. Skye held up her hands. Kangee bent and gathered her sister close, resting her check against the child's baby-soft skin.

Star Walker gave his sisters a hug. "Stay calm. I will leave and find our father."

Kangee watched him walk away with Blaze. They faded into the shadows. She knew they would go up to the cave hidden on the ridge of land where they shared Blaze's cave. From there, they'd shift into eagles or owls and soar over lake and forest together.

"Tired, Skye?" She ran her hands through her youngest sister's silky strands of hair, gently combing out tangles.

Skye's answer was to relax into her sister, letting her small body conform and her eyes close. Around them, voices were hushed as everyone made their way back to their lodges. A small group of men still sat around a fire, the gentle breeze carrying the scent of tobacco from their pipes.

A lump rose in her throat as the scent made her think of her father, and a prick of yearning brought tears to her eyes. Though he wasn't her blood father, over the years, he'd earned the respected title of father and it was her love, and admiration for Conrad Cordell that set her standards high in her search for a husband.

Her arms tightened around her young sister. The worry and fear she'd worked so hard to hide while telling her story returned as she searched the sky, then the thick undergrowth of brush. Did the darkness hide the Shadowed Souls? Not everyone could shift shape for it was a gift given by the spirits of the Earth. But Shadowed Souls took and stole.

They could be hidden in the shadows, watching. She shivered as she turned away from the forest. In her arms, Skye shifted. "Father comes." Skye's sleepy voice was a wisp of sound, but Kangee drew comfort from it.

"Thank you, *Mithan*." There was no doubt that Skye *knew* her father was on his way for the little girl's gifts and talents were many. Unlike Kangee who wasn't so gifted. She was plain, ordinary, couldn't even shift shape to help search for her mother.

Exhaustion was making her feel sorry for herself, so she shoved aside her feelings of worthlessness and gave thanks for her sister and her ability to soothe and comfort.

Turning to the twins, she pointed. "Time for bed." She held up a hand to forestall comments. "Do not argue. Take Skye with you. Your sister is very tired."

Skye shook her head. "Stay. With you."

Kangee eased Skye's clinging arms from her. "I'll be right in, sweetheart. Go now." Skye went reluctantly with the twins.

Taking a few minutes to be alone, to calm and center herself, she walked through the village, tuning out the sounds of families getting ready for bed. She tipped her head back and stared up into the sky. The clouds were gone, leaving the heavens studded with stars.

The moon hung low and heavy, bathing her in its silvery light. Lifting her hands, she silently prayed to Grandmother Moon and hoped that her own grandmother was also gazing up at the moon and would sense her granddaughter's need. Two birds, flying low and silent flew over her. Each dipped a wing toward her.

"Find father," she told them, knowing the birds were Blaze and her brother. "Find father and bring him back." A soft hoot above her head drew her attention. She spotted a third owl.

Help is on its way.

The words echoed in her mind. Kangee didn't question whether she'd heard it or not. The connection between man and the animal world was not so far apart. One needed only to listen.

She nodded to the bird, remembering the feather that she'd caught just that morning. It seemed so long ago. Feeling measurably calmer, she headed to her lodge.

Inside, she found her sisters sleeping on one large pallet on the floor. It didn't matter that there were two above ground beds, her young sisters slept easier on furs covering the floor. And so did she.

Kangee slid beneath the fur covers, careful not to disturb the girls as she settled on her back so she could stare up into the night sky from one of the smoke holes in the roof of the longhouse. The clear sky and bright stars grew larger as they twinkled.

After a while, she turned to her side and closed her eyes but sleep eluded her. As she lay there, trying to keep fear at bay, she heard Night Warrior's shuffling gait as he entered the lodge and made his way to his pallet.

Knowing he was in the lodge close enough for her to breathe in his scent made her feel safe. She thought of seeking solace in her dreams. Normally, like telling her stories, she loved dreaming, even the thought of dreaming. Her dreams were vivid. Colorful. She created them and even controlled them, directing the action as though she stood on the outside and watched. But all that had happened that day made her afraid to close her eyes.

It had nothing to do with Night Warrior's knowledge that she dreamed of him or the fact that he was a DreamWalker and able to enter her dreams. She feared that if she closed her eyes and dreamed, evil would find her as it found her earlier that day.

****

Ardong stretched out tentacles of darkness, reaching, seeking. The night belonged to him. The taint of his evil leached out of the stone. Life around him shrank back and shuddered.

Kangee. He whispered the daughter's name. *Come to me. Come to your mother.*

The power of his voice rode the back of the reluctant wind. What was available to the weak-minded SpiritWalkers was available to him. He was immortal. Powerful. Fathered by Dragon, who'd been given life by Air, Earth, Fire, and Water. The four were as one. One mother. One creator.

He was of the gods, and soon, he'd be free to search out the rest of his soul. And then he would take his place as ruler of the world. Putting aside his plans of vengeance, he concentrated on the girl.

Chapter Seven

Kangee tossed and turned as images skittered through her dreams like leaves kicked and flung by a child throwing a tantrum. She moaned, a low, raspy sound deep in her throat.

The images, those brief, gut-wrenching images of her mother that were gone as fast as they appeared— her mother huddled in a tight ball, the light around her faint and flickering in the shadows of something so dark, so frightening.

She wanted to flee but couldn't leave her mother. She inched forward. "Ina." She wanted her mother to look at her, show herself, but the bluish light grew dimmer.

"Ina, don't go!" She ran toward her mother but barely moved, as though she were swimming against a rushing stream of water.

"Go to her," a voice encouraged. The barriers lifted, and there was her mother, huddled in a blue ball of light.

In the darkness, something moved. It was no more than a sense of something, as though whatever hid in the shadows had no real substance. Yet it was real, the threat to her mother very real, and completely terrifying.

Slowly, she made her way through the inky darkness toward her mother, then came to an abrupt halt when the stench of rotting fish left on the banks of the lake during the hot summer sun struck her.

Horrified, she gasped when thin, dark fingers reached toward her. The air grew so thick she had trouble breathing, the dark, pulsing, and vibrating mass smothering her in—

Evil!

Kangee stumbled back, trying to put as much distance as she could between herself and the raw, hungry, living entity. Something cold and slimy wrapped around her shoulders, pinning her arms to her side.

"Go to your mother. See her. Free her." The voice rolled through her mind, smooth and silky, dripping with sweetness as it enticed her toward her mother.

Unsure, afraid, she didn't know what to do. As desperate as she was to save her mother, something wasn't right.

Her mother. Why did her mother not speak or come to her or fight the hideous monster?

"Go to her." A hard shove to her back sent her stumbling toward the blue light.

She shuddered, and her legs shook. The sickly-sweet smell mingled with rotted flesh turned her stomach, but it was the insidious hissing, buzzing, and that low bone-weakening hum of hate that had her fighting the urge to throw up.

"Ina?" She inched forward. "Ina?" Her voice sounded far away and echoed in her ears as though she both watched what was happening and lived it. She stepped close to her mother and reached out. She was so close. Just a bit more, and she'd touch her mother. Yet, she paused and pulled her hand back.

Why did her mother not respond?

"Go to her, child. She is your mother. Free her. Take her with you from this place. Go! Go!"

The insidious voice relentlessly wrapped her in its dark, dank fingers of blackened sludge. Thinner strands shot up and began twisting and twining around her, weaving a web that made her gag. She needed to get out. Go to her mother and get them both out. She reached out, but before her fingers touched the blue light, it retracted, growing smaller.

"No, chunksi, *my daughter." Eagle Woman's command demanded to be obeyed.*

Kangee stepped back, knowing she needed help.

Night Warrior.

His name shot into her head. He was a shaman, no matter what he said. His powers were great. He'd come if she called, if she found him. He was always there, in her dreams. Turning to go, Kangee cried out when her feet refused to move

She glanced down, horrified at the swirls of darkness moving up her legs, twisting around and around so she couldn't see or move.

"Go to her. Only then will you be free." Over and over the command pelted her. It hissed and growled. Grotesque fingers, shiny, like a clear lake that reflected the light, reached out, but what shone back was unspeakably evil. Dark begetting dark as the web of evil surrounding her began to spin.

"Ina," she screamed and held her hands up to ward off the suffocating blackness descending upon her. Without warning, a creature darker than the deepest shadows appeared with eyes red as blood. Hatred and pure evil buzzed in her ears and bit at her skin like

thousands of angry bees. Kangee fought the monster, trying to escape its gripping hold.

"Who are you?" she sobbed.

"I am Ardong, son of Dragon, banished from your world. Soon, I will be free and all shall know the name of Ardong." The evil spirit laughed with absolute glee. "Go to her. Save your mother. Free her."

"How?" She held her aching head and sank to her knees.

"Take her. Take her. Take her." The words became a loud crashing sound like the roar of thunder overhead.

Cringing, cowering, she sobbed, unable to move under the crushing weight of evil.

Suddenly, she was free. Kangee stumbled to her feet and ran to her mother. They had to leave. "Ina, let's go. We have to go." She reached out for her mother.

"No! Do not touch me. You must go. Get out of here. Wake up! Wake up, chunksi*!"*

The panic in her mother's voice stopped her. She didn't understand. "I came for you. We must leave this place."

She saw her mother's face inside the bluish bubble, saw the tears streaming down her face.

"I cannot leave," her mother said. "If I leave, I free evil. Now go. Do not look back. Do not return." Her image faded.

"Touch her, child. Take her from this place."

The harsh, whispering voice, drowned out her mother's. Kangee put her hands over her ears. "I won't leave you. Mother!" She drew in a deep breath, stretched out her hand, ready to grab and run.

"No! Do not touch her!"

Night Warrior!

Kangee spun around with a cry of relief when she spotted him hovering at the edge of her nightmare. "Come help me."

He held out his hand. "Come with me," he commanded.

"Ina is here. My mother is here. Help me." She begged him to come to her aid. "Please. Help me. We cannot leave her."

"Come to me. You must come to me!"

Kangee tried to go to the young shaman, but evil curled itself around her legs. The more she fought, the harder the grip of the monster until it slithered up her body, then leaped high above her head, a fist of darkness ready to hammer into her.

More afraid than he'd ever been before, Night Warrior entered Kangee's nightmare wholly and rushed toward her. "You cannot remain here." He wrapped his arms around her. She fought him.

Evil wrapped around them, dragging them into the darkness. Night Warrior used every bit of knowledge he had of dream worlds to take them out of the darkness.

Awake, his heart pounding, sweat pouring from his head, Night Warrior knelt on the floor beside Kangee. Her nightmare clung to him. The stench of rotting flesh and pus throbbed in his nostrils and coated the back of his throat.

Though he'd taken them both away from the evil spirit, Kangee thrashed, kicked, and fought against him.

Night Warrior inhaled, allowing her sweet scent to chase away the horrid stench of evil.

"You are safe, *skuya*. Wake now." He dare not

release her until she was awake and aware. Against his bare chest, her heart pounded hard. His jumped in tune to hers.

Still in her mind, he heard her silent screams and knew that while she was no longer in danger, the sickly stench of her nightmare continued to shroud her mind. Fearing he could not hold onto her for much longer or that her screams would break free of her mind and wake everyone, Night Warrior, for the second time that night deliberately entered the dream world, choosing a dreamscape that had once been a favorite, a place he'd often taken—

He shoved all thoughts of that young girl from him. Kangee mattered, just Kangee. In his mind, sunlight, blue skies, and a green meadow replaced the lodge. To his right, came the sound of water. He turned, dived into the small pond, and emerged beneath a waterfall.

He allowed the cold liquid to wash over him and cleanse his mind. Then he reached for Kangee's mind and pulled her into his dream beneath the icy fall of water.

Her screams stopped when the water poured over her head. She gasped, her eyes wide open and wild.

"Safe. You are safe."

She choked, gagged, and her chest heaved as she held onto him. "Where am I?"

"Somewhere safe," he whispered against her ear, turning them so the water no longer pelted them but flowed behind them, showering them with a gentle spray.

"You came for me." She lowered her head to his chest and just stood with her hands on his shoulders, her body pressed against his.

His lips brushed the top of her head, and his arms slid around her waist. "Yes, I came."

As he had every night since her arrival in his village. The ease with which he could enter her dreams both scared him and amazed him. He hadn't DreamWalked since his youth, but now it felt as if he'd never stopped. It consumed even his days, those long days spent in his bed when he'd created special places for them so that when he went to her during the night, he could take her away from her pain and suffering. But this was the first time he'd brought her here, the first time he'd been back himself since the day he'd vowed to never DreamWalk again.

"Where are we?" She repeated, her gaze scanning the pond, the gently swaying trees and rich, green grass blanketing the earth.

Night Warrior didn't need to look anywhere but at the woman he held. He knew every intimate detail of this place because it was his creation—his dreamscape.

"We are in one of my dream worlds. I created this place a long time ago." Memories of the past shadowed his mind and heart.

Around them, birds sang, water splashed, and insects hummed.

Kangee put one hand on his unblemished chest. "It's so peaceful," she said, dipping her fingers into the water. "It beautiful. And so real."

She closed her eyes and ran her hands though her hair to allow a gentle breeze to tug at the dark strands that floated on top of the turbulent pond. After a long moment, she turned so that she could lean against him.

He wrapped his arms around her and pulled her tight, his hands splayed across her abdomen. He rested his cheek against hers and drew in her sweet scent.

"We are in your dream." Wonder filled her voice, and her eyes were wide as she shifted so that she could see him.

"Yes." His lips moved against her soft skin. He tipped her chin up and watched sunlight bath her face and make her eyes sparkle like colored stars. Desire for her slid through his body as his mouth touched the corner of hers.

Twisting around, she wrapped her arms around his neck and surrendered herself to his gentle kiss and explorations. His hands stroked her back and moved beneath her curtain of hair as he pulled her closer.

When the kiss ended, she buried her face in his neck. "I don't want to go back. I wish we could stay here."

Her plea punched him in the gut and drove the air from his lungs. He'd heard those words before. Another dream. Another time.

"No!" He wasn't sure if he yelled the word, and if he had, was he speaking to her or to himself. "We are leaving. Now."

She stumbled out of his arms and nearly slipped on the fine, sandy bottom of the pond. "Wait. What did I do?"

Realizing that he'd overreacted, Night Warrior took a deep breath and shook his head. "I am sorry. You did nothing wrong." He took her hand in his, then glanced around, part of him waiting, wondering if the girl from his past, the one who'd died while here with him was still here? If so, would she show herself or did she blame him for her death, as he blamed himself.

"What is it, Warrior?" Kangee, without releasing

her hold on Night Warrior, was scanning the scenery.

"This place." He shook his head. "I don't know why I brought you here. It's not a happy place for me."

She cupped his face in her hands, forcing him to meet her gaze. "Someday, you will tell me why a place this beautiful, this perfect, makes you sad."

He saw only patience and understanding and realized then that he could tell this woman anything, that she would not condemn him as he'd condemned himself so long ago.

"Yes. I will tell you the story of an arrogant young warrior and a beautiful, sweet girl." He sighed. "Ready?"

Kangee wrapped her arms around his neck. "No. But you are right. We cannot stay here."

"We are back. Wake." Night Warrior's hushed voice pulled Kangee from her dreams.

She opened her eyes. The bright sunlight and waterfall were gone. Darkness once again surrounded her. Panic gathered in her mind until she realized she was on her pallet of furs, on the floor of the lodge. Just another nightmare.

She shuddered. Though the terror had eased, the nightmare left her feeling limp, raw, and achy.

She glanced around. The darkness, broken by the faint sheen of moonlight spilling into the lodge from the smoke holes in the ceiling, revealed the warrior stretched out beside her. His eyes glittered in the darkness, and his breath fanned her face. She inhaled his scent.

"You are safe. A dream," Night Warrior whispered.

A chill shot through her, and her stomach twisted

in knots. "No, it was real."

So real, her shattered mind balked when she tried to focus on the images and meanings. The rawness of her throat confirmed that she'd screamed, over and over yet no one else in the lodge had been awakened. How was that possible? "My mother was there. You were there—"

"Just a dream." Night Warrior's voice came out a harsh hiss of air, but he pulled her closer. "Just a dream," he repeated as though trying to convince them both.

Kangee shook from head to toe. She sat up and so did he. She leaned against him, needing to touch him and ground herself in him. Each breath hurt, and each beat of her heart pounded like the furious river water spewing rocks out of its path.

"You were there," she whispered. "You saved me. Took me away from—"

From what? Fear dried her mouth. She couldn't say it. Her eyes begged him to tell her that he'd been there, had seen her mother trapped by something so evil she couldn't put a name to it.

Not true. She rose onto her knees and faced him, staring into his shadowed eyes. "Say it," she demanded in a low, harsh whisper. "Tell me you saw her and an evil monster."

He gripped her shoulders hard. His left hand traveled up to cup the side of her neck. "I saw both," he admitted.

She slid down, her legs beneath her. "What does this mean? Why did my mother refuse to leave that place?"

"I do not have the answers you seek, *skuya*."

131

"I need to go see if my brother has returned."

Night Warrior grabbed her arm and kept her from standing. "You cannot go there at night. You are not familiar with the path."

Kangee held her tears at bay. Crying would not solve anything, and she was so tired of feeling helpless and sad, but she was so scared that her chest ached and felt as though it were going to burst.

Night Warrior nuzzled her ear. "Breathe, *skuya*. Breathe. We will find the answers."

She swiped at one lone tear that escaped. How was it possible for this evil spirit to invade her dreams and threaten her very life? "You will help me?"

He closed his eyes. "I do not think I have a choice." He opened his eyes and met hers. "Not since the day you begged me to live. For you."

Kangee frowned, but he held up his hand. "Another place, another time."

"Another story," she finished, "that you will one day tell me." She pressed her fingers to her trembling lips. Faint light from the embers of the fire in the center aisle of the longhouse flickered.

She wasn't a DreamWalker like Night Warrior, but she was a storyteller and storytellers were often dreamers. During the day while doing boring tasks, she'd spin a tale in her mind, then continue the story at night while she slept. Her dreams were vivid, lifelike. But tonight was different. It was no ordinary dream or nightmare.

Night Warrior shifted. "I will return to my own bed."

Their gazes met and held. She wanted to ask him to stay but didn't. She'd asked much of this warrior already. Her eyes were full of concern and worry as he limped back to his own pallet.

Before she could settle back on her furs, a loud, long howl rent the air. Another and another followed it.

Kangee cried out. She knew that song, that tone. At once, she jumped up and pushed through the entrance to the lodge. Night Warrior called to her, but she ran out into the night.

"*Ate! Mon père.*" Her father had returned.

Outside of the lodge, a slight movement drew her attention. Three wolves stood beneath the trees. She ran toward them. Immediately, the animals blurred and shimmered. She blinked, and Star Walker, Blaze, and her father were striding toward her.

She threw herself at her father, wrapping her arms tightly around his thick, bear-sized neck. With a sob of relief, she buried her face in his shoulder, inhaling, seeking comfort in his scent of cedar, tobacco, and wood smoke.

Fisting her hands into the soft, well-worn buckskin shirt he wore, she lifted her head and stared up into her father's shadowed eyes. His image blurred as silent tears continued to fall. "*Ina…*"

Conrad tenderly wiped the tears from his daughter's face, then lowered his head until he rested his forehead against hers. "My daughter." He spoke in Lakota. "I have not found your mother." Shame, grief, and despair thickened his voice.

"*Mon père.* She is in danger. She needs us," she said, speaking fast, switching between French and Lakota, her voice urgent.

Conrad's fingers bit into her shoulders. "Where—"

"No. A dream…" She shook her head. "A dream

133

yet not," she said as the hope in her father's eyes faded.

"I saw her, spoke to her, but I do not know where she is." Her voice broke under a wave of helplessness. She'd failed to bring her mother out of that dark, evil place. She'd not only let herself down, but her father and her family.

Conrad held his daughter. This child had stolen his heart from the first time he'd set eyes on her with her big, beautiful jewel-colored eyes. She'd been shy, uncertain, and afraid he'd push her away and ignore her as her real father had done for so many years.

Unconsciously, he stroked her back with his large hand, offering comfort. As a young girl, Kangee had been denied a father's love and had craved it so desperately. The love between them had grown into an unbreakable bond.

Seeing her so distraught now lit a ball of guilt that burned his gut. He hadn't meant to be gone for so long. He stared into eyes so like her mother's and wanted to cry out in pain. Eagle Woman, his heart and soul. How could he survive without her?

"She's alive." He wasn't sure if he was speaking to his daughter or trying to convince himself.

Kangee buried her face into his chest. He glanced over her shoulder and saw the twins and Skye clinging to one another. What was left of his heart crumbled into tiny bits. Pulling Kangee to his side, he held out his arm and swept up his three youngest daughters. For a long moment, he just stood there holding his girls, his world.

"I should not have stayed away so long." He closed his eyes briefly as he drew in the scent of his children, then opened his eyes and saw Chief Two Arrows and Night Warrior watching. "I am sorry to disturb your night."

Two Arrows waved aside the apology. "Your children need you. It is good you have returned." The Chief sent him a questioning look.

Conrad shook his head, and when he spoke, his voice was low and hoarse. "She is alive, I know this, but she is somewhere I cannot reach her."

Kangee pulled away. "*Mon père*, I failed—"

Conrad held up his free hand, his heart breaking. He loved the fact that Kangee, from the day he'd married her mother, had insisted on using the French term for father. He ran a large thumb over her checks, wiping away her tears. "No, my daughter. You did not fail, for if you could have returned your mother to us all, you would have done so, just as I would have."

"She is in the dark…" She shivered violently.

Conrad pulled her close. "Hush now. We shall speak of this with your grandmother."

Once again, Grandmother was right. He'd joined her and the rest of the family earlier. The old woman had told him not to wait until morning, that his children needed him. Especially this child of his heart.

Kangee trembled in his arms. He glanced back at the chief. He spoke near-perfect Lakota so that all could understand him. "My wife's family has arrived. They await us. He nodded toward his son who stood with his arms around Blaze. "I will take my daughters with me to their grandmother who waits."

"We will accompany you," Two Arrows said.

Conrad shook his head. "It is best if we go alone."

The chief nodded thoughtfully. "Your family is welcome."

Conrad turned his attention to his children.

"Come." He set the twins down, kept Skye in his arms, and pulled Kangee close, then led the way into the forest.

****

Restless and edgy, Night Warrior entered the forest, following a path that circled the lake. He walked until he tired, then pressed his back to the trunk of the tree, man and tree in perfect alignment in the night shadows. The shared dream with Kangee left him shaken, but taking her into his own forbidden dreamscape was worse.

Night Warrior shoved aside the painful and bitter memories that threatened, unwilling to remember or think about them for now and focused instead on Kangee and the ties that were tightening between them.

He couldn't ignore the connection between them any more than he could ignore the danger he sensed each time she was drawn into the darkness. He had no experience or any idea how to deal with the evil he'd seen and heard, but one thing was clear. Whatever connected them had begun well before they'd met.

The part of him that accepted that he was a shaman, had always been a shaman, also understood that what was happening to Kangee and her mother was not taking place in the physical world. That meant he needed to travel through dreams.

At the back of his mind, always at the back of his mind, was that hideous voice urging him to accept death, even tempting him with visions of the Spirit World? Then came her voice, begging him to live, demanding that he return to pain and darkness.

For the first time, he admitted his experience was that of a shaman, for a shaman often traveled to other worlds to find answers and needed knowledge. He sighed. It no longer mattered what he wanted. Or even needed.

Kangee was in danger and nothing scared him more than the thought of her succumbing to something so evil as this monster called Ardong. His past belonged in the past, and if he was going to help her, he had to accept that what had made him what he was today was the very past he'd run from.

As a warrior, he expected to battle to the death for his people. Kangee and her family were under the protection of his tribe, and that meant he'd fight to save her or any member of her family. But this had been different. He'd felt the danger to her soul and his as well.

Once again, Night Warrior wished for the old shaman's counsel. The thirst for knowledge that had once driven him as a boy to learn everything he could about the world he'd been born into demanded to know what was happening—to him and to Kangee. He had to find the answers. Not just for him, but for her and her mother.

He was wiser now than that young boy-man who'd allowed his need for answers to spin out of control. As an adult, he'd closed off that part of him and kept a tight rein on his mind, limiting himself to knowledge he needed to fulfill his position as a warrior, a strong leader, a fighter, and a provider. Being not just a warrior, but the best, was all he'd wanted.

Until the day he'd died.

Now his thirst for answers consumed him. His need for answers was as strong as his need to breathe. But this time, it wasn't just to satisfy him. He needed the knowledge for others. Exhausted from lack of sleep and the events of the day, he lowered himself, closed his eyes, and concentrated on clearing and calming his mind.

He frowned when he felt vibrations in the ground. They traveled up his body, up the tree, and into him where he and the tree were one. He pressed his palm to the forest floor and focused on his Earth Mother.

He sensed many people walking with purpose. His brows lifted as he felt the scrape of claws raking into the ground. His brows rose. It no longer mattered that he could feel and sense far more than he should have. He used all that was available to him.

As was his habit, he wore his knife. He drew it from its leather sheath. The pull of torn muscles made him grit his teeth and transfer the knife into his left hand. Standing, he moved toward the intruders.

Once more, his body reminded him that he did not have the use of the warrior's body he'd had weeks before. He ignored everything but the need to scout out possible danger to his people.

He crept and limped deeper into the forest, stopping every few feet to touch the ground or to sniff the air. Even the leaves of shrubs and plants trembled with knowledge of movement.

Night Warrior kept moving forward, following the scent of the intruders on the faint breath of air. The scent grew stronger, and his nose wrinkled when he caught the strong, musky scent that belonged to a bear.

He frowned but moved with more caution toward the approaching group. A slight breeze brought to him a single, sweet scent his body recognized. Kangee. He scented the air again, sure he had to be mistaken, but he wasn't. He'd know her scent anywhere, anytime.

Her image, her sad, haunted eyes slid into his mind, distracting him for a moment, and then he realized that the intruders must be her family. When he caught a whiff of tobacco smoke favored by the trapper, he relaxed.

Surrounded by the nighttime forest, he paused. Would Kangee's father take his children away? That thought settled like a heavy boulder in his belly. He'd grown used to having her around. Her presence calmed an ache that hounded him relentlessly.

He ran fingers over his chest, rubbing away the burning ache, then, needing to see her, to be closer to her, Night Warrior crept forward and spotted his sad-eyed woman standing beside her father with her brother and sisters forming a protective shield at her back. Everyone stood still and silent. As though waiting.

A thick wall of trees protected the tiny glen where the small family gathered. Over time, the trunks had thickened and banded together to form a hidden area accessible by either the small dry creek along one side or the gap facing the lake, on the opposite side where one of the trees had died and fallen.

So tall in life, the dead tree spanned the meadow at an angle, supported by the trees opposite. The thick canopy of branches and leaves blotted out all light but to the very heart of the meadow where tall green grass offered a blanket of softness and a sweet scent that surrounded Kangee and her family.

He made his way toward the creek bed, then leaned against a thick trunk, drawing in the flow of life. He stood there, still and silent, unseen and unheard yet from several feet away, Skye, cradled against her father's chest, lifted her head and looked right at him.

Night Warrior shook his head, unsurprised that the young child knew he was there. It still came as a shock to him that any one person, let alone a small child, could wield such great power. He felt her whisper-soft touch brush his mind and had to admit that he shared a connection with her as well.

He was getting used to SpiritWalkers and their strange abilities, just as he was getting used to the fact that some of those abilities appeared to have transferred into him.

You chose life.

That had been Blaze's answer as to why when she'd healed him, he'd become so much more than he'd once been. He ignored her earlier words, her command to fulfill his destiny. For now, it was enough that he was willing to use his abilities to help Kangee in whatever way was required. Past was past. The future could wait. His concern was with the here and now.

With the hint of a breeze brushing over his chest, he focused on the vibrations beneath his feet. Across the glen, shadows slipped from shadows as a pack of wolves emerged and fanned out around the heart of the meadow, taking up positions just inside the tree line. No one paid them any attention.

Night Warrior straightened, his attention sharp and focused when two wolves stopped close to where he hid. Both animals turned their heads, fixed their deep, golden-orange eyes on him.

He gripped his knife tighter, then nearly jumped when something furry brushed against his leg. Startled, he glanced into the brush to his right. A large bobcat sat looking up at him with intense golden-green eyes.

Night Warrior held his breath, then let it out when the cat turned and strode through the trees, walking without fear or hesitation through the pack of wolves pacing the perimeter of the glen.

He shook his head and wondered if he wasn't caught up in his own dream, but then the entire day would be a dream for it had been a day unlike any other. He swiped a hand over his face, but the sound of voices drew his attention, though he kept an eye on the two wolves who'd taken up positions on the other side of the trees in front of him.

When he saw people emerging from the tree line behind the wolves, along with children, he decided to go. Now that he knew there was no threat to Kangee or his own tribe, he had no reason to stay.

Ready to return to his village and leave the family to their private reunion, he hesitated when a huge, lumbering bear squeezed through the opening between two trees. It carried upon its back an odd shape that, even with his sharpened sight, he could not make out.

He moved closer to the trees blocking his way, then stopped when the two wolves turned their heads and growled, the threat low in their throats, their eyes narrowed slits. He understood. They accepted his presence in the woods but would not allow him to intrude.

As he watched, several warriors strode over to the bear, reached up and lifted down a fur-covered bundle that, at first, looked like a child. The fur parted and revealed a tiny, old woman leaning on a short, thick walking stick. She whirled around, her walking stick pointed in his direction. A blast of air hit him square in the face.

"Show yourself," she commanded in a gravelly, age-worn voice. She lifted one hand and beckoned him with a finger that age had bent and twisted.

Night Warrior hesitated. A low hiss and a nip at his heel startled him. He saw the glittering eyes of the cat. So engrossed in the tiny woman's appearance, he hadn't been aware that the cat had returned. He eyed it warily.

When the cat snarled, he held out a hand. "I'm going," he told it, then slipped through the trees, walking with pride toward the old woman. Squaring his shoulders, chin up, he met the old woman's dark, glittering gaze. She looked to be as old as time itself with her shock of white hair, the wrinkles upon wrinkles and shrunken, stooped body that looked far too fragile to stand upon its own.

"Your name."

He gave her the respect her status as an elder demanded. "*Unci*. I am Night Warrior, son of Turtle Moon of the Turtle clan and cousin to Chief Two Arrows."

Silence fell. The old woman shuffled toward him. In height, she barely came to his chest, making him feel as if he towered over a small child instead of an old woman. In fact, she was no taller than many of the children gathered around the edge of the forest watching him.

She gave a sharp snort. "Why does the cousin to a noble and brave chief hide in the dark? Are you afraid?"

Insulted, Night Warrior glared at the woman. "This warrior has nothing to fear, *Unci*. I do not mean to intrude. It is my duty to protect those in my village. I felt the presence of your people, and I came to see who traveled during the dark of night." He didn't mention that he'd already figured out what was going on and that it had been sheer curiosity that had kept him hidden behind the trees.

"Your hand." The elderly woman held out her own claw-like hand.

Night Warrior held out his hand, surprised at the strong grip of the woman and a bit unnerved by the intensity of her gaze.

"You are one of us, yet not," she proclaimed. "That is the answer you seek."

Before he could comment, she raised her other hand. The bear lumbered forward, then rose onto its hind legs and towered over them. Aware that the woman watched avidly, eyes sparkling with what might have been devious humor, he held himself still but kept his grip on the knife that he had yet to sheath.

"Watch. See what we are. See what runs in your blood now. Then we will see how brave you are."

Kangee stepped forward as though ready to protest, but at one look from her grandmother, she backed away. A hush overcame the dark meadow when the old woman lifted her walking stick and thrust it into the air. The air shimmered and crackled, causing the hairs on his arms to stand on edge. Around him, the air gathered and pulled together near the top of the walking stick where a large, translucent stone glowed. A sharp snap ripped the silence followed by the bright flare of light shooting from stone to clouds.

Light speared the sky, then spread, devouring the darkness. High above, the moon seemed to absorb the light. It grew brighter, sending down a stronger beam of light to circle him, the elderly woman, and the tall bear, leaving the rest of the group in an eerie shadowy glow. Night Warrior was aware of everyone watching him.

"I have seen the power of your people. A SpiritWalker healed me and the young child named Skye saved both my life and that of her sister today. There is nothing you can do that will frighten me. Your show of light demonstrates your power, but it does not scare this warrior." He'd had enough scares this day to last him a lifetime.

The woman laughed, a long, wheezy sound that bent her over. "Spirit. Boy, you have spirit. Let us see how much." She motioned to the bear. "Now," she commanded. The bear pawed the air.

Night Warrior didn't flinch, refused to give the old woman the satisfaction, but kept his wary gaze on the bear.

The edges of the bear blurred, thinned and shrank. Night Warrior blinked rapidly, then stared. Just stared at the tall warrior standing in the place where the bear had moments before towered over him.

The knife in his hand fell with a soft thud and missed his moccasin-clad foot by two blades of grass. He couldn't tear his gaze from the tall, broad-shouldered warrior with those strange eyes that glowed with a silver sheen in the moonlight.

Kangee joined him. He looked at her. "You did not speak of this when you explained what it is to be a SpiritWalker."

She put her hand on his arm. "I did not believe you were ready for this." Her voice was low. Soft. A frown of disapproval marred her features.

He glared at the old woman, waiting for her

explanation, but she jabbed him with one, long finger.

"Not ready," she sighed. "Much work to be done before the boy is ready." She turned to leave.

Kangee sent him a plea that begged understanding. "I am sorry, warrior of the night. Grandmother and my uncle had no right to do this to you."

Her soft, husky voice warmed him from the inside out. Beneath the rays of moonshine, her hair glittered silvery-blue and her eyes shone with apology. "There are many things my people can do, just as there are things they should not do." The look she gave her grandmother was full of love, admiration, and respect. She glanced back at him and frowned. "You are angry."

He went to fold his arms across his chest, then remembered his wounds. He wasn't sure how he felt about the bear. The light flashing up into the sky hadn't shocked him, not after Kangee's storm earlier, but the bear shifting, becoming a man? That was hard to accept yet it happened. How could he understand and grasp that these people could actually shift shape when he barely understood or accepted the changes within him? "I cannot learn about that which I am not told."

Kangee nodded. "You have the right to know the truth. But there are much better ways to explain who and what we are," she said, her tone one of disapproval as she narrowed her gaze at her grandmother. Then she shot her uncle a look of disappointment. "This is not the way of our people."

The warrior shrugged. "I cannot refuse to obey when commanded."

She waved a hand in dismissal. "Free will, Uncle." Her fury slid into a frustrated sigh.

"Night Warrior, this warrior who acted more like a

child is my uncle. Runs With Bear is normally well mannered. Our people do not show themselves to outsiders. It was wrong of him to do so without your consent or without lives being in danger."

Runs With Bear bowed. "You are correct, my niece. I should not have frightened this young man." His gaze challenged Night Warrior.

Night Warrior took one step forward. "There is a difference between being frightened and being faced with the impossible." He issued his own challenge.

Kangee stepped between Night Warrior and her uncle as though afraid of a fight. She glared at the elderly woman. "*Unci.* This is your fault. Do you not have anything to say?"

The woman rocked forward and leaned on her walking stick. She considered her granddaughter's words then narrowed her own eyes. "I have nothing to say."

"*Unci—*"

Without warning, the wizened old woman drew herself up, her bent back suddenly stiff as a board, her amused demeanor fading into coldness. Though she spoke to Kangee, her powerful and sharp gaze held his. "The boy cannot hide from his fate. He will accept what is meant to be, what *he* is meant to be." Her voice was firm. Authoritative.

Night Warrior bent over and snatched up his knife, hiding his wince of pain as he straightened, then sheathed the blade. "I was healed by one of your people, but that does not change who I am." He was not ready to admit to others what he'd already accepted for himself. He also needed time to absorb what he'd just seen. Just how much of him had changed? He wasn't a

SpiritWalker, but he was no longer just a man.

"You wonder," Grandmother said, as though she could read his mind. "It is time for you to accept your true position."

"Free will," Kangee said, her voice low, harsh. "It is his choice."

"Do not worry, child." Grandmother's voice softened. "The choice of how he lives his life remains his." She clapped her hands, and immediately one of the younger warriors stepped forward. "We will sit."

The tall, broad-shouldered warrior lifted his hands, spoke softly, as though to the wind. He shimmered and, in the blink of an eye, he was gone, and in his place was a large tortoise. The ancient woman sat on the hard shell of the tortoise. Everyone but Night Warrior and Kangee gathered to sit in front of her grandmother.

Night Warrior backed away. "I will let my chief know of your arrival."

"No. Stay," Grandmother commanded. "This concerns you as well."

Night Warrior hesitated.

You may run, but if you want answers, stay.

Dumbfounded that the old woman had spoken in his mind, he, his mind numb and reeling with shock, lifted his chin. He'd stay. And get answers.

Chapter Eight

Kangee glared at her grandmother. The tiny wooded glen was silent. "We are taught not to show ourselves to outsiders. You shocked him on purpose." She loved her family but at that moment, she wanted nothing to do with them.

She was tempted to take Night Warrior by the arm and leave. "Was one demonstration of our abilities not enough? This is unacceptable, *Unci*."

Her grandmother smiled with satisfaction. "Your young warrior is brave."

"That was never in question." Kangee turned to Night Warrior. "I am sorry. My family is not normally rude and inconsiderate of others."

Beside her, Night Warrior's heart beat louder and faster than normal. She didn't blame him for being shocked, upset, and angry. Some of that anger was directed at her for not revealing the true nature of her people earlier, and she accepted her failure, but she'd never imagined him finding out in this manner.

In front of them, her grandmother remained unrepentant. She waved her staff. "Sit, children," Grandmother ordered, very much in charge.

Neither Kangee nor Night Warrior moved.

The old woman sighed. "There is much you do not understand, child." Her voice softened. "It is time for the boy to accept his destiny." She glanced around. "Let us begin."

Kangee, after several long moments, sat, the anger leaving her. The grass beneath her was soft and springy, the air moist from the nearby creek on one side of the glen and the lake on its other. She drew in a deep, calming breath as Night Warrior joined her.

"It is not our place to interfere," she said, her voice low. "I am sorry you were upset." Grandmother never did anything without reason, and for her to have revealed the true nature of her people meant there was more going on than Kangee thought and that didn't sit well with her.

"Startled," corrected the old woman, proving age had not dimmed her hearing. She leaned forward, resting her weight on the carved handle of her walking stick. "Is this not correct, Warrior?"

Night Warrior inclined his head. "It is fair to say that I was not expecting to see the impossible."

The tiny woman's stare was intent, then she gave a slight nod. "Good. You have begun to accept the truth of your future." She held up a hand, stopping Night Warrior from speaking. "What saved you, Warrior?"

"A SpiritWalker," he answered.

Grandmother shook her head. "No. *Love* saved you." She looked from one to the other. "Now, enough of this. There is much for us to discuss."

Love. Kangee had a feeling she was well on her way to falling in love with Night Warrior. Remembering how he'd felt against her in that pond with the waterfall, she closed her eyes. She couldn't think about that now. Or the future. Too much change, too many unanswered questions. She was so afraid of what it meant—the dreams, her mother, and yes, the warrior's involvement in her life, for she sensed he was connected to her and to her mother.

Feeling eyes upon her, she gave her grandmother her undivided attention.

"I once told you what your future held."

Kangee frowned at her grandmother. "What does that have to do with—"

One stern look silenced her. Frustrated, confused, angry, and close to tears, Kangee dug her fingers into the soft carpet of grass. She didn't want to talk about her future, not now.

"Repeat what I once said to you," the woman ordered gently.

Kangee cleared her throat. "You once told me I would marry a man of great power," she admitted as she plucked a long, thin blade of grass.

Her grandmother nodded. "What else?"

"I would someday bring twin boys into the world." The thought of birthing twins had always thrilled her. To be blessed with more than one child was a special gift of the gods.

The old woman shook her head. "No, I said you would be responsible for giving life to twin boys who would one day become powerful SpiritWalkers."

Confused, Kangee frowned. "I don't understand."

"There is much at stake for both you and the warrior you defend. The boys I spoke of grow inside your mother."

Kangee's jaw dropped. Behind her, Kangee's father cried out.

"My wife is with child." He handed Skye to Kangee and jumped to his feet. "Where is she?"

Voices rose around them. The full ramifications of

her grandmother's words hit Kangee hard. She was going to have to save her mother in order to save her brothers. Hugging herself, she tried to fight off the chill of despair.

"How?" Kangee's question was swallowed by the raised voices of her family

A shot of light blasted into the air. Immediately, everyone fell silent. Grandmother pointed her stick first at Conrad. "Sit." When all was quiet, she turned back to Kangee. "Your dreams. Tell me of them."

Kangee didn't need to ask how her grandmother knew of her dreams for the wise elder was blessed with many gifts, more than any other SpiritWalker in her tribe. Visions were amongst her strongest of her abilities.

Taking several deep breaths, Kangee organized her thoughts. When she was ready to speak, she opened her eyes and focused on her grandmother.

First, she told everyone what happened with Skye, how the little girl had had been trapped in her vision. "Night Warrior took us to her. He was able to find her through me and he saved her, brought us both out of the darkness." She also told them of her dream, and how the warrior had entered her dream to bring her and Skye back out. She didn't mention that he'd taken them into one of *his* dreams.

Night Warrior shifted, bringing his thigh close enough to touch hers and lend her warmth and strength to continue. "I saw her. I saw *Ina* trapped in a dark place with an evil spirit."

Kangee touched her fingers to her lips to still the trembling. Everyone was silent, as though they all held their breaths. She drew in a deep and shaky breath. "I don't understand. The evil spirit kept telling *Ina* to go. He wanted me to take her and I tried, but *Ina* wouldn't come with me. She told me to leave and never return."

Her throat tightened, her lungs hurt and tears threatened. "Why did she do this?" She pleaded with her grandmother. "Why? Why won't she come back to us?" Squeezing her eyes shut, she brought back the chilling sound of laughter, her mother's frightened cry, the absolute sense of danger, not just to her and her mother, but to all who lived.

Night Warrior rested a hand on her shoulder. *Breathe.* The word whispered in her head.

"I am afraid." She shoved strands of blue-black hair back, then swiped the tears from her face as she struggled to make sense of everything that was happening.

"You should be, child, as we all should be." Grandmother bowed her head, resting her forehead on the backs of her gnarled hands that gripped her walking stick. "My daughter is trapped with Ardong, son of Dragon."

Low murmurs followed the old woman's announcement. Kangee lifted her head. She tried to speak, but her mouth was dry. "Ardong. That is what the monster called himself, but how can that be? He was banished from this world in the time the world came to be." She struggled to breathe. Everyone knew the story of how the son of Dragon had been condemned to death by the gods and how he'd escaped death by shattering his soul. Furious, the gods trapped each piece of his soul throughout the world where they'd fled.

"That is a legend. A story. It isn't true," Conrad

said, his voice harsh and choked with emotion. "It can't be real."

Grandmother tipped her head back. "It is very true, my son. My daughter is trapped with the father of all that is evil in this world. I'd hoped my visions were wrong, but after listening to my granddaughter..." She shook her head and sighed. "This is so."

"We have to find her and free her," he said, staring at his wife's family. His heart thudded painfully when he saw utter despair and grief on their faces. "It's not too late." He held up his soul stone. "She is alive."

Bright Star stood. "If my sister has found Ardong, or a piece of Ardong's soul, then she is trapped. The son of dragon can only be freed if invited back into the world. If she leaves his prison, she gives him permission to leave as well. Once free, Ardong's immortal soul will roam the earth, searching out each piece of himself. He is evil and cannot be allowed freedom."

Conrad frowned. He knew the legend, had heard his wife tell the story many times to their children, but he'd never believed it. He went to the old woman, knelt, and held her hands. "There has to be a way to save my wife."

Grandmother looked sad. "There might be. But the danger is great. I fear the sacrifice too much to ask."

"I will go to her and take her place."

Grandmother rested her frail hand against the side of his face. "It is not you who can save her, my son. There is one person who might be able to save your wife and your unborn sons." She pointed to Kangee. "Your daughter is our only hope."

Night Warrior stood. "She almost lost her life to

that evil spirit. You will not ask this of her."

Kangee stood as well, her legs shaking. Night Warrior steadied her with his hand on her arm. She took a step toward her grandmother. "What must I do?"

"No." Night Warrior got between Kangee and her grandmother.

Kangee smiled weakly. "You cannot stop me, warrior of the night." She addressed her grandmother. "How can I save her? What do I do?"

Grandmother motioned with her hand, and two warriors stood and helped her to her feet. Her shoulders were hunched as though she bore a great weight. "I do not know, child. The darkness hides many evils, but none is more dangerous than the darkness that lives in each of us. I've said what I can for now. It falls to you to find a way to save your mother and your twin brothers, without freeing evil." She sounded weary and sad.

Kangee couldn't stop the tears of fear and helplessness. "And if I cannot?"

"Then I fear for our future. Our people and this world we have been entrusted to protect are in your hands, my child."

The two warriors picked up the old woman and walked away.

Kangee watched in stunned disbelief as her family began bedding down. How could they act as though nothing was wrong when her whole world had shattered, when she was so afraid, she couldn't move? She couldn't stay here, not with them, not with her nerves raw and fear clawing her insides to shreds.

At her side, Night Warrior waited. When her father approached, she shook her head. She'd wanted him to come back and he had, but he couldn't put things right. That burden had fallen onto her unprepared shoulders. "I'm returning to the lodge with Night Warrior."

A small hand slipped into hers. "Story, Kangee." Staring into Skye's sleepy gaze, Kangee picked up her sister.

Conrad sighed. "We will return. He took his twin daughters by the hand and led the way through the trees. Silently, Night Warrior fell in step with her. Thankful that he remained silent, Kangee tried to block her fear, but how was she going to face that evil creature again?

"*Ina.* Dream." Skye's sleepy voice pulled Kangee's mind away from her thoughts and fears.

Kangee sighed and rubbed her cheek over her sister's head. "Yes. I dreamed of our mother." How could she free her mother and save her brothers without setting evil free? Questions whirled like a tornado through her mind.

Skye wrapped her arms around Kangee's neck. "Story. Tell story."

As she walked, Kangee spun a short light-hearted tale for Skye, but all the while, despair and grief tore her heart into shreds.

****

High above, Moon surveyed the land below from her throne in the heavens. Soft as a caress, her ray of light illuminated a lone warrior in the forest. Darkness, blacker than the night and more viscous than the sap running in trees filled him. It ate at him from the inside and formed a thick aura of despair that engulfed the warrior's body and soul.

"He returns to his family." She sighed as the old

warrior made his way through the forest using her beams of light to find his way. When he neared the sleeping village, he stopped and stood in the shadows listening.

"We knew this day would come." Earth rumbled her displeasure from deep in her domain. Once, this man had been filled with light, with good. Now his soul was all but dead.

Air spoke. "What has been set into motion cannot be stopped.

Moon dimmed her light as she and the rest of the gods and spirits watched the warrior lift his hands and whisper a chant in a low, harsh, and gravelly voice. His body shimmered, growing smaller until only a large, luminous moth remained. The moth fluttered high into the protective canopy of leaves, and then dipped down over the darkened villages.

"Can his child do this?" Moon asked the questions of not just Earth, but all the gods and spirits.

"She has no choice." Air's voice echoed around them all, for she was everywhere. "She has no choice," she repeated, sighing.

"She is too young," Moon mused when her light fell onto Kangee sleeping in the lodge. Her heart tore a bit when the woman shifted and moaned ever so softly. She loved these humans and felt their sorrows and their joys.

"It is her time." The low, harsh rumble came from Earth. The ground shook slightly. "She is the only one who can free her mother and save the precious babies."

"But at what cost?" Moon asked.

"That will be up to her," Air said. She too loved the humans called SpiritWalkers, for she and her sisters had created them to keep balance in the world.

"If only there was something we could do," the soft-hearted Moon said.

"Free will. We cannot interfere." Deep inside her domain, Earth felt the continuous struggle between evil and the young woman's mother.

"Mother and daughter carry gifts each of us has given to our children. We can only watch and wait."

Reaching the longhouses, the moth hesitated over the roof of each before moving on. As though finding what it sought, it dropped down the smoke hole of the largest lodge.

In the thin ray of moonlight, Kangee's blue-black hair shone like a bright, molten light. As though drawn to that gleaming light, the large moth hovered inches over Kangee, its wings beating a breath of air across a face streaked with tears. Fluttering away, the moth shimmered. In the blink of an eye, it became once more a warrior kneeling beside his daughter.

Kangee shifted and moaned softly as though she sensed his presence. Silent tears shed in sleep slipped from her eyes, then she groaned and flung her arms out.

The warrior quickly murmured a chant. His form blurred until there was only a softly glowing moth hovering over Kangee before it flitted up and out the smoke hole in the roof of the lodge.

Once the moth was back in the shadows of the forest, it once again shimmered and fluttered to the ground, becoming an aged warrior cloaked in despair from the choices he'd made, condemned to a life of bleakness.

His daughter was the key to gaining power. He'd use her if needed. Deep inside, a small part of him mourned the loss of his family, but his thirst for power kept it buried. He walked deep into the forest and once again shifted, this time into a mangy wolf that raced through the forest.

Chapter Nine

Kangee woke with a start. She stared into the darkness, her gaze darting from shadow to corner, from ceiling to floor, from wall to wall. Nothing moved. Her senses were raw and jagged from everything that had happened that day.

Staring up into the bit of night sky revealed, she realized not much time had passed since returning to the longhouse. She turned her head and found her father. He slept in one of the beds with Skye cuddled in his bear-like arms. Kangee rubbed her arms and wished she were once again a small child able to seek comfort in her father's arms.

Though she was safe in the lodge, surrounded by both her family and Night Warrior's, chills paced up and down her spine like an agitated wolf guarding the borders of his territory. A loud snort burst the quiet. She jumped, then shook her head. Her father sounded like a hibernating bear.

The normalcy of her family should have reassured her, but it didn't. She should have felt safe and protected not vulnerable. She squeezed her eyes shut and focused on her breathing. Deep breaths in, slow breaths out. In. Out. In. Out.

Would the evil spirit, Ardong, return to invade her dreams and her mind? She had no trouble seeing again the red-eyed creature that had radiated hatred and pure evil. She shuddered and pressed a hand to her stomach.

It seemed unreal, as though she were living and breathing a bad dream, but it was real. She'd sought and found her mother and, in doing so, found an ancient evil being, one that had blazed a trail into her mind.

She shifted onto her stomach and rested her chin on her fisted hands as she tried to take in everything that had happened that day—without remembering the horrors of being surrounded by Evil.

Take her. Take her. Take her.

The words spoken by Ardong hammered and echoed. Panic sent her heart racing. Was she remembering or had the shattered soul breeched her consciousness again. She moaned and dropped her head to the fur she slept on and covered her ears with her hands.

The thought of facing the evil spirit terrified her. Yet, if she wanted to free her mother, she'd have to.

Tears gathered at her eyes. She wanted more than anything to have taken her mother from that place when she had the chance earlier. So what if Ardong went free? If legend was right, the son of Dragon had split and scattered his soul. What harm could one piece of one soul cause?

Remembering the hideous monster, Kangee wished she knew more about the legend. She ran a hand through her hair. Over and over, questions circled her mind. How was she going to save her mother and her unborn twin brothers? She sat up and clasped her knees to her chest. Grandmother had said it was up to her to free her mother. How was she going to bring her mother back to her family without freeing Ardong?

Across from her, Conrad snorted again, which both

startled and comforted at the same time. Accepting that she would not get any more sleep that night, she stood. Accustomed to the dark, she had no trouble seeing as she checked on the twins sleeping in one of the top bunks.

One of them shifted, then the other so that they lay in a tangle of arms and legs, much as they must have done when in the womb. Their voices were muffled as they muttered in their sleep. She shook her head. Even in sleep, the girls talked to one another.

She went to the doorway, pulled aside the flap, and stared outside. "*Ina*," she whispered. "How do we free you?"

She thought of her aunts and uncles. Each of them was a strong SpiritWalker and her grandmother, the most powerful of them all, so why did it fall to her to save her mother? She had no gifts or special abilities.

Yet, of them all, she was the one who had somehow connected with her mother. It didn't matter how—visions, dreams, seeking, then finding her. Kangee had sought her and found her.

And Ardong.

Protesting or fighting against the task that had fallen on her shoulders helped no one. She accepted that her grandmother was right. Good or bad, it was up to her. And if she failed?

She gripped the hide door as she faced her biggest fear—not death, not even Ardong. Above all else, she was afraid of failing and disappointing her family, especially the man who'd treated her as his own and her young sisters.

Trying to get away from her thoughts and fears, Kangee slipped out into the pine and cedar scented night. The air, cooled by night, and a misting over the lake helped clear her mind.

Beneath the ghostly canopy of trees surrounding the village, Kangee wasn't afraid of the night shadows. The rustling of small rodents in the thick undergrowth accompanied her as she wandered to the wide stump where earlier she'd sat and entertained the children with stories. Dark shadowy shapes darted into the brush as she neared.

She was as much a part of the night as these small animals, for she was a child of the earth and moved as one with the night world on silent feet. She swept a hand over the worn and smooth surface of the tree stump. Though the tree itself was long dead, its spirit remained to form a connection to the earth, one she had felt when she sat there earlier, telling stories to the children.

Needing to move, needing time to think and calm her mind, heart, and spirit, Kangee slipped through the trees and brush and embraced the chill wind sweeping over her.

Sensing a presence in the shadows to her left, she stopped, drew in a deep breath as she scented the air. Then she relaxed. Just one of the warriors standing guard in the night. Knowing he would not allow her to leave the safety of the village, Kangee grinned like a mischievous child as she planned her escape.

Anything that cast shadows had a spirit and that spirit could be called upon in time of need, including the shadows themselves, which she pulled around her and formed a cloak to shield her presence.

The poor warrior would be left puzzled when she faded from view. She passed him when he neared.

Away from the village, she headed toward the lake.

Reaching the shoreline of the misty lake beneath the light of Moon, she stopped to let the gentle smack of water rolling over land soothe her and draw her closer. A tickle of cold water brushed her bare toes. She shivered. Summer had faded. Soon, the nights would grow darker, colder and longer. She walked along the bank, kicking up droplets of water, making her way to where a huge fallen pine blocked her path.

The giant tree lay partially on land, and partially in the water. Mist drifting across the lake hid the tip of the tree. She followed the thick, tall trunk to its root ball. In the night, the huge hollowed out ball yawned like a gigantic monster ready to swallow anything foolish enough to get too close.

She remembered her amazement when she'd first seen this tree, for the root ball was taller than perhaps four warriors. Beside it, she felt as small as an ant.

She gripped one thick root and climbed until she stood on the humongous trunk, then walked cautiously to the end where the top section of the tree, shrouded in mist, was submerged. The trunk beneath her feet rocked gently with the motion of the lake.

Kangee touched the trunk with the tips of her fingers and drew in the comforting presence of old spirit. A faint breeze brushed over her as she stood and stared up at the full moon and let the energy of the moon wash over her.

Focused on the mist-covered moon, she took several deep, calming breaths, drawing into her the light, the power, the love that was Grandmother Moon. Holding her hands out to the side, palms open to the rays of silvery light, she felt them tingle and grow warm. She let her head fall back and adjusted her feet to keep her balance as the waves in the lake grew stronger and caused the trunk to sway with each wave. Slowly, she raised her arms.

Warmth flowed into her and surrounded her. She turned her palms inward, splayed her fingers wide, and felt the energy forming into a ball that she rolled and maneuvered, swirling the moon's energy into a tight ball.

Playing with the ball with the abandonment of an innocent child, she suddenly realized she was no longer alone. Using pure instinct, she whirled around and with a push of her hands, sent the ball of energy outward.

****

Waves of warmth flowed over Night Warrior like water from the lake roused from its depths by the wind to sweep over land. The sensation was incredible—a heated breath of love chasing away the pain that hounded him day and night.

His mind, blessedly clear of the fog caused by unrelenting pain, accepted and embraced the unexpected gift. He closed his eyes, amazed how his body vibrated with strength.

He drew in the scent of the night—the trees, misty moistness of the lake, and the woman standing high above him. Deep inside him, something stirred in response. His heart—no, the intense feeling rising inside him came from deep in his soul.

Desperate for answers to the questions, Night Warrior's mind shifted to become that young warrior who'd once embraced what could not be seen or explained.

He accepted the gift from Kangee and the power

she so easily and naturally commanded in a way he'd never even imagined possible. He watched as she walked along the trunk toward him.

Limping more than normal due to doing too much that day, he stepped into the cold lake water. "How did you do that?"

Kangee shrugged.

For once, he didn't even think about the fact that he could now see in the dark.

"SpiritWalkers are of the Earth. Air and her sisters, Water, Earth and Fire, created us. Air breathed life into us and we became." She held out her hands. "I am a child of the gods and live as one within our world."

He glanced up at the full moon. The moon was *Wo Wakan,* belonging to the mysterious. Sun, Moon, Sky, and Stars were all considered *taku wakan,* things mysterious and therefore sacred to his people.

"You command the moon as well as the wind?" His voice sounded awe-struck.

Another shrug. "I use what is available to me."

Night Warrior just lifted a brow.

She laughed. "Any who live on earth can touch and feel the energy that is Moon."

Night Warrior shook his head as he watched Kangee. The log even at this point in the water was at least twice his height, and with a light mist gathering and forming a halo around her, she looked more like a god than a human. "None of my people can do what you just did."

Kangee lowered herself to sit. "Powerful shamans and healers know how to call upon the power of the moon."

"Not like this." He had seen his uncle working in

the moonlight many times and he'd never done anything close to what Kangee had managed.

Head to the side, she studied him. "You have it within you to command this power."

He stepped back toward shore. "No. I cannot." His stance dared her to argue with him.

She shrugged again, then sighed as her feet dangled over the side of the log, the water lapping against her toes. "Grandmother said tonight that you are one of us. Your people also call you a shaman. You have the knowledge to do as I just did, for our people can hold the power of Moon in our arms."

Night Warrior eyed the moon. His feet and legs were numb to the cold. There was so much he wanted to know, he didn't mind a bit of discomfort.

"You have much to learn, Warrior."

The sound of her voice swept over him, enveloped him in her youthful innocence and sweetness, and tugged at something deep inside him. Sadness slid into his heart. He had nothing to offer this woman or any other woman. He squared his shoulders and held his head proudly. *Step back, return to the village.* He didn't need more pain, especially that of the heart.

But his thirst for knowledge compelled him to stay. "Show me," he challenged.

She held his gaze. "Will you accept that you can do this and what it means?"

Frowning, he considered his answer. "There is much I can now do that I could not do before our healer gave me back life." He still refused to believe he was one of them. Just as it was easier to tell himself he was not a shaman rather than face and admit that when he'd accepted life, he'd taken the path to becoming the shaman his uncle had once declared him to be.

Tonight, he would not deal with his being a SpiritWalker or a shaman. Tomorrow and all it brought would come much too soon. Right now, he wanted to hold and command the power of the moon with this woman.

Kangee stood and faced the nearly full, glowing moon. He did the same. When she held her hands out to her side, he followed suit. "Close your eyes. Concentrate. Feel the light of Grandmother Moon touching your palms."

Night Warrior did as she commanded. He studied the bright light of *Hanwi*, focused on what looked to be an aged face, and concentrated on the light, on the faint ring around the moon, fingers of light that fanned outward and downward. Toward him.

"Let me feel your warmth and your power," he said in a low whisper. Unexpectedly, his palms tingled and grew warm.

"Hold the moon. See her resting on your palms, feel her weight, her life, her power." Kangee raised her arms.

Concentrating, imagining the moon in his arms, he followed her instructions and mirrored her movements. And felt as though he held something big, heavy, and warm between his hands.

An exuberant sense of accomplishment went through him as he raised his arms. A sudden sharp shooting pain shot up into his injured arm, forcing him to bring his arm back to his side. He swallowed the grunt of pain and stared at his palms with wonder.

"I held Grandmother Moon." His people had their myths and lore, but tonight, he'd gotten his first glimpse into another world. He shook his head, and his lips twisted. "Thank you for this. I fear it will be a while before I can hold the moon on my own." *If ever.*

"I will help."

He shook his head. "Even you, sweet one, cannot fix what is wrong with my body."

Kangee nodded. "Only time can do that. But I can give you the gift of moon. Do you accept?" She waited, her gaze solemnly holding his.

Pride warred inside him. The warrior in him demanded it should be him doing the comforting and offering his help to the woman with haunted eyes and frightening dreams. But once again, his thirst for knowledge won out. He nodded.

She held out her hands. He moved closer and offered up his uninjured arm. She held on with her hands and slid off the log. He stared down at the woman who was but a breath away. "The water is cold. Let us move."

"No. We are grounded by Earth, surrounded by Water as we once were in the womb. The connection to Earth and Water will make this easier. And more powerful."

With Kangee so close that her warmth chased the chill from his body, Night Warrior found it difficult to think, to move, and even to breathe. Her scent beckoned him, urged him to bring her closer, to hold her so tight that he wouldn't know where he ended and she began.

He stared into her eyes, the swirls of color that reflected silver beneath the moon, and he forgot all else. There was just her. And him. The very air around them stilled, as if life itself held its breath.

Reaching up with his uninjured hand, he cupped

the side of her face, amazed at how soft and delicate she felt beneath his large, rough hand. For a moment, she leaned into his hand, their gazes locked.

Once more, something stirred deep inside him, then as though held prisoner, it burst free and filled him with an incredible sense of love being utterly complete.

"How is it that I know you, have always known you?" Warmth from where they touched sent shivers racing throughout his body. He wanted to pull her close, feel her against all of him.

Kangee rested her palm against his face. The air between them crackled with energy. A faint cast of silvery light brightened the surrounding night.

A halo of light that surrounded Kangee and grew to encompass him. It reminded of the strange dream-like world he'd walked in after he died—the fuzzy cocoon of light, the bluish bubble, and the ball of light that had commanded him to life. The light surrounded them, blocking the darkness.

"The circle is complete," she said, awe in her voice.

He stumbled back, slipping on the slick bottom of the lake, but regained his balance. He ignored the chill of air on the side of his face where her warm palm had rested. "What are you doing?"

She took a hesitant step forward and held out her hands. "It is not what I am doing, but what we together have done."

She gave him a sad look of regret. "You are not ready to hear more." Another step brought her closer. "You wanted to touch the moon."

He would rather touch and hold her. And more. He also wanted to flee from what was happening to him—

to them—but he was no coward. Except that he agreed he wasn't ready for any more shocks. Silently, he nodded.

Kangee turned, her back to his chest. The brush of her long hair against his belly sent shooting darts of awareness through him.

"Hold your arms out to the side, like mine." her soft voice lured him into holding out his arms behind hers. He leaned forward, drew in her scent and the warmth of her body so close to his.

Smoothly, she moved her hands so that her palms rested on the back of his hands, their arms twinned. She leaned back, rested her head against his chest. Instead of causing pain to his wounds, warmth that had nothing to do with Moon's guiding life force slid through him. "Concentrate on the warmth and light falling over us."

His chin brushed the top of her head. It took no effort on his part to *feel* her warmth. His gut clenched, and blood pooled between his legs.

"Let the light from Moon enter through your palms. Hold her between your palms."

Breathing slow and deep, Night Warrior concentrated on the moon, rather than the woman resting against him in the moonlight. "I see her beauty, her light, her life." *Along with the beauty of the woman in his arms.*

"Now touch her, let her touch you." She lifted his arms out to their sides and held them there.

Heat swirled inside him. How could he feel the moon when every sense was tuned to Kangee? He focused on her voice, the words she spoke in a language he'd never heard before. Over and over, she chanted.

In his mind, he repeated her words. When she lifted

their arms, he held his breath, determined not to allow the pain in his arm to stop him this time, but he only felt heat swirling across his palms and up his arms. Focusing all his attention on the moon above their heads, he gave himself over to the woman and moon. There was no pain. Just awe as Kangee continued to lift their arms up higher.

Her palms grew hot against his skin. "Feel the ball of energy flowing between your palms."

Amazed, Night Warrior kept his gaze on the moon and imagined that he held that sacred globe between his hands. Heat and energy tingled and pricked his skin. Together, they brought their hands over their heads, her hands sliding down from the back of his hand to his elbows.

The energy pulsed against his hands, and when he rolled his hands side to side or up and down, it seemed as though he really was playing with a ball of light. "I feel her."

"Now, release the power we hold."

Night Warrior recalled how she'd sent that ball of warmth at him, as though tossing it like a child tossed a hoop. Drawing in a deep breath, he first gave a silent prayer of thanks to *Hanwi,* then quickly pulled their joined arms to the side and down. Pure energy flowed over them as the water from his dreamscape had cascaded down over them.

With their hands still locked together, Night Warrior held onto Kangee. She leaned back, and her scent, her warmth surrounded him and made him yearn for more. He closed his eyes with a long sigh. Everything he wanted was here, in her. All he wanted at that moment in life was to hold her tight and keep her close to his heart.

He wanted this woman. More than anything. Including regaining his status as a warrior.

The realization shocked him. With eyes open and wide, he tried to pull his hands free and step away, but Kangee turned around, keeping his hands in hers.

Staring into her moon-shadowed eyes, emotion flowed through him and around them. The colors, normally sharp, clear and distinct were now swirls of silvery, glittering mist with the hint of a rainbow lurking deep in her gaze. He felt as though he were falling deep inside her. Had his life depended on it, he could not have broken eye contact with her. All that mattered right now was Kangee and the aching need inside him.

"I cannot resist," he murmured, lowering his head slowly, giving her a chance to refuse, and hoping she would not.

Faster, with more force than the rushing streams in spring, his insides churned and boiled, and his heart swelled and pounded so hard he could barely breathe. He slid one hand up her back, beneath the dark curtain of her soft-as-silk hair, to cup the back of her neck.

Her arms lifted, her hands sliding over his chest, leaving a trail of liquid fire in their wake. Her fingers inched up his neck, her thumbs stroking up the center of his throat. He swallowed. Hard.

"What can you not resist?" she asked, her husky voice low, a mere whisper of sound.

Night Warrior slid one hand beneath her chin and tilted her head back. "This," he said, bringing his lips closer to hers.

Kangee's breath hitched in her throat. At the first

touch of his lips against hers, hers parted on a deep sigh. One of his hands moved to her jaw.

She leaned into him, her arms tightening around his neck, bringing him closer. For just a moment in time, his mouth hovered over hers with a touch lighter than air. Then his lips moved over hers in a kiss that was demanding yet gentle.

His lips played over hers, teased her. One-minute hard and firm, the next, soft and light. Her fingers slid into his hair and gripped the back of his head. Needing more than this sweet teasing, she pulled him closer. This time, *she* demanded. She kissed him hard, needing to be closer. The taste of him excited and thrilled her.

"More," she whispered.

He needed no coaxing. He pulled her tighter to him and moved his mouth over hers, taking what she offered and gave back that and more. The kiss deepened, grew hotter, and tasted sweeter. Kangee moaned, and when his tongue snaked out to lick at her lips, her knees weakened as desire struck deep at her core.

Holding her tight to him, Night Warrior entered her welcoming mouth and ignited the passion born beneath the light of the moon. He couldn't get enough, and he wanted more. His tongue swept over hers, danced with hers. He was drowning in the incredible sweetness of her mouth. Each soft little gasp or moan drove him harder, faster, and deeper. He needed this woman, had to have her but should stop, put distance between them.

As though she sensed his withdrawal, her tongue darted into his mouth. He groaned, opened himself to her, and encouraged her tentative exploration until he could refrain no longer.

Biting gently, he captured her tongue with his teeth

and suckled. Kangee cried out—not in pain but in pleasure—then he gave her the same freedom to mimic his actions.

The pull from tongue to groin sent shudders throughout his body. When her hips moved against him, stirring him to hardness, igniting a passion that was close to consuming him, he froze. The knowledge that he wanted nothing more than to claim this woman as his own at whatever cost to either of them made him lift his head.

He rested his forehead against hers. His blood sang in his veins, urging him to taste more of this woman who'd so quickly found a way past the walls he'd built to keep him separated from others.

Her hands slid from his neck, but instead of dropping her arms, her finger traced his mouth, lightly playing over his face, as if committing him to memory. Something deep inside opened, like a flower blooming. As though her soul had its own voice, it burst into full song. Everything around her grew brighter, and in her eyes, colors turned to sparks and a wavy aura that seemed to encompass him in the bright colors as well.

"You are the one." Her voice was breathless and wonder softened her features.

The look in her eyes, the love shining there shattered the cloud of passion holding him hostage. He pulled his hands free and stepped away, crossing his arms across his chest. He'd come too close to taking this woman and making her his.

He had to break the spell passion had spun around them. "You should not be out here alone."

He watched the show of color fade from her eyes.

Kangee narrowed her eyes and frowned at his

abrupt change of mood. "I am not alone. I am with you." *As we are meant to be with each other.* What she'd suspected was true. He was her SpiritMate. Night Warrior, her warrior of the night and her dream warrior. Hers.

But she kept that to herself. She and her dream warrior were bonded, mated. The connection that had been between them from the beginning now made sense. Their souls and their hearts had known the truth. She accepted this, but her mate needed more time.

She tipped her head to one side as she regarded the stony set of his mouth. He could deny what he felt, ignore the sparks of emotion flying from her to him then back, but nothing changed the truth.

"You may return," she murmured. "I chose to remain here beneath Grandmother Moon."

"I cannot leave a woman out here, alone and unprotected. You will return to where you are safe."

"I am fine here."

His lips tightened, and she knew he thought of himself as unable to protect her due to his injuries. She wanted to comfort her SpiritMate, but any show of sympathy or recognition of his limitations would not be welcome. Instead, she lifted her eyes to the moon. The ray of light in her soul swelled, grew brighter, and burst into a vast and colorful array of pure joy that longed to break free and dance in celebration.

Hadn't her mother always said she'd know when she found her SpiritMate? But Kangee hadn't understood the depths of feelings that the discovery would bring to her. Was this love? She was sure she loved this damaged warrior who chose to close himself off from those around him.

There is no greater joy in life than finding your SpiritMate—except falling in love with him. For there is nothing so great than the love that will fill you and consume you when you truly discover you love that person with all that you are.

The words her mother had spoken to her on the day she became a woman filled her mind and warmed her heart. She took a small step toward Night Warrior, part of her yearning to throw her arms around him and pull him close, eager to share her discovery.

She searched his face, and she calmed her excited heart and mind for Night Warrior wore no expression. She moved close, keeping her eyes locked with his. Each step forward she took, he stepped back. The hot desire she'd seen in his eyes was gone.

How could he not feel the pull between them, the tie that bound her soul to his? Her mind reached out to his, but he'd closed himself off to her. She could breech it without too much effort, for they were connected, but respect and free will kept her from doing so.

She breathed in a calm, deep breath. "You are my SpiritMate."

Their souls had recognized one another from the first day she'd set eyes on this handsome yet damaged warrior, but with all the worry over her mother, she hadn't noticed the tiny flutters of awareness seeping into her soul.

"No. I am—" Night Warrior closed his eyes as though in pain. "No."

Though he couldn't see it, Kangee sent him a smile of pure love. They were bound. He, an injured warrior, and she, a SpiritWalker with no great talents and little hope of freeing her mother. They each lacked something in body, mind, and spirit, but out of the sorrow and pain in each of their lives, they'd found one another. He belonged to her and her to him.

This was the absolute truth, yet no matter how much she wanted to embrace this wonderful feeling and share it with her future mate, she held back.

Free will.

It was that simple. As his SpiritMate, Kangee respected Night Warrior's need to keep his mind hidden. She sensed in her heart and mind that he knew the truth, had from the beginning when he'd first become aware of her presence within his lodge. He'd known whatever it was that drew them together was special. She chose to acknowledge it. He did not.

She sighed and turned to stare up at the moon. A slight breeze cooled her heated flesh. Shoving her hands beneath her heavy curtain of hair, she lifted the strands off her neck and let the air cool her.

Night Warrior remained still and silent. He would not leave her out here alone, yet the last thing she wanted was to return to the lodge. She'd get no more sleep this night. Turning back to the warrior, seeing deep lines of pain etched around his mouth and eyes, she sighed and closed the distance between them. "We belong together. We are connected and have been since we first met. Deny it if you choose, but it does not change the fact that I speak the truth."

He drew himself up, a movement Kangee knew had to hurt. "I am drawn to you sweet one, but I cannot belong to you or to any other. I will do what I can to help you find your mother. But do not expect more."

He turned and waded out of the water. At the bank, he waited.

Kangee's feet were like ice as she left the water. "I choose to walk." She stalked past him but froze when he stopped her with a hand to her shoulder.

"You will return with me." His voice was hard.

Kangee turned her head and smiled without humor. "I can take care of myself. Release me."

"No." His hand slid down to her arm and pulled.

With a quick strong twisting motion, she freed herself, and when the warrior moved toward her, she narrowed her eyes and drew upon her indignation and the innate confidence in her ability to take care of herself. Lifting her right hand, she shoved her palm outward toward him.

The powerful gust of wind caused Night Warrior to stumble back. He lost his footing and fell, landing in the shallows of the lake.

Kangee stood over him. "I can take care of myself. Do not forget this." Then she walked away.

Before she'd reached the shadows of the forest, she'd faded from view. Night Warrior tried to find her but she was gone. He couldn't even hear her.

Part of him was furious that she'd used her powers against him, but he also saw the humor in her actions. She had spoken the truth when she said she could take care of herself. Respect, along with something he was afraid to name, grew as he sat there, feeling overwhelmed and out of his element.

Chapter Ten

Tendrils of morning fog draped the village with wraith-like moss found deep in the dark heart of the forest. Wood smoke rose from the village, adding a swirling, sullen layer trapped beneath the clinging moisture.

In tune with nature's mood, the Turtle Clan tribe stood in hushed silence, everyone's attention focused on the wall of pines closest to the lakeside of the village. Women clumped together in small groups while men and young warriors stood tall, alert, and silent, forming a protective ring around their women and children.

Word had spread that Kangee's family of SpiritWalkers was due to arrive. Nerves warred with curiosity and excitement. Chief Two Arrows, at the suggestion of Night Warrior, Blaze, and Kangee, had gathered them together and explained that Kangee's family were shape shifters as well.

No one wanted a tragic accident like the one that killed Blaze's parents who'd been shot when they'd taken the form of eagles and were flying low over a lake. The warrior who'd killed them hadn't known they were humans, SpiritWalkers, in the form of birds.

Kangee, surrounded by her family, waited impatiently. Blaze, Star Walker, Travers, and Alex stood to her right, her father and sisters to her left. She shifted her weight from one foot to the other, impatient to talk once more to her grandmother. She needed someone to tell her how she was supposed to fight a Shattered Soul.

As she studied Night Warrior's people, some curious, others nervous and afraid, she understood. To these people, she and her family were myth and legend. Just as she'd always believed that the stories of Shattered Souls, like the one trapped with her mother, were nothing more than a story used to frighten children into behaving.

But they were real. So how was she going to find the courage to not only face that spirit again but also fight it? Her heart pounded and a chill swept through her. This was beyond her. Grandmother expected too much. What if she failed? Scared at the very thought of losing her mother because she was not gifted or talented enough, to succeed at her task, Kangee shivered and pressed her fist into her stomach to calm her nerves.

Hugging her arms tightly around herself, she struggled to breathe and to keep panic from taking over. A firm hand on her shoulder steadied her. She turned her head and found Night Warrior staring at her with eyes that were dark and focused. He stood tall and proud, yet she saw the tiny lines etched around his mouth and eyes and knew that he was still in pain.

Her gaze drifted across his bare chest and the puckering wounds. She grimaced when she realized she hadn't considered his injuries when she'd shoved him into the lake after sharing that wonderful, heart-stopping kiss.

Night Warrior leaned close. "You did not hurt me." His breath skirted around her ear to warm her cheek.

Next time, you might not be so fortunate.

His deep, low chuckle made her grin, which eased her tension. With his body nearly touching hers, she couldn't help but remember the feel of his wide strong shoulders and the long, lean strength of his torso. The injuries to his chest didn't diminish her attraction to him, and just thinking about how her body had come alive when they'd held each other and shared that wondrous kiss sent heat gathering in her belly.

She wanted to turn, slide into his arms, and press her lips to his. To keep herself from giving in to her desires to touch her SpiritMate, she turned her back to him. Pride filled her that this proud, wounded man, refused to stand with hunched shoulders to spare himself pain.

In her heart, she'd already known he was hers—the ties between them were strong—but after sharing that kiss beneath the moon, there was no doubt in her mind or heart or soul—Night Warrior belonged to her.

With him standing behind her, she drew his warmth around her like a soft, comforting fur robe and let it draw the chill from her as she tried to clear thoughts of the future from her thoughts. Yet it was impossible not to think of Night Warrior. Dreams had drawn them together, but what they faced in those shadows could very well tear them apart and destroy them.

A low murmur swept the crowd. A pack of wolves emerged from the dark forest edging the village. Fog drifted around the animals.

"At last." Kangee sighed.

The wolves padded their way down the center of the village, close enough for her to see and appreciate their beauty and grace and the wise intellect in their eyes. Two warriors with spears and bows in their hands followed. As soon as they entered the village, the wolf pack faded into the morning mist and slid back into the deep shadows of the trees.

Kangee, so in tune with her SpiritMate, felt his breath in her hair and the beating of his heart. Like hers, his raced with anticipation.

"They have arrived," she whispered.

Night Warrior shifted so that he stood angled both behind and beside her, so close, her shoulder rested against his chest. He enjoyed the way Kangee's head brushed against his shoulder, the sweep of her long hair sweeping across his thigh, sending shafts of desire shooting into every part of his body and mind.

He longed to put his arms around her, pull her against him, and feel her lips against his. She was soft where he was hard, whole where he was broken, and she didn't care. There was no doubt she saw him as a man, and that made him want her even more, for during that brief moment beneath the moon, he'd felt complete. He'd been a warrior with hope and a future.

The boy cannot hide from his fate. He will accept what is meant to be—what he is meant to be. Her grandmother's words echoed in his mind. What had she meant? Did she refer to his being a shaman or a SpiritWalker? Or both?

He accepted that death had changed him even though he didn't understand why. He couldn't argue that he was no longer Walks Like Turtle, warrior. He'd become Night Warrior—

Night Warrior what? Shaman or SpiritWalker? He couldn't bring himself to admit he was both. He sighed.

It wouldn't be long before he'd have no choice but to admit the truth, but that time wasn't now.

He breathed, once more pulling Kangee's scent deep into his lungs. Her spirit filled him, flowing from his chest to the top of his head and down to his smallest toe. He wanted this woman with everything that was inside him. She'd declared them SpiritMates, and he wished that it could be so. Though he feared his heart belonged to Kangee, he could not give it to her.

"Watch," she said, indicating a tall, slender, wildly exotic woman walking behind the two warriors. Three young children followed. The woman wore a deerskin dress with the waist nipped in. Fringe swayed and touched the tops of her moccasin-encased calves. A fur cape covered her shoulders.

"She is beautiful," he said, his jaw dropping, awe hushing his voice.

A light pinch to his uninjured thigh made him wince. "Yes, she is. That is my aunt. Her name is Moon Dancer. Her husband is Runs with Bear. You met him last night. Moon Dancer is sister to my mother."

One look at Moon Dancer, and he knew what Kangee would look like as she aged.

Kangee's fingernail dug into his side. "You're still staring."

He tugged her hair. "I think today it is allowed." He searched among her people. "Your uncle. Will he arrive as a bear?" He would never forget how the man towered over him with his long slashing claws.

She shrugged and hid her smile. "No one ever knows what form he will take." She tipped her head toward another woman with two small children who'd joined Moon Dancer. The second woman was no less exotic than the first.

"Another aunt?"

"Moonsong, sister to my mother. Her husband died last winter. She has two children."

"Died?" That bit of news startled him. "Your people…"

"We are as mortal as you and your people."

A loud gasp rose from around them. Night Warrior returned his attention to the forest and also let out a gasp of appreciation. A large elk with a huge antler rack had stepped out of the woods. Mist swirled around the animal, parting as it moved forward. Upon its back, Kangee's grandmother sat with her walking stick across her lap. But it wasn't the sight of an old woman riding an elk that had everyone talking in excited whispers tinged with threads of fear. Two sleek, black cats, one positioned on either side of the elk padded silently through a fog that rolled out of the way as the cats moved. Heads down, shoulders and muscles quivering with restrained power, the cats stalked forward.

The smaller of the two cats opened its mouth and growled, baring long, needle-sharp teeth. Instantly, a buzz of alarm sounded throughout the village. Young children who'd begun to venture forward ran back to their mothers.

Beside him, Kangee chuckled. "Trust Grandmother to make an entrance that will become a story to be told and retold." She glanced back at him. "This is how legends and myths and stories are created."

Night Warrior nodded. He'd lived in this village his entire life, recalled the strange things Blaze had done as a child, the fear she'd instilled because of what she did. None of them, including Blaze herself, had had any idea just how different she truly was.

Glancing at his aunt, he wondered if his uncle had known their healer was a SpiritWalker. Given that his uncle might very well be among them as an owl, it would not surprise him to learn the old shaman had known the truth about Blaze.

He still had difficulty accepting there were people who looked like everyone else, spoke the same tongue, lived as they lived, yet those people were not the same. They were as different as the sun from the moon.

After today, no one in his tribe would be left in doubt that SpiritWalkers held astounding power, that they were as Kangee had told him—a separate race. They were *The Chosen.*

"What are those?" He managed to get his mouth moving. He'd never seen cats so large, so black, so sleek, or so powerful.

"They are panthers." Kangee smiled as the graceful animals approach.

Night Warrior could not tear his gaze from the prowling cats. They vibrated with contained life and energy, yet looked ready to explode. He barely noticed the remaining warriors who brought up the rear of the procession and came to a halt until the warriors of Kangee's tribe mirrored the warriors of the Turtle Clan as they too formed a protective ring around the two women and five children.

At the sound of a single sharp clap, two warriors stepped forward smartly to gently lift the elderly woman from the back of the elk. Kangee's grandmother hobbled forward, her back hunched, her fingers thin and claw-like on the carved handle of her walking stick. But as soon as she reached the chief, she straightened her spine and speared the young warrior with her icy stare.

"We are SpiritWalkers. We are of the Earth Dwellers. We are the same; we are different. We are SpiritWalkers," she announced, her voice strong despite her age and loud enough to reach each man and woman and child gathered. "We live among others, a people apart yet merged with those who share this world we call Earth Mother." She finished her speech then stood silently.

Chief Two Arrows gave her a bow of respect. "You and your people are welcome, Grandmother. We are the Turtle clan, though there is one among us who is SpiritWalker." He indicated Blaze.

Blaze took one step forward. "I am of the Air Seekers."

Grandmother nodded. "A powerful tribe. I know of you, child. You are a great healer." Her head whipped around and her fierce stare stabbed Night Warrior. He met the old woman's brilliant green gaze with their patches of brown and yellow. Thin wisps of blue separated the colors, and right now, they held solid resolve.

The old woman approached him. For a long moment, the two stared at one another—an old woman who radiated power and a warrior determined not to show weakness.

Grandmother tapped her cane into the dirt twice. "You have two of *The Chosen* among you." Her voice, her stance, dared Night Warrior to disagree. He remained silent. The elderly woman nodded then returned to Chief Two Arrows.

The low hum of whispering grew louder as speculation rose like water in the lake to slap against the shore. Night Warrior sighed. Though part of him longed to deny the truth he'd been determined to ignore and discount, what she said was true, and he felt a measure of relief in hearing someone say the words aloud. It gave him hope that one day his body would heal, and he'd once again be whole.

Yet the whisper of power, the yearning for power, the thirst for power frightened him. Becoming a SpiritWalker did not change who he was and take away his weaknesses. Instead, he feared his added power would tempt and corrupt him. How could he trust himself?

Grandmother swung her head back toward him as though she'd heard his thoughts. "Fear of repeating the past will keep you from making the same mistakes. Fear will keep you honorable."

Night Warrior couldn't fight this woman. He held himself proudly and nodded, accepting his fate and his future.

She lifted her hand. "You accepted the gift of life. Accept all that life now offers."

Wise Owl stepped forward. "There is room in the lodge of Chief Two Arrows. You will stay with us?"

Grandmother nodded. "I am honored. Thank you." Then her eyes brightened with devious humor as they once more rested on Night Warrior. She clapped her hands sharply. Twice. "See what we are, people of the Turtle Clan, but do not fear us for we join you in perfect love and perfect trust. Let it be known."

The elk stepped forward with a shake of its antlers. The majestic animal blurred, his body shortening, compacting, shifting, revealing a man with shoulders as wide as an ancient tree. He wore a short tunic with fur and fringe, leggings, and moccasins. His knife and war axe hung from a belt around his waist. He nodded once toward Grandmother, then joined Moon Shadow and his children.

Though Night Warrior had known what was coming, the sight still amazed and thrilled him every bit as much as it had shocked him the night before. He shook his head and gave up trying to describe what he was seeing. Not everything was meant to be put into words.

Around him, voices rose and fell as everyone talked at once. There was shock and fear in the air, along with excitement. His people had dealt with Blaze and her healing abilities, especially when it came to his own recovery, then yesterday, with Kangee and Skye. Now that they saw people shifting shapes, he didn't think anything could surprise them. Or him.

Kangee's fingers gripped his arm. "Watch."

Night Warrior followed her gaze to the two black cats sitting among a carpet of swirling mist. The smaller of the two nudged the largest. The animal shook his massive head and stepped away. In another blurring blink of an eye, the panther gave way to a man. This one was younger, with hair the same blue-black as the cat he'd been. His eyes were piercing shades of the sun and moon. He moved apart from his family.

"Dark Star," Kangee murmured. "Youngest brother to my mother."

"And the other cat?" A kernel of longing swept through him. What did it feel like to shift and change shape? To become what one was not?

Kangee laughed. "My aunt, Bright Star. Twin to Dark Star."

But before the remaining black cat could shift, a small girl ran forward. A gasp rang out when the child halted inches from the cat. Unafraid, she lifted one hand and touched the soft nose of the cat. To the relief of those watching, the big cat gently rubbed her face against the child's then stepped away. In a motion faster than any other, the cat shifted and there stood another young woman with blue-black hair hanging past her bottom in a sleek curtain. She stepped forward and picked up the child.

"Your daughter is brave." Bright Star carried the child to her nervous mother, but the little girl wrapped her arms around the SpiritWalker.

The young mother sent the SpiritWalker a hesitant smile. "You are most welcome in our lodge."

Bright Star nodded. "Go now with your mother," she instructed the child. "I will come to see you soon."

Her eyes shining, the child giggled and went into her mother's arm.

Night Warrior blew his breath out as the two tribes merged. His people had accepted hers. "Some family, you have."

Kangee sighed with happiness. "Yes. This is my family," she said proudly as the village came to life. Children came together, and in the manner of children who so easily and even eagerly befriended those who were different, they began chatting. A group of boys ran off while the girls smiled shyly at one another. One girl held out a small, pure white feather. Moving her fingers, she floated her gift to a girl her own age who caught the feather and giggled.

Night Warrior had a feeling life was going to be very interesting for him and his people for however long Kangee's family remained.

He followed her to join his family and hers. It did not surprise him to hear Wise Owl inviting Moon Dancer and her family to stay in their lodge. With so many of his cousins living elsewhere, their home offered plenty of room.

As though a signal sounded, the women from both tribes gathered in groups to fix a shared morning meal. The men of both clans readied themselves to go hunt for the celebration feast to welcome the newcomers that evening.

In the rush and bustle, no one noticed the arrival of a single warrior leading a group from the stream until they too entered the village. A wave of silence fell upon the excited village.

At her side, Kangee heard Night Warrior's hiss of indrawn breath. She glanced up at him, then frowned when she noticed his attention fixed on a new group of visitors. He didn't look happy. In fact, he looked downright displeased.

"Who are they?" Kangee asked.

A large woman in the group broke past the leading warriors. She hurried toward them. The rest of the warriors followed with more caution.

Gray Dove, Night Warrior's younger sister poked her brother none too gently in the ribs. "Tatonga has arrived," she announced.

"Who?" Kangee frowned. The woman heading toward them looked happy. Excited. Determined.

"She is the woman my brother promised to marry."

Kangee couldn't have heard right. She whirled around to look at Night Warrior. "You are to be married?"

At first, she thought Gray Dove was playing a prank, but the stony set to Night Warrior's features said she'd told the truth.

"You didn't tell me about this woman." Kangee's fingers curled into fists at her side, and her chest tightened into a hard knot that made breathing difficult. Surely, she hadn't heard correctly. Night Warrior belonged to her.

"There was nothing to say," he returned grimly.

She shoved past him, taking a perverse delight at his hiss of breath when her action knocked him off balance.

Night Warrior grabbed Kangee by the arm, but as soon as he touched her, the air whirled, pulling the cold, foggy air down and around him. It spun him around, then swirled back into the sky, leaving him sprawled on the ground.

Chapter Eleven

Kangee sat around a large fire in the center of the village along with her family and Night Warrior's family. The cold, damp air clung to her arms, but it wasn't the fog that chilled her to the bone. It was the woman sitting next to Night Warrior. Glancing through the dancing flames of the fire, Kangee glared at both.

Since her arrival, Tatonga had not left his side. She didn't have to touch him to give the impression that she clung to him like moss on a tree. It was in her actions, the looks she sent him, and the way she narrowed her eyes at the other women. Even his mother and aunts.

"Will she not stop talking?" Kangee muttered. Tatonga's mouth moved nonstop.

"Did you say something, *Mithan*?" Blaze couldn't keep the thread of laughter from her voice.

Kangee grimaced and picked at her bowl of venison and greens. "You heard what I said." Blaze's hearing was as sharp as her own, which, unfortunately, allowed Kangee and all SpiritWalkers to hear every single whisper, giggle, and word that came out of Tatonga's mouth.

Unable to stop herself, Kangee watched Tatonga. The woman ate and talked. Talked and ate. She looked as though those two activities were her favorite pastimes. An elbow in her ribs from her sister-in-law made her sigh. "I didn't say anything," she grumbled.

"Didn't have to. You reveal your thoughts on your face," Blaze said.

Kangee huffed out a breath. *Eat. Ignore them.* But when Tatonga shifted so that her knee touched Night Warriors, Kangee clenched her teeth. She was tempted to drop a whirling wind over the woman, suck her up, and fling her deep into the forest.

She sighed and pushed her food around with her finger. No matter how tempted, she would not give in. Not because it was a misuse of her power and not even because her grandmother sat to one side of the couple. It was her own innate sense of fairness.

It wasn't the woman's fault that Night Warrior was Kangee's SpiritMate. The woman believed she had rights regarding Night Warrior. And maybe she did. Kangee eyed Night Warrior. Given any bit of encouragement, she might be tempted to let the wind toss him somewhere deep in the forest as well.

As though reading her mind, Grandmother glanced over, her wise eyes sharp as the tip of an arrow and just as deadly with their piercing stare. Kangee kept herself from squirming. She'd done nothing wrong. Yet.

To her surprise, Grandmother smiled, winked, and then gave a tiny flick of her finger, so slight that Kangee almost missed it.

The sharp pop of fire sent a shower of sparks high into the air. Kangee's eyes widened when a slight shift in the air sent the hot embers toward Tatonga, who was leaning over Night Warrior, so close, all he had to do was put his arm around her to embrace her.

Tatonga squealed and whirled around, scooting away from the hot embers. Kangee choked on her laugh and went into a coughing fit.

Night Warrior also shifted to avoid the sparks falling like stars from the sky. He narrowed his eyes at her.

Kangee shrugged her shoulders, but her grin faded when Tatonga leaned close to Night Warrior, brushing ash off his shoulders.

Beside her, Blaze sighed. "I am sorry, *Mithan*."

Too distraught, too angry, too heartsick to even pretend to eat, Kangee set her bowl onto the ground. She couldn't speak. What would she say? Or even do? Gray Dove had told her that he had called off the wedding, but it was obvious Tatonga refused to release him.

"You need to eat."

Kangee shook her head. "No, I cannot." The sight and scent of food made her feel sick to her stomach. She was tired, worried, afraid, and mad. Emotions churned through her. So much had happened in the last few weeks, the last day, that she found it difficult to comprehend the twists and turns to her life.

She swallowed a yawn. Her sleepless night was catching up with her. She closed her eyes. Sleep. She just needed sleep.

No. Her eyes flew open. She didn't dare. She feared what awaited her in her dreams.

Blaze touched her arm. "I know you are tired. And afraid. But you must eat." She handed Kangee a flat corn cake.

Kangee glanced up at the sky—the grayness, the sullen, sulkiness of the fog had grown thicker instead of thinning and was dropping lower. A small drift of moist air above them swirled downward like a hawk diving for prey. Shivering, her heart pounding, Kangee nearly leapt up, but the sudden flare from the fire sent a blast of hot air upward to consume the cold air.

Her gaze shot to her grandmother. The elderly woman was frowning, her sharp gaze on the sickly yellowish-green wisps of fog that looked bruised.

Kangee glanced around. There were no birds chirping, no squirrels chattering. Not even a breath of wind in the trees. Just a faint, foul taint to the air as though something nasty hid in the fog.

Frightened, she whispered, "*Unci?*"

The wise woman shook her head. *Later*

Kangee's anxiety returned. Everyone around her had gone on alert, except her father, who was staring into the forest.

For the first time since he'd come into her life, he looked old, tired, and beaten. He wanted to return to his search for Eagle Woman, but Grandmother had ordered him to wait.

Tears stung her eyes. She wanted to go to him, throw her arms around him and tell him she'd find her mother and bring her back, but her own fear of failure kept her silent.

Staring around the circle of her family and Night Warrior's, she tried to tell herself she could do this— she had to do this. Family surrounded her. Everything would be all right. It had to be, yet her talents were few, unlike her aunts and uncles who each possessed great power and command of their world.

She glanced at Bright Star. Her aunt sat tall, proud, and silent. She and her twin were among the most powerful in her tribe, second only to Grandmother. The energy and power swept over Kangee, making her wonder why it had fallen to her to save her mother.

She brought the cake she was crumbling with her nervous fingers to her mouth, but before she took a bite, raw laughter, sounding much like her father's pack mule, made her cringe. Her corn cake broke into crumbs and fell to the dirt.

"That woman," she muttered as she picked at the ruined cornbread. Hearing another bark of laughter, she hunched her shoulders.

How could he? She crushed the tidbit of food flat between her fingers and thought back to last night, or was it early this morning? She sighed. It didn't matter. What was important was that what had happened between them had not only *felt* right, it had *been* right.

Calling upon the energy and warmth of the moon had been a powerful act she'd never forget but it had been nothing compared to when he'd taken her in his arms and kissed her beneath the full moon. That moment confirmed what she'd suspected: they belonged. Her warrior of the night was the other half of her heart and soul, her SpiritMate.

Kangee wanted to stand and shout her news to her people for finding one's mate was cause for celebration but another loud, raucous peal of laughter rang out followed by an equally irritating giggle that set her teeth on edge.

She rubbed her eyes with her fingers. Hard. She and Night Warrior were connected by dreams and so much more. She wasn't about to let this woman come between them.

What if Night Warrior refused to accept that the two of them were meant to be? She sighed and mentally ticked off the list of things that she needed to do.

Find and save her mother.

Convince her warrior that they were SpiritMates.
Get rid of one very irritating woman.

"No problem," she muttered.

She ignored the looks from her family and put Night Warrior and the other woman out of her mind. Her mother was all that mattered. She'd just concentrate on finding and saving her.

Except she needed Night Warrior's help. And not just to find her mother or to fulfill what her grandmother had said. She needed her warrior to keep her safe and steady and she needed him to make her heart and soul complete.

Kangee swallowed but the lump in her throat made it difficult. Her stomach contracted and her heart ached. Though it hurt, she lifted her eyes and watched Tatonga press food into *her* warrior's hands. The woman's loud, grating voice went on and on about their wedding and the children she'd give to Night Warrior.

He is my *SpiritMate.*

Agitated, yet needing to appear calm, Kangee folded her hands and set them in her lap. She kept her eyes downcast. Her hair fell forward and hid the tears in her eyes. No matter what she told herself, it hurt to see another woman openly claiming her SpiritMate.

Unashamed, she tuned out all the conversations around her and focused on Night Warrior and the woman. Though he said little, Tatonga chattered nonstop, like the squirrels in the trees. It was wrong of Kangee to invade their privacy, but she couldn't help it and had no one but herself to blame as Tatonga nattered on and on about plans for the wedding feast. When the woman finally stopped talking, she got to her feet and entered the lodge belonging to Night Warrior and his family as though she belonged there.

Even at that distance, Kangee heard her ordering his mother about. Gritting her teeth, Kangee lifted her head and studied the open doorway. A slight breeze in the towering pines loosened more dead pine needles that fell onto the roof with a tiny skittering sound.

Kangee focused on the edge of the roof and the layer of needles that the wind had yet to sweep away. Silently, she called upon the breath of *Wind* to brush the needles into a neat pile then waited.

When Tatonga stepped out with a bowl of water cupped in her hands, Kangee shifted her hands in her lap, and with a tiny, short jerk, the pine needles took to the air, lifted by a sudden, concentrated gust of wind. The dry needles hung as though suspended, then fell right on top of the woman.

Startled, Tatonga jumped back, dropped her bowl, and fell, landing on her backside. The bowl hit the dusty ground and sent into the air a small wave of cold water that, with a bit of help from Kangee, ended up splashing Night Warrior.

He jerked and gave a low hiss of pain. Kangee hid her satisfied smile.

"Not nice, Little Sister." A thread of humor laced Blaze's rebuke.

She shrugged. Petty of her, she knew, and she was careful to avoid her father and grandmother's gazes.

Beside Blaze, Bright Star chuckled and leaned closer. "Clever. Very clever."

Kangee's lips twitched. That small act of rebellion went a long way to easing the tightness in her heart, but when Night Warrior turned his hard gaze her way, her pain speared through her heart.

Kangee tipped her chin upward and glared back. *You are mine.*

I belong to no one.

Narrowing her eyes, pleased that once again, they'd connected in this silent manner, she sent her thoughts back to her SpiritMate. *You do not tell the truth, Warrior. We are connected. If you know my thoughts, then you know this is so.*

Is this not just another trait of your people—to talk without words? Night Warrior waved away Tatonga and her attempts to dry the water from his body with her skirt. *Your grandmother and sister-in-law have both communicated in this manner.* He glanced at Blaze as though checking to see if she heard his thoughts.

Kangee kept her eyes on his, Tatonga forgotten for the moment. *You and Blaze are connected because she healed you. Grandmother is powerful. I think she can communicate with anyone she wishes. But until you, I had never talked silently with anyone except my mother and Skye. The bond between you and I is strong. This is proof that we are connected.* She didn't dare use the word *SpiritMate* again. Not yet.

Night Warrior looked thoughtful, as though part of him was fascinated by this new discovery. *The connection is your mother. Or Skye.* He dismissed her claim that the two of them were connected in any other manner than as a couple.

Kangee sent images of the two of them beneath the moon from her mind to his. She called upon the warmth that had surrounded them and shared it, then added how she'd felt in his arms, how the kiss had ignited a desire for more. She held back nothing, not even the rush of desire that came from remembering their kiss.

Desire and longing left her nearly gasping with need. She shared with him all that was within her. He looked uncomfortable but not convinced, so she flooded his mind with his own reactions, their moans, the feel of his hands on her and hers on him. But in trying to prove to *him* that they SpiritMates, she'd set her own body on fire.

Deny me now, Warrior. Does that woman fawning over you make your heart race? Can she read your mind and feel the blood rushing through your veins? Kangee lifted her chin, daring him to break eye contact. She spoke not just her mind but also her heart. *You belong to me, Warrior.*

Night Warrior couldn't look away from Kangee's wild beauty, the flash of emotions in her eyes that flooded both his mind and body. Each image she shot into his mind left him aching with lust. He tasted her, breathed in her scent, and heard her sweet moans of pleasure as though he held her in his arms. With great difficulty, he kept himself still, giving nothing away on the outside, but inside, he was a quivering mass of need.

Caught and trapped by the fierceness in her eyes, everything around him faded, as though it were just the two of them, as it had been last night when they'd shared that kiss beneath the moon.

In her eyes, he saw the hurt and anger she tried hard to hide. Her pain became his pain for he wanted and needed her more than he wanted to regain his strength and the use of his injured limbs.

Last night, he'd given in to his need to touch her, hold her, and feel her lips against his. He hadn't thought of Tatonga or even to his own reasons for calling off the marriage. He'd acted on the moment and, in doing so, had given Kangee the wrong impression.

I am sorry for hurting you and not telling you about Tatonga.

Gray Dove said you called off your wedding.

Night Warrior sighed. *Yes. My injuries mean I cannot provide for a mate. Those reasons have not changed.* He wished things were different, feared he wasn't strong enough to resist Kangee? He yearned to hold her, taste her, and feel her body against his. With her at his side, he was complete, yet he truly wasn't, and until the day came when he was fully healed, he had no right tying her to him.

Kangee kept her gaze on his. *You will heal and be whole again, for you are a SpiritWalker now.*

Tatonga shifted, bringing herself closer so that she was practically sitting on him.

Across from him, Kangee's gaze burned with a fury that he felt. *What are you going to do now?*

Night Warrior sighed, shifted away from the woman. He winced when Tatonga's voice rose as she berated him for ignoring her.

The woman is overbearing, bossy and loud. Kangee rolled her eyes and looked for a moment as though she felt sorry for him.

Night Warrior stifled a groan. *I cannot argue with that.*

Beside him, Tatonga whirled around to see what had captured her warrior's attention.

"Why do you watch that woman? It is I who will soon be your wife." She folded her hands across her ample breasts and glared at Kangee.

Across from them, Kangee stood. *Remember, you*

belong to me as I belong to you. With a toss of her head, she turned her back on him.

Tatonga glanced at him, her gaze avoiding his raw wounds. "I care not that you are marked from battle or that you will not become chief of my tribe. I am still willing to be your wife."

Night Warrior stood. "You should not have come."

She stood as well. "I wanted to see for myself that you had survived."

"You have seen. My answer is the same. I cannot marry you. It is best that you and your people return." Night Warrior turned away.

Tatonga stepped into his path. "I will not leave. You made a promise. You will keep it. "Do you think I do not see the way you look at that woman? You think to take her as wife instead of me."

Night Warrior rubbed his aching arm. "I cannot marry anyone at the moment." And that was the truth. Though he suspected Kangee was right, that somehow, the two of them were connected and not just by her mother or the evil spirit, he refused to marry until he could provide for her. In the meantime, he had to find a way to get Tatonga to leave. Things were complicated enough without adding her jealousy and Kangee's fury and petty pranks.

"I am not leaving." Tatonga slapped her hands onto her ample hips.

"I will discuss this with your brother. Or my chief will."

He spun around and almost fell on his face when he forgot about his injured leg. Tired of dealing with difficult women when the day had just barely begun, he headed into the forest. He hadn't gotten far before

Kangee's voice slid into his mind.

Warrior. Grandmother has need of your presence.

Night Warrior ignored her. He yearned to be alone. He wanted peace. Quiet. Time to think. Tatonga's unexpected arrival and her determination to wed as planned made him feel like a trapped animal.

If he took a wife, honor dictated he marry Tatonga, but his heart urged him to claim Kangee, as she'd claimed him. He frowned, recalling how she'd called him her SpiritMate. He sighed. The word fit. There was no denying he and Kangee's spirits were somehow connected. He thought of that ball of light and how he'd been drawn to her in death and how now, in life, he wanted to make her his.

Return, Warrior.

The pull of Kangee's voice made him want to turn around and go to her, and because that was exactly what he wanted, he kept moving, feeling like a guilty young boy disobeying an elder.

Behind him, the sound of crashing in the thick brush startled him. He whirled around to see a sleek, black cat emerge. She hissed, held out a paw, claws extended. He froze. Something brushed against the back of his thighs. His heart jumped into his throat when he spotted a wolf blocking his retreat.

It took a moment to realize these animals were Kangee's family, not wild creatures. Glaring into the intense gaze of the wolf, he shifted a step away. "Leave."

The wolf moved with him, and the cat continued to growl. Suddenly, the wolf blurred.

In the blink of an eye, Kangee's father stood before him. "You will return with us."

Eyes narrowed, Night Warrior stood his ground.

Conrad reached out to grip his shoulder with one hand. "Grandmother has gathered us together by the stream. You are needed as well."

"You cannot force me to return," Night Warrior said.

Con rad nodded in acknowledgement. "We could, but we won't. It is your choice, but I would ask you to hear me out."

Glancing from cat to man, he dipped his head. "Speak."

Pacing, Conrad was silent as he gathered his thoughts. The black cat slipped into the brush as though to give them a moment alone. "If it is true that my daughter is the only one who can find and free her mother, my wife, then she needs you. My wife may be lost to me. I cannot lose the daughter of my heart. Come. For her. Do not let her face Ardong alone."

"She's going to try to find her mother again?"

"Yes. Her grandmother has asked her to make contact with my wife."

Conrad's gaze pleaded with him, though the man stood tall and proud. There was no way that Night Warrior would allow Kangee to do this without him. "If your daughter needs me, I will come." Seeing relief mingled with anguish in Kangee's father's features, he put his hand on Conrad's shoulder. "We will find a way to return your wife to you and to your children."

He turned, and strode past the cat and proudly, limped his way back to his village where two women waited—one that he was honor-bound to marry but wouldn't and the other who held not just his heart but his mind and soul.

Chapter Twelve

Beneath the tall stand of cottonwoods that rose as high as the spine of rock, Kangee sat with her legs crossed, hands clenched in her lap. Her grandmother sat on her right, Night Warrior on her left.

The three of them formed a triangle, knees touching while her father, brother, Blaze, and her aunts and uncles sat in a tight circle around them. The cold, damp air seeped through her clothes and into her bones. She gripped her elbows to still shivering brought on not just by the chill but by the fear of failing.

"Relax, child." The voice of her grandmother cut through her fear.

Kangee dropped her hands back into her lap, straightened her spine, and tried to ease the tenseness from her muscles. The silence roared in her ears as she tried to blank her mind and think of her mother. She vowed to do whatever it took to save her mother and her unborn twin sons, but she dreaded confronting that horrible evil creature.

Her grandmother started a low chant. The family joined her, their voices shifting from chant to song. Kangee's emotions fractured and her throat tightened with emotion as the words flowed through her.

"Sing, child."

She wasn't sure she could, but she added her trembling voice to those of her family. All the while, fear of failing assailed her mind and undermined what little confidence she had in herself. Why had her grandmother gathered them? What would the old woman ask of her? Whatever it was, she feared it was beyond her abilities.

A wisp of wind brushed her face, icy-cold against the beads of sweat brought on by fear. A light nudge from Night Warrior's knee steadied her, and when he sang—no words, just tone and rhythm—the tightness in her chest eased, allowing her to breathe. She focused on his voice, his touch, his scent, and the steady beat of his heart until she was calm, centered, and grounded. Then she lifted her voice and sang with her family.

When the song ended, Kangee opened her eyes.

Grandmother pulled two very old-looking leather pouches from her lap. "Children." Her gaze swept from Kangee to Night Warrior. "The two of you are among *The Chosen*. You are also among *The Honored*."

Kangee's eyes widened and her heart raced with both anticipation and dread. All SpiritWalkers were children of the gods and, as such, were given the respected title being among *The Chosen*. But to then be *chosen* from among others of her people was an honor. It meant she and Night Warrior had exceptional powers and abilities that would be used to protect not just their own race, but all Life.

Was she going to learn what her special gifts were? As a child, she'd been told that one day she'd be a powerful SpiritWalker, but she'd never considered she might be among the elite of her tribe.

Her grandmother ran her fingers over the two pouches. "These have been in my care, waiting for their rightful owners to claim them." She speared Kangee and Night Warrior with her sharp gaze. "Today is that day."

From each pouch, she drew out an amber-colored stone hanging from a leather thong. "By accepting these gifts, the two of you accept your new roles as Defenders. When the gods condemned Ardong to death by fire, he split his soul into pieces."

"Shattered Souls," Kangee whispered.

Her grandmother nodded. "The many souls of Ardong scattered and hid from the gods. But they were imprisoned and cursed by the gods. Each piece of soul retains its immortality. Each soul lives and if freed from their prison. Each soul will seek its brothers to rejoin and become as one." She paused to allow each person to absorb her words. "Dragon sacrificed his life for the world by gifting his blood, teeth, scales, and claws to the gods to use against the evil souls of his son." She held up the amulets and motioned to Kangee. "First you, child. Accept this gift from Mother Dragon."

Holding her breath, both eager and nervous, Kangee reached out and took the large amulet that weighed almost nothing from her grandmother. She held it between her hands and studied the dark, orange-yellow stone the size of her fist. She ran the tip of her finger over its edges. Strange. It didn't feel like a rock. Aside from being too light, the texture was smooth and warm. She turned it over and gasped. In its very center lay a single bluish-purple claw. At the base of the claw, two small scales glittered with the colors of a sunrise. On either side of the amulet were two stones. Each shimmered with an array of breathtaking colors.

"The wife of Dragon couldn't bear the loss of mate and son. She cried, her tears turning into stones." The old woman paused but didn't take her eyes from Kangee's.

Kangee touched the gleaming stones. "Her tears?"

Her grandmother shook her head. "Listen to the rest of the tale, child." She took the amulet and slipped it over Kangee's head. "The mother's heart was broken. She followed her mate into death. The gods were moved by the selfless sacrifice of the dragons and vowed their deaths would not be in vain. The mother's blood, teeth, scales, and claws also became powerful tools, and each drop of blood became a Stone of Hope. Legend says her tears and heart-stones are among the most powerful of all the sacred objects."

Around her, the silence was absolute except for the indrawn breath of each person looking upon the amulet.

"*Unci...*" Words failed her.

"You child, have been honored by Mother Dragon. Like the Stones of Hope around your neck, your greatest gift is hope." Grandmother turned to Night Warrior.

"You, warrior, offer protection and knowledge." She leaned forward and placed an amulet around his neck. The stone looked identical to Kangee's except that his claw was reddish-orange and much larger. Behind the claw lay a large scale that shimmered with the colors of a rainbow.

Kangee wanted to say something but couldn't break the hushed silence. She couldn't believe she'd been honored in a way she'd never dreamed possible. It also scared her. What did this mean?

Her grandmother held out her hands. She and Night Warrior obeyed by placing their palms on top of hers. Grandmother turned Night Warrior's hand over, palm up, and placed Kangee's hand on his. She sandwiched their hands between her hands.

"The two of you are a mated pair; your souls exist as one. Dragon and his mate gave their lives to protect this world and all who live in it. They have passed this task to you. You are both Enforcers. Champions. It now falls to you to seek out Dragon and enforce the laws of our people, and the gods." She pulled her hands away.

Before either could absorb her words, the old woman pulled an amulet from around her neck and removed the flap of leather that covered it. The yellow stone was the same as the amulets that had been given to her and Night Warrior, but in its center sat an eye that resembled the eye of a lizard.

Her grandmother sat in silence, her eyes closed, her hands cupping the amulet. No one moved. Or breathed. She gave a small nod, then opened her eyes, her sharp gaze holding Kangee's as she held the amulet up. Kangee gasped, as did everyone else. The center slit of the snake-like eye glowed with an eerie greenish light.

"Our family has been entrusted with three sacred objects."

Kangee couldn't take her eyes off the glowing Eye of Dragon. An intense wave of power poured into her. She gripped her own amulet and cried out when it grew hot in her palm. Unable to take her hands off her gift or her gaze from The Eye, she reached for Night Warrior's mind. *The heat. Do you feel it?*

Beside her, Night Warrior didn't move. *Yes. I—*

A sharp glare from Kangee's grandmother silenced the couple. "We three are DragonSeekers as well as Guardians of the Past and Defenders of the Future. I cannot tell you how to use your gifts. I know only that the Eye of Dragon revealed to me who would receive them and when. That time is now."

Kangee didn't know what to say. She'd never seen the eye of the dragon her grandmother wore, had known nothing about it or the amulets she and Night Warrior each possessed.

Her grandmother lifted her hands high. Immediately, those in the outside circle began a low chant. "It is time. Close your eyes, Granddaughter."

Kangee, comforted by the weight of the amulet and the rush of power in her mind, obeyed.

"Storyteller of the Earth Dwellers. Open your mind to the darkness. Let it swirl and become."

Breathing in slow, deep breaths, Kangee focused on the back of her closed eyelids, but like a piece of blackened hide, there was nothing there—nothing she wanted to see. Especially what she suspected her grandmother wanted her to see.

"You are a dreamer. Asleep or awake. You dream."

Kangee frowned as she let the tone and rhythm of the chants seep into her. She was a dreamer. A *day*dreamer. Whenever she was faced with a mundane task, her mind wandered off to whatever world pleased her. Lately, those worlds centered on Night Warrior, which made her feel guilty. Her mother was missing, her young sisters suffering, her father gone, and instead of finding ways to help her family, she kept escaping into her own worlds where everything was as she wished it to be.

A sharp clap brought her mind back to her grandmother's words. "Connections are made during dreams."

Wisps of fog brushed against Kangee's arms. She

smelled it, felt the moisture sliding against her skin, but instead of being cold, it cocooned her, keeping the warmth of Night Warrior, her grandmother, and her family around her.

Kangee sighed as she concentrated on the darkness of her mind. Connections. Her. Night Warrior. They'd connected from the first night in this village. In their dreams. *Dreams.* Night Warrior was a DreamWalker. Maybe it was his gift that her grandmother referred to. It couldn't be her. Her dreams were the dreams and hopes of a foolish young woman.

With no effort, the window of her mind opened as though a beam of sunlight had burst through the darkness. She stood at the top of the mountain with beauty spread out before her.

Night Warrior's arms snaked around her, drew her back, drew her close. Kangee tipped her head back into the hollow of his shoulder. His scent—pine, cedar and dark forest—flowed around her, held her in its sweet caress.

His head dipped toward hers. She lifted one hand and stretched until her palm rested against the back of his neck. She pulled him close, then lifted her lips to his.

The tender kiss made her sigh. His arms around her made her feel safe, secure, and loved. She wanted more. Much, much more. She turned around, ran her fingers up his smooth chest, and pressed herself flat against him. "Again," she murmured, her fingers sliding through his long, dark hair.

"We cannot." But he did. He bent his head and kissed her. Tenderly, gently, until she thought she'd crumple into a boneless heap at his feet. Her hands tightened. Her mouth demanded. For just a moment, the kiss went from gentle to an explosion of need, as though he needed and wanted her as much as she needed and wanted him. Then he pulled away.

"No," Kangee whispered. "Do not stop."

He rested his forehead against hers. "We must, *skuya*," he said, admitting his love and adoration of her.

"Why?" Touching him, kissing him kept the fear at bay.

"We are not alone." He lifted his head.

Kangee's head jerked around. In her dream world, she turned to see her family gathered around them, their voices rising and falling as they chanted and sang. For her.

Horrified, Kangee's eyes shot open. Her dream world faded, and she realized she was still sitting in the middle of the family circle with her grandmother on one side and Night Warrior on the other. Not on the mountain. Not alone with Night Warrior.

And one look at him made her want to curl up and wither away. His eyes were soft, slumberous, and filled with longing. His lips were full, as though he'd just been kissed. She drew in a deep breath, and his scent filled her lungs. Her dream had seemed real.

She bit back a groan. She was supposed to be seeking her mother, making that connection so that her family could save her, and instead, she'd drifted off into one of her silly, childish daydreams. Staring at her hands, unable to face any of them, especially *him*, Kangee wished for the earth to open and swallow her whole.

Fingers beneath her chin forced her head up. "You are a dreamer." Night Warrior stared into her eyes. His own were wide with discovery.

"I am sorry," she said miserably. "Sometimes I cannot help it. I know I should be thinking of *Ina*, dreaming of *Ina*." She tried to turn to her grandmother, but Night Warrior did not release his hold on her chin.

"Do not be sorry. That was very enjoyable." A thread of humor wove through the awe in his voice.

You cannot know what I dream. Humiliated, she spoke silently to Night Warrior.

Night Warrior grinned sheepishly. *I can. I do. I was there. On that mountain, kissing you.*

How—

"You are both dreamers," Grandmother announced, breaking into their private conversation, making it obvious she knew what they were talking about. "It is the way of our people to allow our young to discover their gifts on their own, then guide and train you. I have waited long for you to realize dreaming is your gift."

Kangee jerked free and stared at her grandmother as though the woman had lost her senses. She shook her head, unable to accept something she hated and felt was a curse was in reality a gift. "What I do is childish. Foolish."

Grandmother held up one hand. "I will say this once. You are a dreamer. That is your gift, and you must use this gift to save your mother. There is no time to allow you to find this out for yourself."

She turned to Night Warrior. "You are a shaman. It is that gift that makes you a strong dreamer as well. Shamans have the ability to travel to other worlds. We gather information we then use for our people. You turned your back on your heritage once. Denial does not change what we are. Accept your truth, accept yourself fully and completely, for this is your future."

Her knowledgeable gaze moved from one to another, then latched onto Kangee. "Dreams will save your mother if you have the courage to follow your true paths. You must dream. Both of you. Together." She shifted her gaze to Night Warrior. "Resist your path no more for it is up to you to keep our child safe. Dream with her."

Kangee tried to absorb all her grandmother said. They were Dreamers, but how could dreams save her mother? She wanted to ask, but her grandmother lifted a hand.

"Sing. For them." Then Grandmother gripped Kangee's knee hard, her sharp nails digging into skin. "Dream. Of your mother. Let your heart find hers." She clasped her hand around the Eye of Dragon. "Find her to allow me to see what you see." She closed her eyes, her back straight, chin up, lips moving in an almost silent chant.

Kangee trembled and shook. Around her, her family had their eyes closed as they chanted and sang. For her. She tried to swallow, but her mouth was dry, as though she'd swallowed fistfuls of fine sand.

How was she supposed to dream of her mother? Last night had been a nightmare. It had come to her in sleep. She hadn't sought and found her mother on purpose. How could this be a gift? Gifts were used with purpose and intent.

Or were they? Those with the gift of visions didn't ask for the visions that came. Was it that way with dreams as well? It made sense, even if she didn't like it.

She glanced at Night Warrior, looked into his dark eyes, and saw once more a hint of golden stars glittering deep within. Her mate. Her SpiritMate. She calmed somewhat.

"How?" she mouthed.

He held his arms out to her. "Together," he whispered in her ear.

Kangee let him pull her onto his lap. It mattered not who saw or who might have protested the intimate closeness. She needed this man, this wounded warrior. He was her warrior of the night, so she settled into his embrace.

Her back lay flush against his chest. He crossed his feet in front of hers and wrapped his arms over hers, his fingers gripping her elbows.

"Close your eyes," he murmured. "And dream. I will follow."

****

Ardong's frustration grew. The woman who shared his prison had grown weak, her blue shield faint. He'd been forced to stop his attacks. If she died here, in his cell, all hope of escape died with her, and Ardong needed her alive, needed her strong enough to leave so he could go free.

He paced and beat against the walls. Where was the girl? He needed the daughter to dream, to return and take her mother from this place. He laughed. The harshness of it vibrated inside the rocky prison and drew a shuddering gasp from the silent woman whose spirit had curled into a tight ball.

"Foolish woman. You condemn not just your own life but the lives of those you carry within."

The spirit of the woman quivered but she did not speak.

"I will be free. If you will not free me, then your

daughter will," he said cruelly.

"Leave her be." Eagle Woman's voice sounded faint.

"Then go to her. Go to your husband. Go to your children. Give your unborn children the gift of life."

Silence.

Furious that she continued to deny him, Ardong, son of Dragon, rightful ruler of this world, his freedom, he turned his attention to the faint path he'd discovered between mother and daughter. There was nothing there for him to find.

Dream.

He needed the girl to dream.

****

Night Warrior closed his eyes and focused on the woman sitting so close that he was aware of each and every breath. His own breathing remained steady, which, considering he was purposely setting out to DreamWalk, surprised him. Once, many, many years ago, entering the dream world had been as easy as drawing fresh air into his lungs. It had taken no effort on his part.

The power of it had been as intoxicating as honey to a bear. There, in that shadowy, misty world, he walked with guardians of the earth or flew with the winged creatures, learning all he could from the spirits who shared that higher plan of existence with him. Knowledge had been part of what had compelled him into other worlds. It was fun and powerful. As he grew older, his ability had grown so that he had the power to influence not just his own dreams but also those of others. To go where he wished, do what he wanted.

A slice of pain pierced his heart.

Power. So much. So tempting. So real.

Stay with her. Do not leave her alone.

The harsh, cold voice was a slap to the back of his head. Setting aside his past, the regrets, and the sorrows, Night Warrior focused on Kangee. He held her tighter, drew in her scent, listened to the steady beat of her heart, then let himself go.

It was that easy. Just let his mind go, focus his thoughts to where he wanted to travel. Kangee. The wish of his heart. He saw her, breathed her, felt her. Then he was with her, a shadow in her mind and a whole man in her dream world.

She turned to him in the swirling dreamscape that tunneled ahead. "Stay with me." She held out her hands.

Night Warrior could do no less. He took her hands, drew her close. "Always, *skuya*." Always. He smoothed the hair from her face and stared into her wide eyes. The swirls of color were gone, and her eyes were clear, crystalline.

He turned her in his arms so she faced forward. She trembled but took two tentative steps.

"Mother. *Ina*. Where are you?" Her voice shook as she walked.

Night Warrior followed close enough to jerk her out of harm's way if needed. DreamWalking was not without its risks. As he well knew.

"I can't find her," Kangee whispered as they walked through images her mind projected.

"Concentrate. Pull into your mind your last image of her, of her surroundings."

Kangee reached back and took hold of one of his hands. "I'm scared. Don't leave."

"Never. I am always with you." He spoke the truth. Good or bad, like it or not, he was connected to this brave, wonderful woman who saw him as a whole man. He stroked a hand across his chest. There were no wounds, no scars, and no pain. He couldn't believe that, in Kangee's mind, he was strong and able.

"As you will be once again."

Night Warrior drew in a deep breath and let his worries, fears, and thoughts of the future fade. There was here. Now. And this woman. He'd do whatever it took to keep her safe. "Focus now. Let us do this."

Kangee stopped walking. She touched her amulet.

He felt the power seeping from her as she put her energy and effort into reconnecting with her mother. Holding his sacred amulet, he did the same. Around them, the swirling air faded, grayed, then darkened, as though they had stepped into the black heart of a cave. They walked in silence until they spotted a faint wavering light ahead.

"*Ina?*" Kangee stopped.

On full alert, Night Warrior scanned the darkness. He saw no monsters. No evil. When she started forward again, he wanted to put her behind him, but he resisted the overwhelming instinct to go first. This was her dream, and he was there to help and protect. Not lead or control.

Kangee drew courage from Night Warrior's presence, grateful to have him close. Taking a deep breath, she concentrated on the tight bond between mother and daughter. When she neared the light, she knew her mother was alive, but her heart sank. The light that was her mother's spirit had grown smaller. Fainter.

The urge to run to her mother was tempered by the fear of what awaited her in the darkness. *Evil.* It was here. The Shattered Soul that belonged to Ardong, son of Dragon. He lurked in the shadows, a cat ready to spring and trap its prey.

As she and her warrior approached her mother, she kept her fingers twined with his. It didn't matter if he thought her weak.

"Not weak. Never weak."

His words brought a small, faint smile to her lips. "Nor are you, my warrior of the night."

She moved forward, closer to the light, to her mother. She didn't speak. Not yet. When the light that was her mother's soul brightened, she moved faster.

A low hiss of sound had her whirling around. She faced the dark mass that oozed out of the shadows. She took a step back until she was up against Night Warrior. He put his hands on her shoulders.

"Let her go," Kangee demanded. "Let my mother return to her family."

"I do not want her here," he said. "Take her. Take her and go."

Kangee frowned and glanced back at her mother. "*Ina?*"

Still no answer. Dropping Night Warrior's hands, Kangee took small steps toward the ball of pulsating light. She closed her eyes and concentrated. "Mother. Talk to me." She put all the love and command she could muster into the plea.

"She does not love you," Ardong whispered. Darkness, like a wall of mud, slid between Kangee and Night Warrior.

Kangee whirled around, her eyes darting

frantically, searching for Night Warrior, but she saw only the oily dark mass of Ardong.

"No." She shouted the words. "You are wrong. You are evil."

Yellowish eyes burned bright. "Yes. Yes." The words were a hiss of sound. "I am evil. Take her. Take her from this place. Take her from me. Save your mother, child." The voice crooned in her ear. "Touch her. Free her. Take her with you and go from this place."

"Where am I? Where are we?" If she could figure out where her mother was, maybe she could learn of a way to get her out.

The evil menace swirled, a huge black roiling mass that spun like a whirling cloud around her. Faster and faster until the darkness consumed her, pulled at her, made her feel as though her entire body was being pulled apart. She tried to cry out, but the tunnel of wind swept away her breath, left her unable to draw in air.

Then, as suddenly as it disappeared, Kangee found herself standing in a wooded patch of trees. Alone.

Kangee's heart pounded against her chest. Where was she? What had happened?

"See the place where your mother hides."

The words were a painful jab in her mind. Realizing she was still in her dream world, she studied the new dreamscape of forest. She moved, searched.

Had her mother shifted and merged with one the trees? She touched each tree she passed. Nothing. Not even the hum of life. Because it wasn't real.

"Take me back to my mother." She shouted the words.

"She is here. Find her."

"Where?" Frustrated, Kangee turned in a circle. Searched. Sent her senses flaring out, seeking. But there was nothing. Not even the reassuring sounds of wildlife. She backed into a large boulder wider and taller than Night Warrior.

"Yes," Ardong hissed. "Feel her, go to her."

Kangee turned and ran her hands over the rough stone. "*Ina?*" There was something here. Not life. But something that sent fear skirting up her arms and down her spine. Around her, the peaceful image of forest blurred around the edges.

"Go to her. Go to your mother. Take her from this place." The low hiss filled her mind and chilled her soul.

Kangee touched the stone. First with one hand, then two. "Mother. I've come for you."

She let her body fall away, it was her dream, she could do what she wished, and though she hadn't ever managed to merge her spirit with that of any other spirit on her own while awake, in her dreams, she saw herself as part of the rock, becoming the rock, entering the rock. Then without warning, she was back in the blackness, surrounded by evil. And she knew. Her mother had merged with the stone.

How was that possible? Then she remembered that anything with a shadow also had a spirit. Rocks, stones, and mountains might not be life in the way her people knew, but each cast shadows when in the light. Therefore, they had spirits available to SpiritWalkers.

She faced the boiling mass that gathered at her back like a menacing storm.

"Your mother does not love her children," the insidious voice hissed. "Your mother hides. She is a coward."

"No. She is brave to be here with you." Kangee wanted more than anything to be wrapped in her mother's loving embrace. Unable to resist, she reached toward the light. "*Ina*. My brave mother."

"No." The weak voice of her mother startled Kangee and took her breath away. "Do not touch me, child. You must not touch me."

Kangee knelt. Though her mother's spirit lay in a tight ball, Kangee understood that her mother was as one with the spirit of the rock *and* the Shattered Soul. They were all one yet separate.

"I will find a way to take you from here."

"I cannot leave, daughter. Ever." Eagle Woman's voice was a low, wisp of sound. "I did not ask permission to merge with one of Mother Earth's creations. Had I done so, I would have been warned of Ardong's presence. If I leave, I break the curse of the gods and free this evil soul. Know that I love you and that this is my will. My choice. Now go and do not return."

The mass of Ardong whirled and tried to blot out the sight and voice of her mother. It screamed and howled and frightened Kangee. The despair and determination in her mother's voice broke her heart.

"I want to save you," she screamed.

"Yes," Evil said in her ear. "Touch her. Take her. Save her." The cloak of darkness wrapped around her and chilled her very soul. The press of evil forced her closer to the warmth of her mother. Slit eyes, a putrid shade of shimmering yellow, stared at her from the other side her mother. "Take her from here. Take her with you when you leave. Do it. Do it."

"No. Do not set Ardong free," her mother whispered. "I...choose...to...stay. Go. Go now."

Kangee covered her ears with her hands. Around her, an angry, loud buzzing sound grew and drowned out her mother's voice.

"Take her. Take her. Now. Now!"

The high-pitched screams hurt her ears. "I don't know what to do," she cried out. Screaming, she tried to block the insidious voice of evil hissing in her ears as she tried to fight her way back to Night Warrior.

"He is gone. He has left you here. Go to your mother. She needs you. Her babies need you."

Kangee fought to leave, but the mass of evil wrapped around her, refusing to let her go. "No. He's not gone. He'd never leave me." The thought of being alone with this evil creature buckled her knees. Night Warrior didn't abandon her in her time of need.

"But he has." A faint, translucent window opened in the dark wall of evil. Kangee searched for her warrior but couldn't find him. There was nothing there. She was alone. "Night Warrior," She screamed his name, unable to believe he'd abandoned her to the evil soul. "Help me. Come back! Come back!"

She fought waves of dizziness and sickness. The surrounding darkness became a tight band around her chest.

"Turn around, look at your mother, and see your brothers. Save them."

Kangee stared at her mother's spirit and, for the first time, became aware of two tiny fluttering balls of light in the center of her mother's aura.

Her heart stopped. "Mother," she whispered, reaching out, her mind fuzzy, her only thought was to save her brothers from being consumed by evil. She'd forgotten what her grandmother said about twin boys, and seeing them now, she had to do something, anything.

"No. Do not, *chunksi*. Do not—" Eagle Woman's voice broke off when a sizzling ball of fire hit the protective wall around her.

"Save them." The glowing eyes turned red, grew larger, brighter, and a yawning hole opened, over her mother as though to swallow the spirit of her mother and her twin brothers.

Kangee tried to fight her way out. She had to find a way to save her brothers in a way that would not free Ardong. She pulled her amulet from her tunic and remembered that she was honored among *The Chosen*, that it was her duty to protect her world from the evil of Ardong.

"I will not free you," she shouted. "I will not free you." She screamed the words over and over. It hurt to say them, felt as though she was stabbing herself in the heart, because it meant she was condemning her mother to death along with her unborn brothers. But she couldn't violate her mother's free will.

A dark fist of evil reached out, wrapped around Kangee, and pulled her forward. "You are weak. Like my father and my mother and the gods who created us. If you will not save her, save them, then you will die with them.

Chapter Thirteen

Trapped behind the slimy blackness, Night Warrior kicked and punched, trying to reach Kangee, but he could not get past the twisting wall of black fog that had come between them. He heard Kangee scream.

"Kangee!" Fear rose up his throat and burned. "Where are you?"

The harder he fought, the thicker the dark mass grew. It coiled around him like the thick rope of a snake's body as it readied itself to choke its victim. The screaming continued, sending his heart racing.

"I won't lose you," he shouted, finally admitting that she was the reason he'd lived. She was the light in his soul, and he belonged to her. He remembered her declaration of love at the lake and how she'd declared them SpiritMates. Night Warrior put all he had into the fight to save the woman who'd saved his soul.

"Kangee!" Desperately, he reached for her mind and found emptiness instead. Terrified of losing his mate to this evil entity she faced on her own, he calmed his mind and his body and did what he'd always done so well. He dreamed.

Closing his eyes, he let the darkness smothering him swirl up and away until he saw light. Great colorful streaks slashed across a soft, dreamy blue sky. Then he reached out and snatched Kangee out of her dream world and pulled her into *his* dream world.

Choking on the breath of evil, she fought him. She scratched and she bit, but it didn't matter. She was alive. He had her. He held her. He loved her.

Moaning, Night Warrior pressed kiss after kiss to the top of her head. He fisted his hands in her hair, tangled his fingers around the soft strands and just held her tight. "You are safe, *skuya. Thehila.*" He loved her.

He whispered the words over and over, comforting them both. When he thought how close he'd come to losing her—

He squeezed his eyes shut and allowed himself to just savor the truth. He loved this woman. Loved her mind, body, heart, and soul. She was the light that saved him from the darkness. She was the reason he'd lived.

As though just becoming aware of him, Kangee gasped. "You left me. You weren't there. Ardong said you left me."

"Shh. I was there. I never left. Ardong lied. You are safe," he murmured. "I almost lost you." Not physically, but spiritually. Her soul, the very essence of her spirit, had been threatened, and he'd reacted. He hadn't thought. Hadn't planned. Just did what he needed to do.

In his arms, Kangee drew in a deep, shuddering breath and huddled closer. "I was so scared. I thought you were gone. I thought I was alone." Her breath hitched.

"Open your eyes, *skuya.*" He lifted his head and brushed her hair out of her eyes.

Afraid of seeing the black mass of the evil spirit, Kangee opened her eyes warily and found Night Warrior's eyes on hers. She breathed a sigh of relief.

"Stars, I see stars," she whispered, focusing on the sparkle in his eyes. The gleam of gold in their dark depths steadied her. It was like looking up into the inky blackness of the night broken only by pinpricks of starlight.

She slid her hands up over his wide, strong chest and around his neck and ran her fingers through his long hair. Strands of his hair fell forward, brushed against her. "We're safe," she murmured, needing to hear the words aloud.

"Yes. Safe," he assured, pulling her up so she sat.

Without letting go of him, she shifted her head to study her surroundings. Swirls of blue sky and soft white clouds eased her aching eyes. And trees. Tall, wide canopies of green. Pulling away, she glanced at the carpet of thick, lush grass. Everywhere she looked, there was color. It was quiet. It was peaceful. It was safe. No darkness. No monsters. No hideous being.

Only beauty.

He gently turned her in his arms. She placed one hand on the grass. The sweet smell of it eased the aches in her body. She drew in another deep breath. A spray of moisture misted over her. She turned her head, saw that they lay beside a small pond where the gentle trip and fall of water bounced over a rocky slant of ground then fell into the pond. Tiny droplets rose into air and sparkled in the sunlight. The water-song soothed her bruised mind. She recognized it as the same fall he'd brought her to last time.

Shifting back to the warrior, she realized he'd saved her. Again. Her warrior of the night had taken her from the dark into the light.

"Somewhere safe, *skuya*." Night Warrior wrapped

his arms around her, breathing in her sweet scent. He no longer felt helpless. Here in the dream world of his creation, he was strong. Still, in that dark, evil place where Kangee had been taken from him, each scream had emphasized his weakness, and he hated the fact that the evil spirit had been able to separate them so easily.

He buried his face in her hair. How was she going to save her mother? How could he keep her safe while she did it? He shoved the questions aside. Right now, all that mattered was calming and soothing her. He murmured softly as he stroked her hair, her arms, and the sides of her face.

His lips brushed across her forehead, then feathered soft kisses over her face, down her nose, beneath her eyes. Using his thumbs, he tenderly wiped away the streaks of tears.

"*Ina*." Kangee's fists rubbed her aching eyes. "You took me from her before I could save her."

"No choice." Night Warrior had obeyed his instincts, and as soon as he'd sensed danger to Kangee, he'd reacted by taking her out of the grasp of that monster. He ran his fingers through her hair, gripped the back of her neck, and tugged gently until she looked at him. He stared into her tear-ravaged features.

"Trust me." Even as he whispered the words, a ball of fear slammed into him. Could he trust his own judgment, his use of that power? What if he'd stopped her from rescuing her mother just now?

Gentle fingers feathered over his face. "I trust you." Kangee pulled his head to hers. "Touch me. I need you to touch me."

Night Warrior could do nothing other than obey for his shaken heart needed her touch as much as she needed his. Lowering his head, he brushed her lips with his. Lightly. A soft tease, then his mouth moved over hers. He breathed in her breath, the sweet scent of moonshine and flowers. Her lips parted on a sigh of pleasure, and her arms wrapped tightly around his neck, pulling him closer, tighter to her.

He meant to keep the kiss light. Gentle. Sweet. But when her mouth met his, moved with his, heat and desire twinned together and rose to arrow through his body and settle in his groin, a hard ache. He loved this woman and yearned to make her his. Only his.

Shifting his upper body, he covered hers. He planted his elbows on the ground, lowered his arms so that his hands cupped her face.

He wasn't sure who was doing the consuming as the kiss deepened and hardened into desperate need. His blood pounded through his veins. He wanted this woman, had to taste her, feel her, with the same primitive need as his body had of air.

Pulling his mouth from hers, he trailed mouth along her jaw and down the curve of her throat, lingering on the wild pulsing beat in the soft hollow of her throat. Breathy sounds of pleasure vibrated against his lips. Her fingers dug into his hair and held him to her.

Between them, her deerskin tunic hid her curves. He wanted to feel her skin against his, her heat melding with his. Night Warrior shifted to his side, pulling her hard against him. One leg draped over hers, and he slid one hand over her back and followed the curve of her spine to the gentle swell of her buttocks, then up to the side to rest in the hollow of her narrow waist.

While he stroked her, Kangee's hands were a soft

caress over his chest, his back, then skimmed over his muscles until her fingers lingered in the band of his loincloth. Then she reached up and pulled his head to hers. There was no hesitancy when she pressed her lips to his. Consumed by his own desires, he reclaimed her mouth with a fierce intensity.

To his intense pleasure, she kissed him back, her lips not only moving with his, accepting all he gave, but also taking and demanding in return. A low moan filled the air, his as an aching need for this woman grew. He wanted more. So much more. His tongue slipped into her welcoming mouth. He stroked and wooed, groaned when her lips closed around his seeking tongue and suckled, pulling him deeper into a swirling pool of love.

His hands slid downward, stroked along her thigh, then up along bare skin to caress her nicely rounded bottom. He pulled her tight against him so that his swollen manhood throbbed against the center of her heat. The touch of her, the scent, and taste of her tore a low, rumbling sound that came from deep inside him.

Kangee had never suspected that a simple touch or kiss could ignite a storm of feeling. She kissed Night Warrior, closed her lips around his tongue. The sensation was strange but enjoyable, so she let her own tongue explore the moist cavern of his mouth. His moans and harsh breathing surrounded her, ignited her own need. Her hands imitated his.

The firm, muscled flesh of his shoulders, the gentle swell of his lower back, and the smooth feel of his buttocks beneath his loincloth. She had no idea touching a man could be so pleasurable. When he pulled her tight, so that they touched from chest to groin, she moved against the hard length of him.

Something deep inside her melted.

Her hips shifted, seeking, finding. Keeping her mouth against his, claiming him as he claimed her, she pushed him onto his back and followed, covering his body with hers. Tearing her lips away, she nibbled her way along his jaw and found the strong beat of his pulse. She ran her tongue over the spot and suckled lightly, tasting.

He groaned and did a quick reversal of positions. "You are mine," he whispered.

"As you belong to me," Kangee breathed. Above their heads, the tree blurred and shifted, became a tall cottonwood covered with tiny flowers. As they kissed, sweet-scented petals fell from the sky like a soft, summer shower. The sweet scent covered them and formed a blanket on the surrounding ground.

The soft sound of song filled the air, the chanting growing louder until it broke into the haze of passion. Night Warrior lifted his head and glanced around.

Kangee took several deep breaths and her hands fell with a thud to the grass. Her eyes were wide with horror. "My family. They are calling us back." Her voice was thick and sultry.

Night Warrior wanted to protest. He rested his forehead against hers. His lungs burned with each ragged breath, and he ached, his manhood hard and throbbing.

"A dream." He'd forgotten this was just a dream.

"But real. For us." Kangee's fingers brushed his face.

Flowers—Kangee's flowers—covered them both, and he knew then that this dream belonged equally to them both.

He smiled. "Our dream, but we cannot stay. We must return."

Kangee sighed. "Only if we come back. It's so beautiful."

Night Warrior stood and pulled her up with no effort, for his body was flawless, strong. He was the warrior he'd once been. He wanted nothing more than to hold her by the hand and walk once more as a proud warrior with his woman at his side, but no one more than he knew the dangers of remaining in the dream world too long.

****

"Return now, child!" The sharp command jolted Kangee.

At once, she was awake and aware. She opened her eyes, saw her family, felt the silence within the circle that was thicker than the wall of moist air surrounding them. Tension buzzed, though no one spoke. She knew they waited for her to speak.

Behind her, she felt Night Warrior's heart beating. His warm breath and the scent that belonged only to him filled her lungs as she took several deep breaths. The memory of flowers and kissing beside a stream rolled away, shoved aside by the darker images of her mother and the evil spirit.

Panic set in. So close. She'd been close enough to touch her mother.

"Speak of what you can, child." The gentle voice of Grandmother swept over her.

Kangee, conscious of her family watching her, seeing her cradled so tightly against Night Warrior, shifted and moved to sit beside him, once again forming a circle within a circle. Her eyes misted as she stared at her grandmother. "I saw her. I spoke to her, to *Ina*. I know where she is." She glanced at her father who sat so stiffly and so pale. "*Mon père*—"

The mere thought of her mother succumbing to the evil darkness spilled the tears from her eyes.

"Tell all, child."

Though the command came from her grandmother, Kangee held her father's pleading gaze. His handsome features looked haggard. "She merged with a rock and is trapped there, with Ardong. Her spirit...she is weak."

Conrad leaned forward. "Where, daughter? Tell me where she is." Conrad's voice cracked with emotion. He stood. "I will go there."

Kangee stared into her father's eyes, seeing his desperation. He knew the place, so did her brother for they'd battled the enemy there, right before her mother had taken refuge to save her own life. She could see it but wasn't sure where it was. "I can see the place. The rock is—"

"Say no more." Grandmother turned to Conrad. "Sit," she said, her voice sharp as a knife slicing through bone. "If you go there, you put us all at risk."

Torn between obeying her grandmother and giving her father what he needed, Kangee met her father's gaze helplessly. "I know where she is, but I don't know how to get her without setting Ardong free. He tried to trick me and frighten me into doing his bidding." She covered her face, ashamed that she'd failed not only her father but also herself and the rest of them.

Grandmother reached out and tapped Kangee on the knee with her gnarled hands. "I did not expect you to free her today, child."

Kangee glanced up. "I don't understand."

The elderly woman held up the Eye of Dragon stone. "Through your eyes, I saw what you saw, heard what you heard. I hoped to learn something to help you."

"And did you? Do you know how—"

Her grandmother shook her head. "No." She sighed.

Kangee's heart sank, but before she could say anything, her father jumped to his feet.

"You risked my daughter?" Conrad exploded, his face turning dark red.

Kangee couldn't meet his gaze. She'd wanted so much to bring her mother back to both of them, to all of them. She studied her hands, twisting her fingers together. "I was so close I could touch her. I should have brought her back, but *Ina* wouldn't let me."

"Because that would have set Ardong free," her grandmother said.

Nodding, Kangee ran her hands up and down her arms. Night Warrior drew her into his arms and warmed her.

"*Ina* said it was her choice. Free will." Part of Kangee wanted to be proud of her mother, but she hated and even resented her for being willing to sacrifice her own life and the life of the babies. *We need you, Ina,* she cried silently.

"Your young warrior saved you," her grandmother said.

"Yes."

"She cannot go back. The danger is too great," Conrad said as he paced outside the circle. "I cannot lose my wife and my daughter." Murmurs rose from the others.

Grandmother clapped her hands, one sharp smack of palms that brought instant silence. "Sit," she commanded Conrad and pointed to where he'd previous sat in the family circle. She waited until everyone was still, silent.

The fog dripped from the trees and slid across the stream. Kangee shuddered when she remembered thinking that Night Warrior had left her.

I was there. Never left you alone. Night Warrior's voice in her mind was soothing, and calm.

I know. A trick. It was a trick. She believed him, but it didn't help when she once again recalled the faint, twin lights huddled deep in her mother's body. Her brothers. How was she going to save them?

"I am tired. I need to rest." Grandmother pointed her staff at her son. Dark Star rose to help his mother to her feet.

"Your grandfather and I never found any of Ardong's Shattered Souls, but in a vision, I knew you would, my child. I wept, for I knew this task would be difficult." She sighed heavily and shifted her gaze to each person watching her. "We are all Guardians of our People. And our past. We cannot ever forget the past. This is the task of every SpiritWalker."

Grandmother turned away. The old woman waved her hand, and the fog swirled upward to merge with the gray sky.

Kangee stood when her father walked past her. "*Mon père—*"

Conrad turned back. He gave her shoulder a squeeze. "Later." He strode off, away from the village, away from his family with his shoulders hunched with grief.

She bit her lip to stop from calling him back. He needed time alone. Besides, there was nothing more to be said. Not now. Not yet.

From the corner of her eye, she saw Tatonga push her way past the warriors who'd made sure her family remained uninterrupted. At that moment, the other woman did not matter. Night Warrior was hers. She had no need to fear the presence of another. Like her father, she wanted to be alone. To think. To try to figure out how she could win against an immortal evil creature.

"We will find a way, *skuya*." Night Warrior moved close.

Kangee shook her head, her throat too clogged to speak. She headed in the opposite direction of her father.

Night Warrior tried to follow, but Wise Owl stopped him by putting her hand on his arm. "Let her be. For now."

Hearing Tatonga's heavy tread, he sighed. "I cannot marry Tatonga. My heart belongs to Kangee. If Tatonga refuses to accept this, I risk war breaking out between our tribes."

He watched his sister waylay the woman and sent her silent thanks. Beside him, his aunt sighed. "You will talk to your chief. He will figure out a way to keep peace." She lifted her hand and stroked the side of his face. "My husband would be proud of you."

"How do I help her?"

Wise Owl took his hands in hers. "Your answers lie in the past and in the future. Only by accepting both will you find peace. I see in your eyes that you have at long last accepted your future, but you have yet to forgive yourself for the past."

Night Warrior shut his eyes. "What if I cannot?"

"Then you will fail. Not just yourself but the woman of your heart." She glanced up into the trees. "Travel the wheel of the west. Look to your emotions. Your feelings. Seek out your dreams. And journey. You are not just a shaman. You are one of them."

He opened his mouth to speak, but Wise Owl held up her hand. "The energy of the west flows. Never floods. Ride it. Learn from it." She turned. "Walk this old woman back to her lodge."

Night Warrior left the stream with his aunt.

Behind him, the owl that was the spirit of the old shaman, swooped down, talons outstretched as he plucked a reddish squirrel from the ground as it scampered up the thick trunk of a tree.

Chapter Fourteen

Red Flower cursed as pain from the owl's razor-sharp talons ripped through the thick pelt of fur along her spine. How foolish of her to forget that while in the form of the squirrel, she was just as vulnerable as that animal to its predators.

She struggled to free herself. Sharp talons dug deeper. The slap of a tree branch against her face as the owl glided through the forest added further insult. Resisting the urge to struggle and scream, she forced herself to relax her body, the body of the squirrel, and thought hard and fast as she was carried higher into the canopy of the forest. The ground below fell away.

She cursed her predicament. She was cautious, overly so, sly and clever. She prided herself in her ability to sneak and spy and gain useful information or objects. But after seeing those twin amulets, the legendary dragon claws and a scales, and the dragon eye the old woman had, it had been all she could do to remain silent and still and not give her presence away.

Zirgis would be pleased. As would their master. He'd reward her well. *If* she survived her act of carelessness.

Clearing her mind of everything but the need to regain her freedom, Red Flower reached out with her mind, let herself see the owl, feel the great bird. As though the owl felt her mind probing his, he tipped his head down, and for a moment, she found herself staring into round, golden eyes.

Immediately, she tried to take command and make the owl return her safely to the earth below. She did not ask permission to merge her mind with his. Nor would she wait to see if the owl willingly freed her once he realized she was a SpiritWalker, not a squirrel.

Only the weak sought free will, and Red Flower was not weak. What good was it to be powerful, to be chosen by the gods, if one had to rely on the will of those beings that were inferior? So sure of her own command of power, the strength of her will over those weaker than her, it came as a cold shock when her mind encountered...nothing. There was no energy to tap into, no mind to seize and control.

The mind of the owl was a dark void.

Her heart nearly stopped when she realized this was no ordinary owl. If it had been, she'd have been able to take over the bird's mind with her own.

Thinking fast, Red Flower kept her fear at bay. Fear made one act stupidly, foolishly. As did becoming too excited to think. This owl, with its talons digging painfully into her back, had to be another SpiritWalker, one who'd sensed her presence as she'd scampered from the concealing cover of brush out into the open to run for the tree.

But how? She shook off the questions of who and how. It didn't matter. Regaining her freedom and living to deliver her astounding news was all that was important at that moment.

She scanned the forest below and the air above her. She needed an eagle. A mind merge with an eagle could free her from the owl. The moment she began scanning the skies, the owl, without warning, went into a steep dive. The blur of greenery rushed past as the brown earth-tones grew larger.

Red Flower screamed, the sound of her petrified squeal whipped away by the wind. Unexpectedly, the owl flared its wings, lifting its body. Her dangling legs had torn through the top leaves of the trees during the dive and once more scraped against branches as the owl once again took to the skies.

Her heart in her throat, she calmed her breathing. She needed to shift shape, become larger so the owl would be forced to drop her. Trouble was, she was so high in the air. She did not relish falling to her death.

Spotting an eagle soaring high above the lake, she reached out with her mind. *Help me. Free me—*

Her cry for help ended in a strangled squeal as the night bird went into another swooping dive, dropping like a boulder, shooting through the forest, then soaring over the lake. Fear paralyzed her as her tail dipped down into the water.

A flash of silver below was her only warning before a large opened-mouthed fish broke through the surface of the water and clamped onto her tail. Another scream tore from her throat, this one filled with rage rather than pain. How dare this bird, or SpiritWalker, do this to her. She was a powerful woman. No one treated her in this manner.

She twitched her tail angrily. The fish fell back into the lake. At the same time, the owl flapped its great wings, ready to soar again.

Seizing her chance to escape, Red Flower chanted in her mind. She willed the pain aside so she could concentrate wholly on visualizing herself back in her own body. She felt the change, willed it, embraced it. A force, like a punch to the gut, knocked the air from her lungs. Her body went numb, as though it no longer existed. She chanted. Prickles of awareness pierced the numbness and traveled along her bones and through muscle and flesh.

One moment, she a weak, helpless squirrel, the next, she was Red Flower, head woman of her tribe. And was dropping like a rock from the heavens as the owl had no choice but to release her.

She hit the surface of the lake nearly flat on her back. The impact shoved the air from her lungs, and the water as she went under buried her curse. She cried out, feeling as though she'd landed on a bed of rocks.

Dazed by the impact but a strong swimmer, she immediately kicked, twisted her body, and used her arms to regain the surface where she coughed, choked, and gasped. Above her head, the owl swooped low, talons outstretched. She gulped air then ducked beneath the water. The owl's talons skimmed the surface, closed onto her hair, and ripped the strands from her head.

Resurfacing, Red Flower tried to shout, to curse the owl, but all that came out was a gasping cough. She hurt. From the top of her head to her legs where the branches had scraped her raw. She glared at the owl soaring in a careless circle overhead. It let out a loud, long screech, then folded its wings and shot across the lake to the forest.

Furious to have been caught so off guard, she slapped her palm against the surface of the lake. "Die! You will die!" she screamed out at the retreating owl. She'd find him and show him who was powerful. No one treated her in this manner.

Filled with fury, driven by the thirst of revenge, she lifted her arms and called to her mind the spirit of the eagle. Once again, she did not ask permission. She was SpiritWalker, superior to all, including the spirits of the world. So she took.

She embraced the change.

She sank below the surface. Her arms, held high, blurred, then stretched and pulled back. Her legs shortened, her body shrank, became smaller, lighter, more compact. Then she was on the surface, her wings flapping and slapping at the water.

She ached all over and knew she was bleeding. She needed to return to her tribe with her news and get her wounds tended. But not yet. Thoughts of revenge gave her the strength to lift herself out of the water.

Red Flower took to the air with a shrill screech. Small droplets of blood fell like rain and pinged onto the bright blue surface.

****

Night Warrior watched the eagle circling high above the village. Shrill screeches tore through the air. Frightened children ran for their mothers. The women gathered close. Men, gripping bows and arrows in their hands stood in silence.

All the SpiritWalker men were on alert. Night Warrior knew they also felt the waves of anger and hatred that emanated from the bird. He'd never seen an eagle act in this manner.

Dark Star slid up beside him. "It is not an eagle." The SpiritWalker warrior held his bow in one hand, and one arrow in his other.

Night Warrior kept his gaze on the bird. "A Shadowed Soul?" He shot the other man a questioning look.

Lips set in a firm line, Dark Star nodded. Air escaped from his flared nostrils. "Reach out with your mind, touch the mind of the eagle. Tell me what you feel?"

Night Warrior wasn't sure what Kangee's uncle meant but tipped his head back and concentrated on the bird. His focus narrowed. His mind cleared. He shut out the hum and buzz of his people gathered and watching until the bird was all that he saw, heard, and felt.

Suddenly, as though a part of him joined with the bird, he felt the wind sliding over his wings and ruffling his chest feathers. The sharp click of talons opening and closing and the snapping of the eagle's beak spoke of barely contained fury.

"The bird is angry." He didn't take his eyes off the great bird. "Why?"

When Dark Star didn't reply, Night Warrior turned his head. Dark Star had his eyes closed. Lines of concentration bracketed his mouth and formed furrows across his forehead. "Deeper," he said to Night Warrior. "See into the mind, the heart of what flies up above us."

Unsure what the warrior meant, Night Warrior concentrated again on the eagle circling above. He felt the raw power and cold fury that consumed the bird. He reached out with his mind and caught hold of the anger that shot through the air like bolts of lightning.

Why are you angry? He let his thought travel. He didn't question what he did or this new awareness. Just acted upon some instinctive drive. He lifted his good arm and held his hand high, as though reaching for the bird. This time it wasn't his new abilities he sought to use but the old ways his uncle had once taught him.

Slowly, his mind darkened as though a cloak had dropped over him. A trail of red burned through the black. He followed the drops of blood. They were small, but like tiny seeds, they swelled and grew into the size of stones then merged. Formed. Each step he took him into a world somewhere between the dream and waking worlds, the trail of blood grew into a moving stream that suddenly swelled and threatened to crash over his head.

"Who are you? Show yourself?" For a moment, Night Warrior feared he was back with the evil spirit holding Kangee's mother prisoner, but then he heard a woman's low, hateful laugh.

"You have what I want. Give it to me, and you shall live."

Night Warrior lifted a brow. He kept hold of the thread connecting him to the eagle above and went deep into the bird's mind until an image of a woman appeared. Her dress was torn, tattered, and stained with blood. Her bare legs bore angry scratches and welts. She held out her hand. "I want that which you were given." Her eyes, glowing with hate and greed, fastened on the amulet he wore around his neck.

Night Warrior's hand fisted around his amber stone. Was he in a dream world? Or had he somehow connected with this woman? "This is not real."

The woman shrugged. "Does not matter. I see you as you see me." She jumped at him, her hands the talons of the eagle as she tried to snatch his amulet from him.

Night Warrior jerked himself out of the trance. He swayed. A strong hand on his arm steadied him until his mind cleared and he regained his own balance. He stared into Dark Star's watchful gaze, then nodded.

"It is not an eagle, but a woman in the form of the bird." Lifting his good hand, he clutched the sacred amulet that rested warmly on his chest. The dragon scale, if he believed grandmother, glittered and shimmered in the afternoon sunlight.

"Who is she?" He felt strangely shaken from the encounter with the woman.

"She is one of us no more. She is a Shadowed Soul."

"Red Flower."

Dark Star lifted a brow. "Yes."

Night Warrior frowned. "Your niece told me about her." He held up the stone. "She wants this?" He could not take his eyes off the circling bird. The entire village had gone eerily silent. The amulet suddenly felt heavy in his hands, around his neck.

Dark Star nodded. "Yes." He stared hard into Night Warrior's eyes. "Guard it. Guard yourself." He turned to go.

"Wait." Night Warrior took several deep breaths. "Why does she want this? What is its importance?"

Dark Star shook his head. "It is not for me to explain. Grandmother will tell you in time. In the meantime, stay away from her. Do not approach her on your own. Not in your mind or in the forest." He paused. "Or in your dreams."

With that, Dark Star's arms shot out to his sides, his bow and arrows dropping. Palms facing, he jerked them up and together in one loud clap.

Above their heads, a resounding roll of thunder echoed through the cloud cover surrounding the eagle. With a shrill shriek, the bird shot across the sky like an arrow set lose from its bow. Flashes of light chased the bird out of view.

****

Kangee sat on the sandy shore, knees drawn tight to her chest, arms wrapped around her legs to still the shivers racking her body. Here, near the lake, without walls of forest to trap much of the dense moisture, the fog billowed and scudded across the water, like waves. Clouds above her head mirrored the mist rolling on top of the lake.

She usually relished the blending of air and water, the soft caress like the sweet kiss of a mother's lips on her skin. But today, the air was different. It seemed heavy, and the fine mist coating her bare arms felt slimy. Even breathing was difficult, as though she was forcing air into and out of her lungs.

Dread made her shiver. So much had happened. Too many changes now that she was alone, she had a lot to think about. But what first?

Dreams?

"No." She lowered her head to her knees and squeezed her eyes shut. "Not dreams. Not her mother." She couldn't risk letting Ardong into her mind. Not when she was so vulnerable.

Her mind turned to the revelation that she was a DreamWalker and an honored member among *The Chosen.* She lifted her head, catching glimpses of gray-blue water with tiny white caps as gusts of wind swept water toward shore.

"DreamWalker," she breathed out. "I am a DreamWalker." It didn't feel real or even right that dreaming could be a gift from the gods. She'd always viewed that part of her as a curse, a childish behavior

246

she'd never outgrown. To learn it was her gift astounded her and made her shake her head.

She should be thrilled over this discovery, but like all SpiritWalker gifts, dreaming had its dangers, as she'd learned during that last encounter with Ardong. She shuddered against the darkness whirling in her mind, tried blocking her mother crying and begging Kangee to go. To leave her behind.

"*Ina*. Mother. How can I leave you?" Kangee covered her face with her hands. Tears squeezed from her eyes and flowed between her fingers.

Free will.

Her mother was willing to give up her life and the lives of her unborn babes and never see her other daughters or her SpiritMate ever again. No. Not acceptable. Kangee lifted her head. There had to be a way to save her mother, but the thought of going back into the darkness to face Ardong terrified her.

Dreams. From nightmare to beautiful. The dream world she'd shared with Night Warrior had truly been beyond wonderful.

Dream Warrior.

Deep inside, the words rose and images slid through her mind of the kisses they'd shared on a soft mat of green grass with cottonwood petals raining down over them.

Her heart sped up, and a rush of desire warmed her from the inside out. She touched her lips, closed her eyes, and smiled softly. Night Warrior. Dream Warrior. A DreamWalker. Like her.

He'd saved her. He'd swept her from fear and the brink of death to a different threshold, one that left her on edge and needy. For him. Sighing, she crossed her arms, rested them on top of her knees, and wished Night Warrior was here with her, sitting behind her with his arms wrapped around her.

Chewing on her lower lip, she glanced back toward the village. What was he doing? Was he with Tatonga? Kangee didn't worry about the other woman. Night Warrior would not marry her. Not now, for Grandmother had confirmed that she and Night Warrior were SpiritMates when she'd presented him with one of her people's most sacred objects.

Kangee held her breath and pulled the amulet out from under her dress, the length of leather long enough that she could study the sacred dragon claw without taking it off her neck.

Hesitantly, and lightly, she traced the curled claw that lay embedded in the amber stone. Holding her palm flat, she stared in wonder at the sacred amulet nearly as large as her hand. What did this mean to her, to Night Warrior? How would this help free her mother? And what about the Shattered Soul, Ardong? There had to be a way to save her mother but not release the Father of Evil.

The snap of a twig startled her. Kangee closed her fingertips over the amulet and jumped to her feet to stare into the forest at her back. She took a couple steps backward, toward the lake. Her eyesight sharpened as she searched among the tree trunks and thick brush. She didn't see anything but she felt something, someone.

"Who's there?" Her voice quivered, for there was no doubt in her mind that she was no longer alone. She took another step back, ready to run toward the village when she heard voices in the distance along with the crackle of dried leaves being stepped upon. She knew those voices and relaxed.

Without warning, a large black bird flew out of the forest toward her. She ducked, felt the scrape of its talons in her hair, before it circled around and went into another dive.

Kangee sent a blast of air at the bird, whirled around, dropped, and rolled. Spotting the bird a few feet away on the sandy shore, she jumped to her feet, ready to call up a windstorm.

Just as she lifted her arms, two figures emerged from the line of trees. "Got enough wood here to keep us warm for a while," Blaze called out as she and Alex slid from the forest and dropped to their knees on the sandy soil where just moments ago, Kangee had been sitting.

Heart pounding, Kangee stared at the bird, heard its cry of fury as it rose into the air and circled the forest from high above before shooting across the sky and out of sight.

"Kangee?" Alex paused in her arranging the wood into layers to make a wide, tall pyramid. "What's wrong?"

Kangee let the amulet fall to rest just below her breasts and took a deep calming breath. "You two frightened me," she admitted, which was only partially true. "Guess I'm a bit jumpy." She returned to the tiny log-lined area that formed a natural half circle. In the center, where Alex worked, the soil carried evidence of many fires.

"I'll gather some leaves to start the fire," Blaze said.

Not wanting any of them to go into the forest alone, not even where they could see one another,

Kangee motioned to one of the logs.

"Sit, sister." Facing the line of pines, she lifted her hands and using her mind, pushed a gust of wind toward the fallen leaves littering the forest floor. Leaves immediately skittered across the ground and slowly fluttered upward. At knee level, they chased one another in a small, tight circle. With a flick of her fingers, Kangee pulled the tiny cyclone of leaves toward her.

A wind broke over the three women and tossed their hair around their heads, then the whirling column of air grew smaller and tighter as it hovered over the stacked wood. Alex laughed and reached into the swirling leaves to grab a leaf.

"Sure wish I could do that, cuz."

Kangee smiled and with a quick hand motion, released her hold on the current of air. It dispersed and dropped the leaves. Blaze grinned. "You have good command over Mother Air."

"It is all I seem to have," Kangee said wistfully as Blaze held her hands over the wood. Thin bright streaks of light shot downward from her palms and with several small pops, smoke rose from the center of the woodpile. "You have many gifts." She knew from her brother that Blaze commanded great storms of wind, clouds, and even thunder and lightning if she lost control of her emotions. "You also shift shape and mind-merge." She still held out hope that one day the spirits would bless her with that gift as well.

Alex leaned over and blew gently at the tiny flame while feeding it with tiny twigs.

Blaze sat back on her heels and stared down at her palms for a moment. Then she picked up a small pebble and rolled it between her hands. "Until I met your brother, I had no idea what I was or that I had family. A real family."

"You can do much more than I can," Kangee murmured, watching Blaze polishing the stone with her hands and mind.

Alex slid a knife from her boot and began whittling away at a piece of wood. "You both do amazing things. Me? I am boringly normal."

Kangee rolled her eyes. "You are a warrior woman, Alex, and I pity those who cross paths with you." Her cousin by marriage dressed like a trapper in baggy britches, a loose buckskin shirt, and old, worn boots. She kept her black hair short and moved with the silent grace of a warrior stalking prey.

"If that is so, why does my father insist on leaving me with the women instead of taking me with him when he traps or goes for supplies?"

Kangee shrugged. The woman was slim as a willow, tough as a reed, but she was still a woman. "Uncle Albert protects you. From other trappers. He worries."

"He shouldn't. I can take care of myself." Alex's voice was hard.

"I know you can," she reassured. Alex refused to take on a woman's role. She wanted nothing more than to be out hunting. And protecting. Doing. Not sitting.

Alex smiled wryly. "Then convince my father I am a warrior, that I should be walking the land with him."

Kangee tightened her hand around the amulet. Noticing Alex staring at it, she held it out so that both women could get a closer look. Awe clogged her throat, kept her from speaking. As did fear. The owners of such sacred tools carried a great duty and responsibility to not only their people, but to the world.

Breaking the silence, Blaze leaned back. "What does it mean?"

Kangee sighed. "Those who hold a claw from Dragon are Guardians of the Past. More than that, I do not know yet. I had hoped it would help free my mother, but it didn't." She shoved back the memories of that dark place and Ardong.

"Night Warrior has one as well," Blaze said.

Nodding, Kangee clung to the knowledge that she wasn't alone, hadn't been alone. Night Warrior was there, had been there, and would always be there. He was a powerful shaman in his own right, and somehow, when Blaze had healed him, he'd become a SpiritWalker.

Alex tipped her head to one side. "You are a storyteller, Kang. You keep alive the history of your people. That is a guardian of sorts, right?"

Kangee thought for a moment, then nodded. It made sense. She was a storyteller. And a dreamer, a DreamWalker. "But how will those save my mother?"

No one spoke, for no one knew the answer.

Chapter Fifteen

A thick band of cedar and brush hid the cave entrance used by a tribe of Shadowed Souls. The tangle of foliage low to the ground added another layer of protection as did the deliberately strewn branches that covered the hole. A large dragonfly hovered over the entrance as though deciding whether to enter or not for there were several large holes in the cover that would allow an insect passage.

The insect shot up into the air with wings shimmering in the dull, gray afternoon light. It followed a long, narrow, rocky ridge of land known as Dragon's Spine. The forest, as though hoarding its secret, had formed a nearly impenetrable wall along each side that neatly shielded the bumpy, jutting ridge. Reaching a tiny fissure, the dragonfly landed, then blurred into a small, dark blob as iridescent wings stretched and widened into the black wings of a tiny bat that then crawled through a crevice.

The bat dropped down into the total darkness of the narrow chimney. It zipped around nodules of rock, flew past shallow indents and wider openings that twisted ever deeper down into the bowels of the earth.

Meeting bats on their way out to seek the dusk, it clung to the rough stone. Soon, more would emerge from the caverns in a cloud so thick, it would darken the sky. The bat continued its controlled, downward plunge until it came out into a large cavern where it easily avoided the sharp, pointed rocks that hung from the ceiling like dragon teeth.

Leaving the cavern, the bat shimmered and blurred as Zirgis released the spirit of the bat. He bent his fingers and made a fist as the transformation that took mere seconds, almost too fast to consciously feel, completed. His feet hit the ground. Long practice at shifting gave him the ability to go from flight one moment to a smooth, steady stride the next.

The weight of his body, the rough, hard floor beneath him, and the dismal darkness surrounding him made Zirgis sigh. He loved the freedom that came from zipping and soaring through the air, unfettered by weight, unbound from the constraints of the human form. Of all the flying forms, the thrill of flying in the dark, trusting the bat's ability to see not with its eyes but its ears, was his favorite.

An angry, shrill yell echoed through the cavern. He winced, then moved with purpose down the tunnel where a single stone bowl of glowing embers provided enough light to allow him to see. Reaching a low opening, Zirgis ducked low.

Cold rolled off the stone, slid over his shoulders and around his waist and legs, coiling around him like a snake squeezing prey. His eyes, once a bright medley of earthy colors had faded with time and deeds, swallowed by the shadows lurking in his soul.

But he still had his sharp sight that pierced the darkness. "What is wrong?" He strode into the cavern. Another bowl of embers gave off enough light to see Red Flower lying naked on a stone slab padded with bear fur. His gaze took in the raw, angry-looking puncture wounds and ripped flesh along both sides of her spine that the healer was cleaning.

"Owl. Foolish girl. Got caught in the body of a squirrel."

"Not an owl," Red Flower said, her voice harsh. She lifted her head and sent the woman a look of intense dislike.

"Explain." Zirgis watched as the older woman smeared ointment across his mate's back.

Red Flower hissed in pain. "I do not know. It looked like an owl, but I could not touch its mind." She thumped one fist on the bear hide. "It dies." Her eyes, like his, had lost most of their color. Fury flashed like bolts of lightning in their depths.

Both of his brows shot up. "A SpiritWalker?" His heart raced. The family of his wife was among the most powerful of all SpiritWalker families.

Shaking her head, Red Flower frowned. "No. Not one of them or one of us." For the first time, she looked worried. "I felt no life. No spirit. I could not control its mind."

Zirgis glared down at the stubborn woman. "You were told to stay away." Fury deepened his voice. "If the owl had been a powerful SpiritWalker, you would not have been able to control it. You are lucky to be alive."

Hands on his hips, he strode to the opening to the section of cave he and Red Flower shared. Her news worried him. The Earth Dwellers were powerful. Until banished, he and Red Flower had belonged to that tribe, until she got caught trying to steal the Eye of Dragon.

His jaw tightened, as did his stance when he returned to where Red Flower lay. "Your talents are many, but your lack of patience and finesse will cut short your life.

Red Flower was the youngest adult among the Dwellers of Dark. She also had uncanny luck when it came to stealing, and that made her one of the most valued, gifted members of their tribe. Zirgis fingered a tiny medicine pouch attached to a leather thong tied around his waist and hidden from sight by the hide flap of his breechclout.

"Not your concern," she threw back. She grabbed a small, silver flask and took a deep pull of the fiery liquid.

"Put that away." His voice was harsh. He grabbed it and tossed down. "You know better than to drink the white man's poison." One of her favorite pastimes was to steal from trappers. Their cavern was filled with shiny treasures.

Ignoring her furious protest, he narrowed his eyes at her. "You are good at what you do."

"The best," she agreed, her voice haughty and confident.

Zirgis drew in a deep, regretful breath. Once her eyes had been the most amazing shades of blues and greens. The colors had long since faded, as had her youthful beauty.

"You taunt and tempt life. You deliberately flaunt your mortality." Disgusted and afraid for her, Zirgis headed for the entrance before he said too much.

"Don't go."

He spun around. With one sharp gesture, he motioned for the healer to leave. He waited while the woman gathered her supplies. Red Flower picked up her dress, stood, and pulled the dark hide over her head.

She sent him a heated look as she shook out her long hair and walked over to him to rest her palms against his chest.

He shoved her against the cold stone wall harder than he intended. "I gave up everything for you."

Red Flower smiled slyly, then looped her hands around his neck and moved suggestively against him. "We are good together." She tipped her head back and licked her lips. "We are powerful. Soon, we will be able to let all know of our strength, that we survived. We have grown stronger. Smarter. More cunning."

Zirgis grabbed a handful of hair and tugged as he sought to wipe the satisfied expression from her face. "A wise man, or woman does not live long if they underestimate the enemy. Remember this."

He kissed her. Hard. Drew blood. Hearing her moan of pleasure, he turned away. "Enough of this. What did you learn? You look far too pleased with yourself."

She pulled her hair over her shoulder and began braiding the long, black strands. "You were right," she said, her voice a low, satisfied purr. She motioned him closer and lowered her voice to less than a whisper sound. "The old woman had the Dragon Eye." She sat on the stone bench and drew her legs up beneath her. "But that is not all. She had two other amulets. Claws."

He lifted a brow, glanced over his shoulder toward the passage beyond the room, and hurried close to her. He kept his voice low as he gripped her shoulders. "You are sure?"

Red Flower leaned forward so her lips were a breath away and nodded. "Not one sacred amulet. Three." She nearly squealed the words.

Zirgis frowned. "I knew of the one. His blood hummed with excitement. He'd seen the Eye of Dragon once during a ceremony and had never forgotten the power it radiated and the way it seemed to call to him. He hadn't seen it again, but he'd told Red Flower about it. It had been that object she'd been after when she'd stolen the power stone by mistake.

"You and I will take the amulets. And you will have the Eye of Dragon," she whispered, leaning in close, her eyes blazing with both greed and lust. "You shall become our chief, and I shall rule at your side."

He gripped her by the shoulders. "Quiet. No one must know of the Eye of Dragon. Especially—"

Zirgis whirled around. His head lifted and tipped back as he scented the air. Striding to the entrance, he stood with both hands on the stone walls and felt a rhythmic thumping.

"We have been summoned." He pulled Red Flower to him, his mouth close to her ear. "You have done well," he said, then turned and led the way through a maze of tunnels that ended in another, much larger cavern. A small fire in the center did nothing to dispel the chill in the air.

"You are late," a low, gravelly voice complained.

"Red Flower was injured." Zirgis joined his leader who sat with a robe draped around his shoulders. His skin was as gray as the walls of the cave, and deep scars and ridges of burned flesh marred his chest, neck, and arms. His face, long and narrow, carried the same scarring from nose to chin.

"You have news." His voice scraped the air like two rough stones.

"Yes." Zirgis met the blood-red eyes of a man who

looked more monster than human. The shrunken pupils and protruding, snake-like eyes repulsed him, but he was careful to keep his face blank and devoid of all emotion. The creature's body was old and worn, but his mind was sharp, powers strong.

He turned his gaze to Red Flower who swallowed audibly. "I heard of your foolishness." A silent rebuke hung in the air.

She lowered her head as though ashamed. "I am sorry."

"You are not. What did you learn that was worth risking your life?"

Red Flower shrugged off her false cloak of shame. "The old woman had two sacred amulets, claws of Father and Mother Dragon. She gave them to the warrior and the woman who is daughter to Zirgis. She called them DragonSeekers."

The shrunken man straightened. Across his lap, lay a thick, tall staff. He rubbed two fingers over the large yellow stone that tipped the staff, then held it out over the fire, revealing a stone so deep a red it looked black except in the fire. It pulsed as though alive. "You will get them and bring them to me." He caressed the stone.

"There is more," Zirgis said. "My daughter is a DreamWalker, as is her mate. They will try to free my wife without releasing Ardong."

Beside him, Red Flower turned on him. "I am your wife," she said, her voice rising. "Not that old woman."

"Fight later. This is very good news, my friend." His leader held up his staff. "The woman must be forced to leave. She cannot be allowed to sacrifice herself. I have a plan."

He grinned. The motion pulled at the taut scarred

skin of his face, transforming his mouth into an ugly travesty of a smile. After giving his orders, he closed his eyes and sighed. "My soul must be set free. We must join." He opened his eyes and waved. "Go. I must rest."

Zirgis pushed Red Flower out. Though he knew better, he turned and saw his leader shimmer. Where the man had sat, a colorless dragon now lay on the stone floor. The staff lay clutched in its sharp talons.

****

Night Warrior sat with Tatonga and her brother. Chief Two Arrows sat beside him. The meeting between them had not gone well, not that he'd expected differently. He couldn't blame Tatonga for being angry, but he couldn't change what had happened.

"You refuse to marry me so you can have *her*," Tatonga's face was red, flushed with fury. She crossed her arms over her ample chest and glared at him.

Night Warrior also saw the sheen of tears in Tatonga's glittering dark eyes and felt worse. "I do not wish to hurt you. I had not met Kangee when I sent my brother to you with the news of my injuries." He kept to himself that he *had* met her, but in *death*, and that Kangee was the reason he'd chosen to live.

"You do not tell the truth." Tatonga lashed out. "I—"

Her brother held up one hand, cutting her off. "But you now choose that woman over my sister."

Night Warrior did not hesitate. "Yes."

Tatonga let out a scream of rage. "You bring war to our tribes."

Chief Two Arrows intervened. "Much has happened since my cousin was injured. He is now our shaman, an honor held by my father before he died. This position has always been his, but until the attack, he did not accept it. He cannot fulfill his promise to become chief to your people, even without the other woman. The gods have made this clear. His place is here, among our people."

Sitting straight and proud, despite the pain in his chest, Night Warrior inclined his head. "My chief and I hope to avoid war. I cannot change what has happened that led to this."

"Then I will become the wife of a great shaman instead of chief," Tatonga said.

"I am sorry," Night Warrior said, shaking his head. "My future is bound to this other woman. I am not the same man I was when I proposed an allegiance between our tribes. Death changed me. It changed what was, and it changed my future."

Tatonga stood. "Then you will not know peace in your new future."

The men got to their feet as well. Tatonga's brother inclined his head. "We will leave when the sun has returned." He followed his sister.

Two Arrows turned to his cousin. "I will arrange a meeting with their father, the old chief, and see if we can avoid war between us."

Night Warrior didn't bother apologizing for there was nothing more to be said. The two men returned to their lodge.

Chapter Sixteen

High above the trees, the sky remained sullen and gray. Night Warrior sat in front of his lodge with his family and Kangee's. A large fire burned, providing warmth to stave off the chill.

He felt unsettled and on edge. Part came from the guilt that he might be the cause of war between his tribe and Tatonga's. The rest from Kangee and the pressure on the two of them. Though the weight of the amulet he wore was slight, the responsibility it brought weighed him down. So much rested on not just him, but on Kangee. His biggest fear was in failing her, of not being able to give her whatever she needed to save her mother.

Chief Two Arrows dropped down beside Night Warrior. "It will do you no good to worry over the future."

Night Warrior sighed. "I accept that it was not meant to be." He loved Kangee, accepted the connection between them on a deep, spiritual level, though he still had doubts over his ability to provide for her. He frowned. "My reasons for calling off my marriage to Tatonga still exist for even Kangee. I should marry no woman."

"As shaman, you hold a position of honor and greatness in our village. Higher than your chief," Two Arrows said. "Our warriors will see to your needs and those of your family. This is the way of our people. We take care of those we honor." He pulled out his shiny new knife and began cleaning and caring for the blade.

Night Warrior accepted the truth of his cousin's statement. As shaman, he could expect payment of his services in food and hides and anything else he or his family might need. But for a man used to hunting and providing for his own needs, he wasn't sure he could sit back and let others provide for him. He sighed again. Pride had no place in his life, and he was going to have to accept that his life had changed.

"I will miss my old life," he murmured.

Chief Two Arrows nodded. "So you have at last accepted your future."

"Yes." For the first time, Night Warrior made the admission aloud. A blanket of peace settled over him. He glanced down at the amulet resting against his chest, amazed that he had in his possession something so old and valuable. The responsibility of this gift humbled him, and he hoped he could live up to the expectations and responsibilities expected of him. He looked over to where Kangee's grandmother talked with his aunts. He wished he knew more about his new role.

She glanced at him as though she felt his eyes on her and gave him a small nod.

You'll do.

A third, deep sigh escaped. "I'll do," he repeated, needing to hear the words aloud.

Around him, the men shared hunting tales while the women chatted about meals, clothing, family, and so many more topics that he couldn't keep up. Thankfully, no one paid him any attention, which left his mind free to think about Kangee. In so short a time, she'd ensnared him, first with her sad eyes and sweet voice, then with her bravery and her humor.

Though they hadn't spent all that much time together during the days, they were together during the night. They had long talks, took long walks, and offered each other comfort. He scanned the village but didn't see her. Remembering the eagle, the anger of the woman once known as Red Flower, Night Warrior grew worried. Was Kangee all right? He reached out with his mind. *Where are you?*

Instantly, an image of the lake formed in his mind. *We are returning. Did you miss me?*

He smiled. A*lways, skuya. Always*.

He glanced upward. The cloud cover had thickened, but instead of gray or even black rain clouds, the sky looked bruised with yellowish-greenish-purplish clouds. With no hint of wind, the air seemed to wallow and sulk and felt oppressive.

The acridness signaled that more than a normal storm was in the making. *Hurry. Do not linger*, he warned.

We are here.

Night Warrior spotted her, along with her cousins, as they entered the village. He sighed with relief. She moved toward him with grace—the sway of her body, the fringe of her tunic, and the curtain of her hair. He wanted to hold her, feel her curves against him, and run his fingers through the silky strands.

He needed to breathe in her scent and taste her more than he needed air and food. She was his life. Without her, he was an empty shell. She greeted her grandmother, and he saw the deep bond of love between them. He let himself drink in her beauty and sweet nature. Reaching out, he felt her unease, her shallow breathing as she settled between two of her aunts. Like him, she didn't take part in the conversations.

What is it?

She glanced around. *How can everyone act as if nothing is wrong?*

What would you have them do?

She sighed, frustrated. She shook her head. *I don't know. I can't just sit here and pretend that everything is normal.* Her heart raced

Breathe.

Can't—

Night Warrior felt her fear.

Not ready. Mother—what if I fail? Time is running out. Can you not feel it?

He nodded. *Yes.* He sent an image of warmth to Kangee, a warm funnel of air shimmering with a faint rainbow of color. *You have been given what you need to do this. You must trust the gods who created you and believe in the powers they gave to you.*

Kangee closed her eyes. *Thank you.*

Believe. In yourself and in us.

Across from him, Kangee opened her eyes and stared into his. *I am still afraid.*

Night Warrior closed his own eyes and thought only of her. *It is okay to be afraid. Being afraid is a warning. Fear tells us that something is not right.*

So much is wrong.

Acknowledge your fear, but do not give it free rein. Listen to it, then use it to guide you and help you. I do not understand all that is being asked of us, but together we are strong. Besides, there is no one more

stubborn or determined than you or more loved. Use that. All of that.

Kangee smiled softly. *Thank you,* she said again.

A loud war cry made her spin around. There, at the opposite end of the village, a large group of warriors sat in a wide circle. One warrior stood in the center. His arms were miming a fight, and his voice echoed as he recounted his brave deed.

What happens next?

Night Warrior also focused on the storytelling, his keen hearing easily allowing him to listen to the story. Yells, good-natured jeering, and laughter from audience participation filled the air. He scanned the busy village. Women had gathered to work, visit, and gossip. Kangee's family, those not sitting with her, mingled with his people or sat in the storyteller's circle. A group of young girls surrounded Kangee's aunt, the one who'd arrived as a black panther, as she told stories.

And everywhere he looked, children ran and played. *We wait,* he said to Kangee. *We embrace this time where all can act as if all is normal.*

She sighed impatiently.

Across from him, Kangee's grandmother stopped in mid-conversation to Wise Owl and pointed at him. "If the two of you must talk, go elsewhere. I cannot concentrate."

Kangee was horrified to be caught talking with him mind to mind, but Night Warrior nodded respectfully. "I am sorry we disturbed you, *Unci.*" He stood and held out a hand to Kangee. "Come."

She went willingly and eagerly. They strolled around the village. She heard giggling and shifted her gaze to a group of girls close to her own age who were staring at her unmarried uncle. They were clearly taken by the young, handsome warrior.

Drawing a deep breath, Kangee felt as though she'd aged years instead of weeks. It hadn't been that long ago that she too had acted in that silly manner. Now? She felt old. Far too old to engage in such flirting or silly behavior. But then she smiled. She had found her mate.

Drawing in a deep breath, she caught not just Night Warrior's scent but the feel of him, the hum of energy he radiated. She indulged herself and watched him from the corner of her eye when he bent down to greet a small boy who'd run up to them.

His long hair was loose, hanging over his shoulders, covering most of the wounds on his bare chest. In the grayness of the day, he looked pale and weak, but in their shared DreamWalks, he'd looked like a man who was ready to fight for not only his own survival but also that of his people.

She stared at his rock hard belly when he stood and turned back to her. She shifted her gaze down past the flap of his breechclout, then ran her gaze over his strong, muscular calves, thick thighs, and the long puckered gash that looked painful still. She lifted her eyes to his and sucked in her breath. In the space of a look, he made her forget everything but the heat simmering deep in her center. She wanted to feel his arms around her and his lips over hers. She wanted him. Close.

Heat rose in her checks, and she tried to turn away but couldn't. A picture of green grass along a gently flowing stream flowed into her mind. It didn't take much effort to see them there as before.

Do not tempt me, thehila, woman I adore."

Kangee smiled and playfully, deliberately, saw herself twirling in a circle on the grass. Around her, the wind joined her, became one with her as she danced along the stream. *Catch me.*

I shall do better. Night Warrior grabbed her hand and drew her into the woods, away from the village and the noise.

"Where are we going?" The sounds of the village had faded and twilight smudged the forest.

He turned his head. "Somewhere we can be alone." He limped over the uneven ground, and several times, he had to let go of her to shove branches and brush out of their way. When he finally stopped, he turned and held out his hand. "I want you."

She went into his arms. "As I want you."

"Then you shall have me, and I, you." He pulled her down beneath a thick tangle of branches and roots, then into a dark and secluded area, a cave formed by trees and shrubs all woven together. Beneath them, ferns formed a soft mat.

"I have somewhere special I want to take you. Will you come?"

Kangee thought this cozy spot perfect, but she nodded and let him pull her onto his lap so she sat with her back resting against his chest. She leaned her head back onto his shoulder.

"Ready?" His breath was warm on and in her ear. His lips feathered over her ear and along the side of her neck.

Sucking in her breath, her body shivering, not with cold but need, she let her head fall to the side to give him free access. "Yes," she breathed. She emptied her mind of everything but him. She focused on Night Warrior, on his touch, his body, his breath, and the beat of his heart until she felt herself simply drifting.

"Open your eyes," Night Warrior whispered in her ear.

Though she knew what to expect, it still came as a jolt of surprise to find them elsewhere. Instead of the dark hole of shrub and tree, she found herself in a dark cavern of stone. A large fire pushed aside the shadows, and beneath her, the soft mat of ferns was gone. The ground was hard and sandy. She allowed Night Warrior to help her to her feet.

"Where are we?" She turned in slow, complete circle, then stared up at the ceiling where stones glittered and reflected the flames of the fire.

"A place I used to visit with my uncle." He strolled around, touching the walls.

Kangee held her arms out and spun slowly. "It is the most beautiful place I've ever seen. She touched a wall and felt the hard, smooth surface of the stones embedded there.

"Is this a real place?"

Night Warrior's gaze grew distant. He shook his head. "I don't know. I've been here so often that it feels real." He smiled with sadness. "The first time I came here was with my uncle. He used to bring me here, to teach me the ways of the shaman and tell stories. It was our favorite place to meet."

She wandered around the cavern. Two, small, nearly translucent stones lay on a flat boulder near the fire. She picked them up. One was in the shape of an owl. The other a raven. Both hung from leather thongs. She held them up. "What are these?"

He joined her, his expression one of wonder and sadness. "My uncle and I carved these during our visits. He claimed the owl as his totem so he carved the owl. I carved the raven. We left them here as he said they belonged here, that one day, they would be needed—"

He broke off, his eyes going wide, his fingers trembling as he touched the carved owl, then the raven. "He said they would be needed yet this is not real…"

Kangee placed her hand over his, overcome by the emotion in his eyes and voice. "Your aunt believes your uncle's spirit is still here, in the form of an owl. He was a great shaman from what I've heard," She remembered the owl feather and each sighting of the owl since her visit.

Night Warrior picked up the raven, a stunned look on his face. "Your name means raven. I carved this for you." Wonder filled his voice.

"And he carved the owl for you." As though something in her had waited all her life for this moment, she scooped up the two stones and held them up. Then she placed them on her palm and held her hand out to her mate. Deep inside, she felt as though a ritual as old as time itself was guiding her when she spoke the words that filled her heart to near bursting.

"My people give each other gifts of stones. When we bond, they then become our soul stones. We do this to honor Mother Dragon and her love for her mate and for us." With her gaze holding his, Kangee drew in a deep breath. "Will you accept my gift to you?"

Night Warrior nodded, his eyes dark, with just a hint of golden light in their depths.

She couldn't take her eyes off his. "I am yours and you are mine. I give myself to you. Only to you. You are the other half of my heart and soul. You are my SpiritMate."

Something inside Night Warrior shifted at her words. He placed his hand on top of hers and felt the warmth of the stones between their palms as he spoke the words in his heart. "You are mine, as I belong to you. I give myself to you. Only to you. You are the other half of my heart and soul. You make me complete."

The stones grew hot. The warmth flowed up his arm and spread throughout his body. When he lifted his hand, both stones glowed with life. The owl had become a translucent brown with threads of blue and green woven through the stone. The raven was now glossy, a bluish-black with pinpricks of gold. A tiny golden star glittered on its breast.

Tears of joy slid down her face. "We are now truly mated," she said, wonder and awe filling her voice and shining through her eyes. "Our souls are bound. These stones are a symbol of what we are, what we share, but they are also ancient, part of Mother Earth and each of her sisters. These soul stones hold their own powers and are now connected to our souls."

She took the owl and slipped it over his head. He did the same her. For a moment, they stared at one another.

Night Warrior was so moved, so in awe over what had just happened that he couldn't speak. He'd felt the change in him as he spoke the words, as if a rope had wound around them, binding them.

"We are husband and wife," Kangee said with a huge smile.

"Not quite yet." He too smiled, a bit wickedly. He

took her by the arm. "Come."

She followed her warrior, and when they rounded a tall stone pillar, Kangee stopped and gasped. In the ground, surrounded by big boulders, steam rose from a pool of water and drifted high up into the cavern. The air flowed, keeping it warm but not suffocating. She walked to the edge of the underground pond and leaned down to put her hand into the steaming water.

Standing, she turned to him. "It's beautiful. I've never seen anything like this." More shiny and glittering stones decorated the walls, but the ground where she walked was smooth, flat. Another fire added light to dispel any gloom.

Night Warrior walked toward her slowly, the heat in his eyes flaring. Reaching out, he cupped the sides of her face and lowered his head. "I want you."

Kangee melted into him, her arms sliding up his chest and around his neck. She tipped her head back and offered her lips to his. The kiss was gentle, a slow exploration. She followed his lead, mirrored the movements of hands and mouth. Her heart raced with his, and her breath grew just as ragged.

When his tongue slid past her lips, she eagerly gave herself over to him. Her tongue, tentative at first, met his and, encouraged by him, grew bolder as they danced the dance of love. She explored and tasted him, stroked his lips, his teeth, then teased his tongue into a game of chase.

He groaned. She moaned. His hands slid down her arms, over her back and down along the curve of her spine and over the rise of her buttocks. Her fingers traced a path down his back, then dipped beneath his loincloth, sliding her hands over the smooth, taut flesh of his buttocks.

He bucked his hips forward, pulled her up onto her toes, and gripped her buttocks hard to keep her pressed against him as he circled against her center. She nearly screamed as waves of pleasure gripped her. Her head fell back. She needed more, wanted more, had to have more.

"I want you. All of you." Night Warrior leaned forward and nibbled her ear. "Here. Now," he repeated, his breath hot in her ear.

Kangee groaned. "Yes." The word ended on a strangled scream when he lifted her and set her onto his throbbing manhood. Though he still wore his loincloth, she felt his need, his hugeness, and her own need exploded painfully.

Carrying her to the edge of the pond, Night Warrior let the woman he loved slide down the front of him, a slow, painful tease to his overheated body. He wanted to tear away the barrier between them and take her now. Right where he stood. Instead, he stepped back, untied leather thong around his waist, and let the cloth fall.

He proudly revealed himself and watched her eyes grow wide. "I belong to you."

Kangee smiled and, without hesitation, took the hem of her tunic in hand and pulled it over her head. She stood proud before him, bathed in firelight and steam. Night Warrior looked. And thought himself a fortunate man.

Her small breasts were tipped with the rosy kiss of the dawn, the nipples protruding as though crying out for his touch. His eyes traveled down to her narrow waist and the flat belly that drew his attention to where black curls hid her center.

He slowly walked to her. She met him halfway. Keeping her gaze locked with his, he reached out, filled his palms with her twin breasts, and closed the distance. His manhood brushed her curls, then slid up her belly to pulse against her. "I cannot wait. I want you now."

She shivered against the cool air brushing over her skin. She glanced around, disappointed to see that the warm cavern was gone. Night Warrior still held her, still felt hard beneath her.

"I want you here," he said. "I want you for real, not in a dream."

She got to her knees and turned to face him. "Here then." Once more, she pulled her tunic over her head and watched as he slowly removed his loincloth. Unlike the cavern, it was dim, with no light to chase away the shadows. But her eyes spotted something gleaming against his throat.

Reaching out, she touched the owl stone she'd placed there. Her hand went to her own throat, and she felt the tiny raven he'd carved for her when he'd been a boy.

"They are real. What we did was real," she said, her voice hushed with awe.

Night Warrior, on his knees, pulled her to him. "Then let's finish it." He tipped her chin up. "I love you, Kangee. *Thekichila*. Light of my Life. Light of my soul.

"As I love you. Take what I freely offer." Kangee lowered herself to the ground, pulling him with her so that his body covered hers. Her legs separated, allowing him to slide between.

"You saved my life. It is because of you that I

returned to life." He bent his head and kissed her long, slow, and deep.

"I love you, my warrior of the night. You are my Dream Warrior." She ran her hands down his back, following the dip of his spine down to the warm, hard flesh of his buttocks. She dug in, pulled him to her, and lifted her hips to feel more of him.

He explored her body with his hands and his mouth. She arched back as he suckled at her breasts, tasted her, and she reveled in the feel of his mouth on her. He slid one hand between them where he pulsed and throbbed against her.

His fingers slid into her curls and found her moist, heated center. He touched her. Beneath him, she bucked. Her head lifted, and she buried her face in his shoulder to muffle her cry of pleasure.

Kangee had never felt anything so wondrous. He stroked her, slid his finger into her, and brought her so much pleasure, she thought she would fly apart and break into hundreds of pieces.

Her breathing grew ragged. She moaned. He whispered words in her ears, but with the roaring of blood throbbing throughout her body, she couldn't hear him. Everything inside her focused on his hands, his fingers, and the incredible sensations centered where he touched.

His touch grew demanding. "Let yourself fly, *thehila. Thekichihila. I love you.* Give in. Let it happen."

She didn't understand, but it didn't matter. Her body knew exactly what to do. With a cry that he swallowed in a deep, sweet, tender kiss, her lower body went rigid and she exploded, flying into the air, shattering into bits and pieces of light that flashed and sparked.

Wave after wave of pleasure took her. Before she was finished, Night Warrior had moved over her, spread her legs, and was poised to enter. "Accept me. All of me." With one hard thrust, he breached her, entered her.

Kangee, still riding her own pleasure, barely felt the tearing pain as the feel of her SpiritMate inside her made her want him, want what he could give her with his male member, instead of his fingers.

Together, they rode the waves of pleasure.

Chapter Seventeen

Much later, back in the cavern, in the pool of warm water, Kangee smiled at Night Warrior. "I wish we could stay."

He closed his eyes as he remembered another woman who'd said the same thing to him. Kangee put her hand on his shoulder. Despite the heat of the water, he felt chilled inside.

"What's wrong?"

Sighing, he pulled her close. "There are dangers in the dream world." He didn't want reality to intrude. Not yet. He wanted to savor this special time when it was just the two of them. No past, no future, just here and now.

As though she sensed there was more to his statement, she cuddled close. "You speak as though you know this from experience. Will you tell me?"

For a long moment, Night Warrior remained silent. Then he nodded. "I will tell you the story of a young man who thought he knew more than anyone. He was arrogant." He leaned his head against the rock and prayed that she wouldn't think badly of him.

"I will listen to this story," she said, pulling his arm around her.

She gave him the courage to speak of something that up to now, only two people knew—his uncle and his chief. They alone knew of his shame and reason why he'd refused the role and honor of shaman for so long.

"I had just become a man and there was a girl. She lived alone with her father. I met her a few times when our tribes gathered. She was very unhappy. She did not come from a loving family. Her mother had died birthing her, and her father blamed his daughter. He used her in a way that fathers should never use their daughters."

Night Warrior fought his old hatred against the man who'd died at his hands when he'd been old enough, strong enough, to give the girl the vengeance she deserved. Beside him, Kangee waited patiently.

"Whenever this girl needed me, I went to her, and in our dreams, I took her away. We did this for a long time. Sometimes every night. One day, she told me she didn't want to return. Her life was so bad, she no longer wanted to live. I told her we could not stay and took her back. And though I promised to help her, to come for her and take her away, I had to leave her in order to do so.

"The next night I felt her need again. The strongest I'd ever felt. I went to her immediately and pulled her into our favorite dream world." He glanced down at Kangee. "The place I took you."

"What happened," Kangee asked, reaching up to smooth the lines gathered on his forehead.

"When I told her it was time to go, that I was leaving that morning to come for her, she said it was too late, that she was staying. I didn't understand until I tried to return her." He let out a long, soft sigh.

"She truly meant that it was too late," Kangee finished for him.

"Yes, during our time together, she died. I found out later that she'd eaten something poisonous. She knew she'd die while she was with me. I had felt her pain and thought it was her father causing it."

"You blamed yourself." It wasn't a question. She turned and faced him. "It wasn't your fault."

"I never told anyone about her and what was happening. If I had gone to my uncle or our chief, perhaps they could have saved her. My silence condemned her and killed her." He sighed.

Kangee rose to her knees. "No. Her father was to blame. And she made her own choice. Free will. You might have been able to help her by talking to someone. You'll never know, but I know you gave her what you thought she needed at the time, because that is who you are. Then and now." She ran her fingers down the side of his face. "That has to be enough for you."

"Until you, I hadn't been back there. I was young and arrogant. I thought I could care for her and protect her. I planned to marry her when I had earned the right to take a wife." Night Warrior reached out and pulled his mate to him. His SpiritMate.

The words thrilled him and sent a glow throughout his body that warmed him from head to toe. "Thank you, Light of my Life," he whispered, grateful that she'd come to him in death. He bent his head to kiss her, then froze when vibrations reached him. Part of his mind always remained alert and aware of the physical world when he dreamed. He reacted.

Abruptly, the scenery changed and once again, Kangee found herself sitting with Night Warrior on the floor of the forest. They had dressed before returning to the cavern, and he was fully alert, his mind scanning the area as he crawled out of their cozy love nest and stood, his body tense.

"Stay close."

She sent her own senses flaring outward. The forest was quiet. Too quiet. No sounds of birds overhead, no scurrying in the underbrush and the absence of insects left the world eerily silent. Every sense screamed danger.

"We need to return," she said quietly. "Now."

She let him take the lead. He knew the forest well. She scanned the bushes, the treetops, and the shadows. It wasn't night, yet the clouds were swallowing the light and the thickening of the air made breathing difficult. This was not an ordinary storm brewing.

Each step they took toward the village, her sense of danger increased. They moved through the forest as fast as Night Warrior was able with his injuries and were almost to the village when a flock of raven dove out of the trees.

One flew at Kangee.

"Watch out," Night Warrior shouted as he struck out and knocked the bird away as its talons scraped along her neck.

She ducked, then turned to wave her hands at another bird trying to get the amulet from Night Warrior. She sent it head over feet into the trees.

One by one, the birds dropped to the ground and shifted until half dozen warriors and one woman stood, blocking their path.

Night Warrior placed himself in front of Kangee but she took her place at his side. *We stand together. You cannot fight them, not in the ways of a warrior.*

Then tell me what to do. I will not allow anything

to happen to you.

"What do you want," Kangee demanded.

The woman strutted forward. She eyed the amber amulet on Night Warrior's chest, then the one hanging from Kangee's neck. "We want what you have."

Shocked, Kangee recognized the woman's strident voice. She might have been a young child when Red Flower was banished, but with her own role in the proceedings, along with Red Flower's screamed threats, Kangee had never forgotten the young woman.

"Red Flower." She stared at the woman who was nothing like the girl she'd last seen. Her beauty had shriveled like fruit gone bad. And her eyes were colorless. Staring into them, Kangee felt as though she could see right through her.

Red Flower lifted her brows, her features remaining hard. "You remember me. Good, you will pay for getting me banished." She waved her arm and sent a blast of wind at Kangee and Night Warrior.

Kangee blocked the blast with a wall of air. The air currents smashed together and sent a wave of leaves, rocks, and twigs flying. "It was your actions that got you banished. Leave. There is nothing here for you. If you stay, you condemn yourself to death."

In their charge to the race of SpiritWalkers, the gods gave her people the task of meting out justice to those who used their powers against others. Staring into the woman's eyes, Kangee knew Red Flower had long ago lost her soul, which made her one of the condemned. Kangee had never killed but wouldn't hesitate to do so to keep her mate safe.

Red Flower laughed. "Your *daughter* is fierce, Zirgis." She stood shoulder to shoulder with a tall, older warrior.

The woman's words pierced Kangee's mind and heart. She glanced at the man standing beside Red Flower but didn't recognize him or any of the others. "My father died long ago."

Laughing wildly, Red Flower shook her head. "You foolish child. He was banished. With me."

Kangee stared at the shadowed soul. Not a trace of recognition or emotion showed on his face or in eyes that were just as colorless as Red Flowers. He was tall, thin, and his gray hair hung in strings down his back. His face, like Red Flower's, was pale, gaunt, his eyes sinking deeper into their sockets.

He put his hands on his hips and grinned without a trace of humor. "You have grown into a powerful woman, my daughter." His eyes were devoid of emotion.

Cold dread poured into Kangee. Her father couldn't be a Shadowed Soul. The woman was lying because her father died in battle. That's what her mother, her family, had said.

Disbelief warred with shock and even betrayal as Kangee stared at Red Flower, but when she thought about it, remembered back, it made sense. No one ever talked about him, his brave deeds, retold stories that featured his bravery or even whatever gifts he'd possessed.

Kangee had no choice but to accept the truth, especially when Red Flower put her arms intimately around her father and kissed him in a way that told Kangee they were lovers or mated.

"He's mine, was always mine," Red Flower sneered. "I took him from you and your mother." She looked pleased.

The sight made her sick. Anger and hurt warred when she realized he'd chosen Red Flower over her and her mother. And it hurt deeply to know that he'd chosen the dark side of their world. He was not worthy of the honor of being her father though the shock of seeing him alive shook her more than she cared to admit.

The heat from her growing anger built inside her. She shook with emotion.

Keep calm.

Night Warrior's voice steadied her. She didn't dare let her feelings cause her to lose control. Her first priority was getting them back to the village and warning the others.

She tipped her head back and met her father's colorless gaze. "You are not my father. Not since the day you left. You are a Shadowed Soul, and you share the same fate as Red Flower if you do not leave."

Once again, Red Flower swaggered forward, leading the group ever closer. "Give us what we want and we will leave."

"No," Kangee and Night Warrior both said.

"Then we will take from you what belongs to us."

Each of the Shadowed Souls lifted their arms. Air swirled around the forest. She couldn't deflect a wave of air this big or powerful so she called up a small whirling mass that surrounded her and Night Warrior. She kept it small and tight. When the attack hit, the rocks and small branches smashed against her air column, and the debris zipped away, shot into the forest like arrows from their bows.

Red Flower, having to duck to avoid the small missiles, smiled nastily and waved her arms.

Overhead, Kangee heard a creak. "Look out," she shouted, yanking on Night Warrior, pulling him out of the way as a large branch broke and fell.

"We need to get help," Night Warrior shouted.

Kangee felt his pain and had to block her own fear. He was no match against the warriors advancing on them, and he didn't dare try to run for the village. He was in no condition to fight even one Shadowed Soul.

Frantic, she built her anger and fear, her resentment of her father and his abandonment of her. She pulled her love and willingness to do anything to protect her mate into a tightly focused ball of energy in her mind. Then she swung her arms to her side with a cry of outrage and brought them sharply up above her head. Her palms came together with a sharp clap. A bolt of lightning shot up into the sky followed by a rumble of thunder that shook the ground. She prayed her family would see and come in time.

Red Flower laughed. "You can't stop us." She tossed her own arrow of light at a tree. It exploded.

Kangee and Night Warrior were thrown to the ground, but before the tree fell on them, a blast of air stronger than Kangee had ever seen, picked up the tree and sent it skimming over the forest.

She glanced around and nearly sobbed with relief when she saw Dark Star running toward them. A pack of wolves ran past him and surrounded her and Night Warrior. They shifted and in the blink of an eye, Kangee's aunts and uncles stood ready to fight.

The forest exploded as rocks, small trees and shrubs, branches, and tree trunks flew through the air. In the flurry of fighting, Kangee saw Red Flower shift shape and fly through the trees. Her father followed.

One of her aunts tossed stones after her, but the pair made her escape.

Bright Star pulled Kangee and Night Warrior up. "Get back to the village. Now."

"No, we fight." Kangee jerked away, then winced when a blast of thunder ripped through the air.

"Do as I say," Bright Star shouted. "Your man cannot fight, and you both are too important to our tribe. Go!"

Night Warrior grabbed Kangee. "She is right."

Debris exploded around them as Kangee and Night Warrior ran for the village.

Chapter Eighteen

Fleeing the scene of battle went against everything Night Warrior believed in, had trained for, had lived for, but he needed to get Kangee to safety. She came first, and if that meant letting her believe *she* had to save *him*, he could live with that.

Running now, with the screaming and yelling and sounds of fighting behind him, was the hardest thing he'd ever done. He was a warrior. It was his duty to fight. To defend. It didn't matter that he was injured or that he was now a shaman. He possessed a warrior's heart and each step away from the battle was a struggle.

As much as he hated to admit it, Bright Star was right. He was of no use to these people, had no idea how to fight against warriors who blasted trees or called up bolts of lightning or gusts of wind. He fought his pride but reminded himself that when it came to the woman he loved, swallowing pride was a small sacrifice.

Night Warrior blocked the pain in his thigh and the burning in his chest. He kept Kangee in front of him in case anyone came after them. Twice Kangee turned back when a loud explosion rocked the ground beneath their feet, and he had to shove her forward. "Don't stop," he shouted. "Move!"

He closed his mind to the pounding of her heart and her sobbing breaths. He tasted her fear, but he kept them moving. Twice he fell. Twice he swallowed his pride, and twice he allowed Kangee to help him to his feet.

Hearing and feeling movement ahead of them, he stopped and yanked Kangee behind him, then sagged with relief to see Two Arrows, his brother, and the warriors of his tribe running through the forest toward them. Warriors held their bows, arrows, and lances high.

Kangee grabbed his arm. "My grandmother. My sisters. We need to protect them."

Night Warrior shouted to his chief. "We stay with the village." With the amount of power and energy thrown off by the battle between the Shadowed Souls and SpiritWalkers, the arrows the warriors shot off could be flung right back at his own people.

The men protested. Night Warrior held up his hand. "Your weapons won't be of use against what the SpiritWalkers are fighting."

Chief Two Arrows glanced up into the sky, nodded, then ordered his people back to the village.

Night Warrior and Kangee, with the warriors behind them, ran to the village center. Instead of the busy bustle of activity, every man, woman, and child stood frozen, their attention on the sky where lights flashed.

"Go to your lodges," Night Warrior shouted.

Women and children obeyed. A small boy fell. Kangee ran forward, scooped up the boy, and handed him to his frantic mother. Night Warrior kept his eye on Kangee as the two of them helped the old and the young to safety.

Working with his chief, they stationed warriors

around the perimeter of the village, then Night Warrior gathered the elderly men and boys who'd refused to go hide and gave them the task of guarding their lodges. He turned to check on Kangee, saw her turning in a frantic circle, heard her calling out but couldn't make out the words with the loud, thundering battle taking place.

He rushed over, put his hands on her shoulders, and made her face him. "What is it? What is wrong?"

Her eyes were wide with fear. "My sisters. I can't find them." Kangee fought him off as she scanned the village. "They aren't here, and they aren't in the lodge."

Night Warrior looked but didn't see any sign of them. "Let's check the lodge again."

Kangee was afraid and sick with it, but she followed him to the lodge. At the entrance, Travers and Alex stood, weapons drawn. Inside, Night Warrior's family sat in one area. Her grandmother sat calmly nearby with her great grandchildren gathered close. The twins and Skye weren't there.

"Where are they?"

"They must be hiding in the forest," Night Warrior said, sounding worried.

Kangee turned to go back out, but Night Warrior grabbed her arm. He cocked his head and listened. She heard it as well, screams that came from behind the lodge. She rushed out the back entrance. Blaze and her brother were running down the path between forest and village toward the twins who were screaming hysterically.

Kangee ran to meet them and gathered them close. "I got you. You're safe," she said, tears of relief sliding down her cheeks. She glanced around. "Where is Skye?

Where is your sister?"

The girls were hysterical. She shook them. "Look at me," she commanded. "Tell me where Skye is."

"A woman—"

"And a man. Took her."

Kangee frowned. "Who? Where?" If one of Night Warrior's people had taken Skye to safety, why were the twins out here?

"Into the forest," Anika sobbed.

"Skye didn't want to go." Andre added. "We tried to stop them, but we couldn't."

Night Warrior stepped forward and held out his arms, gathering all of them. "Let's get them to the lodge." His glance was wary as bolts of lightning continued to blast the air.

Kangee rushed the twins to her grandmother. The woman sat with her eyes closed, her hand cupping the Eye of Dragon that glowed as though alive.

"*Unci!*"

Her grandmother opened her eyes. "They have Skye. Red Flower and your father took Skye."

A wave of sickness hit Kangee. "No. Not Skye." She turned to Night Warrior. "We have to go after them. I have to get her back."

"No," her grandmother said.

Kangee turned and dropped to her knees.

Her grandmother's eyes were hard, her features set as though in stone. She held up the hand holding the Eye. "I see through Skye's eyes for she will one day take possession of the Eye of Dragon. I have called my children back to us. The Shadowed Souls came for Skye."

"We've got to go after them."

"Skye is unharmed. We wait."

****

Kangee tried to calm her fear and frustration. Why had Red Flower and her father taken the little girl? She'd tried several times to connect with her sister but failed each time. And Skye hadn't reached out to her either.

Her stomach clenched, and she hurt everywhere. She glared at her family. "What are we waiting for? We need to find Skye,"

Around her, everyone was waiting but for what? Night Warrior put his hand on her shoulder. For once, his touch, his presence didn't calm her. Frantic, she went to her father.

"I have to go with you," Kangee said as she watched her father and brother getting ready to go after Skye.

Her father's features were grim, his movements mirroring those of the warriors preparing for battle. "You heard your grandmother. You are to remain here."

Kangee shoved her hair out of her eyes as she stormed back to her grandmother. "I need to help find her. She is my sister."

Her grandmother clutched her staff in both hands. "You will be where you are most needed, Granddaughter." Her features were set.

"What good can I do here?"

Lifting her chin, Grandmother speared her with a long, hard look. "You will dream. You will free your mother and end this. Her time grows short."

Kangee stumbled back. "I'm not ready. I don't know what to do or how to do this."

The old woman's eyes turned bleak. "Then we will

have lost this battle." She closed her eyes.

Tears streamed down Kangee's face. Her knees buckled and she fell. Everyone depended on her. Especially her father who avoided looking at her. None of them said the words. They didn't have to.

Behind her, Night Warrior knelt and wrapped her in his arms. She rested her head on his shoulder, and looked on as one by one, each member of her family shifted into a wolf, panther, or eagle.

Finally, only the twins, Dark Star and Bright Star, remained. Each flanked Grandmother who slowly and proudly got to her feet, her staff held out before her.

"You know where to go. Go, but do not show yourselves until you receive my signal."

The wolves and panthers shot into the forest and the birds took to the air. Kangee turned back to her grandmother. "Now what?"

Grandmother's features softened as placed her gnarled hand beneath Kangee's chin.

"Go where the two of you will be alone, then wait. When the moon is high and at her fullest, I will send you a signal. Then dream. Together. Find your mother and save your brothers. Do not delay."

Chapter Nineteen

Night Warrior led Kangee away from the village. It would take her family time to reach the area where her mother hid inside the boulder. That time was both a blessing and curse for it gave them time to try to figure out how to free her mother, but it also gave them time to worry. He glanced at Kangee. She hadn't spoken since her grandmother gave her instructions.

He pulled his SpiritMate close. This sad-eyed woman was his. They had joined their souls in the manner of her people. When this was over, he planned to make her his wife in front of his people, and he vowed to spend the rest of his life keeping the sadness from her eyes. But right now, all he could hope to do was to ease her burdens and share her grief.

He leaned down and pressed a kiss to the top of her head. "We will succeed," he whispered. "We will win."

Kangee didn't answer, didn't react. She'd closed herself off as though she were already grieving for her mother and facing a life sentence of guilt for failing. He gathered his own determination and focus. They would not fail. He wouldn't let her fail. He glanced around them. They were nearing the lake.

Where could they go where they'd be alone and safe. A dream world? The caverns? No. Dream worlds were great places to visit, somewhere special that the two of them would share, but he didn't ever want to use them as an escape from reality.

When they drew abreast of the giant downed tree that lay in part in the lake, he realized he'd fallen in love with her here, the night she'd shared the moon with him. He glanced up to the high perch of land above them and made his decision. The top of the ridge was perfect. They would be alone. And safe. They would be up high, far from the forest and the dangers that lurked.

No one would reach them without his being aware of it, and it wouldn't matter if they came as man or beast or in any other form a Shadowed Soul might shift into in order to attack them. There were two accessible paths to the top. One from the west that was a series of hand and foot holds that sloped upward. There was no way he could manage that in his current physical shape. The other path led from the south. It also led to the cave Blaze and Star Walker used.

He hadn't been to the top of the ridge in a long time, not since the Healer made the cave her home. He stopped and pointed. "We'll go up. We'll be safe. And alone."

Kangee frowned, and then shook her head. "You can't make that climb," she said, her eyes lifting to his.

He cupped her face in his hands. "Sweet one, with you at my side, I can do anything." Unspoken was that the reverse was also true.

She sent him a sad smile, the smile that had haunted his dreams while he healed, the smile that made him want to get to know her, and the smile that broke his heart.

Seeing it now made him even more determined to see that she would not fail. They would not fail. "Go ahead of me." If he slipped and fell, he didn't want to risk knocking her off the narrow path.

For Night Warrior, the climb was slow and torturous. His thigh burned, his arm went numb, and his chest felt on fire. Halfway up, he stopped to rest on a narrow shelf.

From the vantage point, he saw forest spread out below. A river of sharp pointed treetops formed a path through a forest peppered with trees, some that looked arrow-thin, others with wide spreading canopies and everything in between for as far as he could see.

In the summer, the forest was all shades of green—light, dark, blue-greens and green-yellows—all blended with the browns of trunks and branches and ripening cone-shaped fruit. With the warm months fading, most of the greens had given way to orange, yellows, and reds mixed in with those trees that would remain green throughout the winter.

Far below him, he saw the stream and the spot beneath the cottonwoods where he'd sat with Kangee and her family when her grandmother had given each of them their amulets. It followed the arm of the stone ridge then snaked along the juts and curves of the land out of sight.

They continued to make their way up to the cave opening, then farther, just past the cave to where the ridge flattened out. She paced from one side to the other. Breathing hard, he leaned against the rounded side of the cave. The climb had left him shaking and tired. Taking a moment, he stared out at the lake. The surface mirrored the clouds above, gray and dismal. Above and below.

He closed his eyes, concentrated on his body,

calming screaming muscles, slowing his pounding heart, and easing the pain. Normally, there was the sound of twin waterfalls that came from below, but the lake was low and the stream a mere trickle. After a few minutes, he glanced around. From this great height, he could just barely make out the tops of bark-covered lodges.

He wondered what the signal would be. A fire? A bolt of lightning? He wished he'd asked. Pushing off the rock, he went to Kangee. She was staring out toward a cleared area of forest and the garden where his tribe grew corn, squash, and beans.

He turned her gently toward him. "I am here. Let's talk."

Kangee threw her arms around him. "No, not yet. Just hold me." Her fingers dug into his head. She pulled his mouth down to hers. "Hold me. Love me."

Night Warrior felt the desperate edge to her kisses. "Slow." He wanted to be gentle with her. She was so fragile, he was afraid she might break.

"No." Her hands were all over him, sliding between his loincloth, freeing him. He sprang to immediate life. "Here. Now." She thrust her hips against him.

He pulled her back with him until he was braced against the side of the cave. He lifted her, helped by her own jump into his arms. Her tunic slid up around her waist, and his good arm cradled her bottom. His other arm snaked around her back.

"Hold on," he groaned as he speared himself inside her with one quick, hard thrust.

She moaned, then kissed him, devoured him, as though they only had this one time together. He pulsed inside her. She moved her hips and clung to him. He lifted her until he nearly pulled out, then let her slide back onto him. He circled his hips, grinding against her until she sobbed aloud. "I need you. All of you."

Night Warrior lowered them to the ground. He slid partway out.

Kangee cried out, then arched her back when he thrust back inside her with hard and fast strokes that set her on fire. Heat flared, building, building, building. Her center throbbed, her hips bucked, and she screamed, her palms pressed into the ground as her hips lifted higher, met his, grinding into his as pleasure erupted.

As soon as the spasms slowed, Night Warrior rolled them so that she was on top of him, their bodies still joined. "Again," he said. "Take me. Ride me."

Kangee, still with the edge of desperation in her movements, took him at his word. She rode him hard, feeling the heat and pressure building. This time, when her release came, he came with her. Her scream and his cry mingled and echoed over the lake.

Above their heads, the clouds burst. Rain poured over them.

Night Warrior rolled them over so he could block most of the rain from hitting her in the face. He stared down at her. She cried and cried. And the clouds, the world, and even he cried with her. He whispered to her, murmured, tried to soothe her.

Finally, her tears slowed. "I'll fail."

"No. You won't, because *we* won't. He used his thumbs to wipe the water and tears from her face. Above them, the rain turned to a fine mist, then stopped.

He kissed her softly, tenderly, taking his time. The time for being desperate was over. Now was the time for healing. For gentle loving.

****

A fire glowed and crackled on the ridge. Kangee sat cradled in Night Warrior's arms, her back against his chest as they had sat when they DreamWalked surrounded by her family. This time, there was no chanting, no singing. It was just them. They were on their own.

Surprisingly, Kangee no longer felt alone or abandoned as she had when they'd first left her grandmother. "I hurt you earlier." It embarrassed her that she had been so demanding. And even rough in their loving.

Night Warrior chuckled. "No, *thehila*. You did not. You satisfied me in a way that no one else has ever done."

She tipped her head back and looked at him, then smiled. "I liked it gentle, too," she added, then went back to staring out over the lake. The rain had cleared the sky, revealing a bright world above filled with twinkling stars. The moon had risen and hung low over the silvery sheet of the lake, and overhead, an owl soared.

Kangee sighed. Their time was short. Her anxiety was slowly rising as the moon rose and grew fuller. After making love several times, they'd dressed and talked as the light of day gave way to night.

"We still don't know what to do, how to save my mother." She brought one of his hands to her cheek.

"We'll know what to do when the time comes." Night Warrior nuzzled her neck.

She let her head fall to one side. "How can you be sure?"

"I trust your grandmother. And my uncle." He indicated the owl that had taken up watch at the very top of the cave. It stared down at them. "How can we fail with such wise souls watching over us?"

"You believe that the owl is your uncle's spirit?"

Night Warrior chuckled. "I do. I wish you could have met him. He was powerful. It does not surprise me that he is still here, watching over his family." He moved his hands to her shoulders and rubbed.

Touching both the soul stone and amulet, she hoped he was right. It still amazed her that he'd carved this stone for her so long ago. The stone felt warm and a low hum of energy within the stones grew stronger, as though it was telling her that time was drawing near.

As it rose, the moon became larger and closer. She felt something in the air. Her amulet had grown almost too warm to touch. Behind her, Night Warrior was on alert. She knew he held his amulet. She felt the heat it gave off.

As one, they shifted so they stared out toward the village, waiting for a signal from grandmother.

A loud screech from the owl startled them both. They turned their heads, saw the bird jump into the air and soar down, its great span of wings flaring up. It shimmered and became the ghostly image of an old, proud warrior.

It is time. The words echoed in their heads.

"Your uncle," Kangee said, her voice low and soft with awe.

Night warrior pulled her close and nuzzled her neck. "That is our signal. Ready?"

Kangee drew in a deep breath and held tightly onto his arms. "Don't leave me."

"Never. I will be there with you the whole time. Trust me. Believe in me. In us."

"Then I am ready." She put her trust in the man she loved and closed her eyes. He did the same.

She focused on her mother, on her spirit, on the place she knew her mother to be. She saw both the physical place and the darkness within where her mother had taken refuge. Then she was there, walking down a long, dark tunnel. She shuddered and turned her head. "Night Warrior?"

"I am here with you." He materialized beside her and held out his hand.

Kangee took his hand, held on tight, and kept him close as she walked through the darkness. Then she spotted the faint blue light, just like before. As they neared, Kangee realized her mother's spirit had grown weaker. She stopped before getting too close and glanced around. Deep shadows hid terrible things.

"Mother," she called. "We are here to save you. Do not speak. I will find a way to take you with us without freeing Ardong. Your family is also here. We are all here."

She spoke bravely and prayed she spoke truthfully. She had no idea if her father and the rest of her mother's family were there waiting for Kangee to—

She sighed. To do what? She had no idea what she was going to do. Before she could do or say anything, she heard the harsh cackle of Ardong echoing around her.

"You've returned. Good, good. Your mother grows weak. Soon it will be too late for her."

"If she dies here, then you will never go free." At least, Kangee hoped that was so.

"But you won't let her die. You are here to save her." Ardong slithered out of the darkness. His red eyes glowed, and he had formed his shadowy body into that of a tall man who towered over both Kangee and Night Warrior.

Unwilling to be intimidated, Kangee thrust out her chin. "I will save her."

Ardong laughed. "Then take her. Take her before she is gone." His voice turned sly. "If she dies, there are others who know where I am. They will come. They will free me. Maybe I'll kill her right now." A ball of fire burst into flame. He tossed it from hand to hand.

Kangee thought of the girl Night Warrior had taken with him into the dream world and how she remained there, trapped forever. She shook her head. "No. As long as the body of my mother remains here, so does her spirit, for her soul will be here. Forever. With you."

Ardong let out a furious roar. "Then take her." He threw the fireball down, then made another and another and tossed them at her.

Lifting her hand, she created a blast of air and sent the fire back. Jagged bolts of lightning followed the balls of fire. Once again, Kangee formed a shield around them until the tantrum was over.

Ardong lost shape as he became a snake of darkness. He wrapped himself around Kangee so that she couldn't feel Night Warrior. Couldn't see her mother. She was cold. So cold.

"She's dying. You're too late. You will fail your mother if you do not act now," the hideous voice threatened, the words a hiss of sound in her head.

She panicked when Ardong kept up with his threats. *Night Warrior!*

I am here, Light of my Life. His voice broke through the anger buzzing.

I'm cold. So cold. She needed to see him, feel him.

A wave of warmth slid through her. *I've got you. Trust yourself. Trust me. He's trying to scare you.*

I am scared. But she felt braver knowing he was there, with her. With effort, she calmed her mind, then spoke low and soft. "Stop or I will leave. If my mother dies, you lose all hope of freedom."

At once, the black cloud shifted and moved away, forming this time into a dragon. "What are you waiting for? Your people are here. The woman's mate is here. They wait for the woman. My people wait for me. End this. Now." Ardong screamed the words.

"I won't let you go," Kangee said.

"Then you sacrifice not just your mother and your unborn brothers." A crafty, sly look came into his eyes. "You sacrifice your sister."

One wall of the stone prison turned red, then became translucent, as though it were no longer there. She reached out, then pulled back when she spotted Red Flower and Zirgis standing just an arm's length from her. Her father held Skye, with a knife to the little girl's throat.

"Oh, no," Kangee cried. She rushed forward. "Skye!" She cried out to Night Warrior. "We have to go to her."

Night Warrior held her tightly. "It is a trick."

"No trick," Ardong said. "Let me go, and she will not be harmed." He chuckled wildly and bounced off the walls of his prison.

Kangee was torn. How could she choose? How could she live with herself if she failed and lost not just her mother and her brothers but her sister as well? Too many choices. Too big a burden.

She felt a soft brush across her mind. *Trust your grandmother as I trust my uncle. The answer is here. It is within us.*

As though aware of Kangee staring at her, Skye suddenly smiled. *Story, Kangee. Story.*

Kangee sagged against Night Warrior. How she wished she could lose herself in one of her stories. Just take herself off to another world, her own world, where everything was as she desired. She longed to dream of happier times and places.

A sudden thought came to her. Dreams were nothing more than stories told by the sleeping mind. While asleep weren't they real while you lived them? Hadn't the girl Night Warrior tried to help chosen to stay in a dream world? To her, it had been real.

Kangee fingered her soul stone. It was real, yet it had come from the cavern of their dream world.

She glanced around, remembered how she'd nearly died here. Because she'd believed the danger to be real and wasn't this place, this horrible place as real to her as the lodge or the mountain where they'd made love?

She grinned with relief. *I know what to do.*

Night Warrior leaned forward and wrapped his arms around her. *Then do it. End this.*

She turned to Ardong, letting fear and uncertainty show. "I cannot allow you to claim the lives of my family. I will free you, but only if you come with me to a place of my choosing, far away from my family. I won't let you harm them."

Across from them, her mother let out an anguished cry. "No, Daughter. You cannot do this."

Ardong let out a triumphant laugh that drowned out her mother's voice. "Free me, take me from this place. I will come."

Kangee glanced at her mother's spirit. "You come with me, of your own freewill? You promise not to harm us or return to harm my family?"

"Take me, and I promise no harm." Ardong whirled around and around.

She sent Night Warrior an image, felt his approval. Hoping she was doing the right thing, she took one last look at her sister and nearly choked on a gasp. Skye's small body suddenly blurred into a dark shadow that dropped to the ground and became a tiny, black rat.

Red Flower and Zirgis dove after the rat as it scurried away from her captors. Overhead, a large owl went into a dive and scooped the rat up. Two arrows flew in, one for Red Flower, one piercing Zirgis in the chest.

Kangee nearly fell to her knees with relief at the clear signal Skye and the old shaman had just sent. With the image of a place in her mind, clear and as real as she could make it, she grabbed hold of Night Warrior's hand. *Now!*

At her command, Night Warrior reached out with his mind and yanked her, Ardong, Red Flower and Zirgis into their newly created world.

Chapter Twenty

Suddenly free of his dark cell, the Shattered Soul of Ardong flew through the air. Where before everything had been black and colorless, the world was now so bright a blue that it hurt his eyes. Everywhere he looked, there were rainbows of color from the green of the world below to the bright golden sun above his head.

He soared through the sky, flew through tree tops, spreading and stretching his wings and whipping his tail side to side as he yelled and screamed his jubilation. He shot himself high up into the blue sky and zipped across the heavens.

After a time, he just spun around and around like a whirling tornado. He was free. Freedom. The taste of it was intoxicating. There was so much he wanted to do, so much time to make up. What first?

He dropped out of the heavens, ready to let the world know that Ardong, son of Dragon, was back. He opened his mouth and roared. Pleased by the stream of fire, he whirled and danced with glee.

First, he'd start a fire. Before being imprisoned, he'd loved watching the earth burn. Then he'd fly through it and watch the helpless humans run. He slowed, dipped his head, and searched for the perfect grove of trees, but the trees he'd just flown through were gone.

Puzzled, he flew in a circle. Where were the trees? Was he flying upside down? He whirled, flipped, and turned.

Nothing above. Nothing below.

The world had suddenly turned colorless and empty. There were no trees to burn, no mountains to stand upon so he could survey his kingdom, and no volcanos to cause to erupt.

Nothing.

He spotted the woman and her warrior standing in a bubble of color. Furious, he flew at them. "Where are we?" He bounced off the bubble and flew around them. The only color he could see was trapped within that bubble or shimmering on his own body.

Movement below drew his attention. A man and woman stood below him, looking as confused and bewildered as he felt.

"What does it matter? You are free," Kangee said, smiling. She lifted her hands. "This is your new world, the one you freely agreed to come to."

Kangee was no longer afraid. The warmth from the amulet she wore seeped into her, and she allowed an inner wisdom to guide her.

The son of Dragon flapped his wings. His talons clicked angrily. "This isn't the place you brought me to. Where are the trees, the sky? Where are the humans and other beasts created by the gods?"

She studied the long reptilian body that shimmered with faded color in the dream world she and Night Warrior created. The beast's yellow, snake-like eyes with their red slits no longer frightened her. "You flew out of the world I created and entered the world you now call home willingly. Free will. You chose to leave this world."

Ardong shrieked with fury and flew at the woman but couldn't burst the bubble filled with color and life. Everything he'd wanted, everything that he believed to be his right was there, with the woman.

"This isn't real," he screamed.

"It is real, because you believed it to be," Night Warrior said. "You accepted it as real, and now you will live within it."

Kangee pulled the amulet from around her neck and held it out, then took the one Night Warrior handed her. "Father Dragon and Mother Dragon, your parents, sacrificed their lives to protect the world from your evil. We honor their love for each other and this world in that we condemn you to this place forever. We are Guardians of the Past. This is our judgment. So be it."

She held up both amulets. A flash of bright light flew across the colorless sky, pulled all the colors out of Ardong and spread them across the heavens where they hung in a ribbon of color.

She stared at the dragon's gray body. "Each time you look up, you will be reminded of all that you had and all that you lost. This is the price you pay for choosing evil."

Ardong tossed ball after ball of fire at them, but the flames fizzled, sending their colors high above.

From below, Red Flower let out a screech. "I didn't choose this."

Kangee glanced down. "You made your choice years ago."

She stared into her father's stunned gaze. "Shadowed Souls, you were given a second chance at life. You chose to walk your dark path. I condemn your souls to this place. You will never leave, never cause pain or harm to another living creature. Your bodies will be destroyed, just as you destroyed your souls."

Above them, a flash of light drew her attention. It was a signal from her grandmother and that had to mean her mother was safe. As was Skye.

Night Warrior put his arms around Kangee's shoulders. "It is time for us to go."

She turned to Night Warrior and placed his amulet back around his neck. "Take me home, warrior of the night. Take us home."

As soon as they returned to their bodies on the ridge of land above the lake, they silently hurried down the mountain. Talk would come later. With only the light of the moon to guide them, the climb down was difficult. Though she wanted to hurry and even rush off, Kangee patiently waited for her mate. In part, because she was afraid.

What if the dream world they left had simply been just that—another dream? What if nothing had changed?

"They are safe," Night Warrior said behind her as they hurried into the forest.

"What if—"

He stopped, pulled her into his arms, and kissed her tenderly. "Trust and believe. You did it. You saved your mother."

She leaned her forehead on his chest and breathed in deep, calming breaths. "No. *We* saved her. I know we did. But—"

"—you need to see for yourself," he finished for her.

"Yes," Kangee lifted her head to look at him.

"Then let us return." Night Warrior took her by the hand.

A loud screech broke the eerie silence of the night world.

Kangee whirled around and cried out when an owl flew toward them with a small rat clutched in its talons. "Skye!"

She ran toward the owl, hands held out. The owl slowed, flared its wings, and let go of the rodent. She caught tiny black rat and cupped it gently. The wings of the owl brushed the top of her head as the bird soared back into the trees.

"Skye." It had to be Skye. She couldn't have dreamed this. Carefully, Kangee knelt and set the rodent down. "Return to me, *Mithan*."

In the darkness, the rat blurred, blending for a moment with the shadows of the night. Kangee blinked, and there she was. Skye.

"Oh, my lovely, sweet sister. You are truly gifted," she said to the little girl who just sat there, staring up at her calmly, as though nothing had happened to her.

The child held up her arms. "Story, Kangee. Story."

Laughing and crying, Kangee pulled Skye into her arms and hugged her tight. "I told a story, Little One. A good story, too! Let's go. Let's get back to our family."

"To *Ina*." Skye put her head down on Kangee's shoulder.

Night Warrior held them both. "Now do you believe?"

"Now I believe

****

Night Warrior watched Kangee pace. Her family

had not yet returned with her mother. "They'll be here soon enough. Come rest."

Kangee shook her head. "I can't."

He didn't blame her. He too was restless. They were outside his lodge. Skye and her sisters were inside, with his family and Kangee's. Leaning against one of the lodge poles, he folded his arms across his chest and lifted his brow when he realized he'd done so with no pain. Testing his body, he put his full weight on his injured leg. Very little pain.

He smiled, satisfied with the knowledge that he'd soon be pain free and whole. A short while ago, that was all he'd wanted. To be whole. To be the warrior he'd always been.

Now? It wasn't so important. Yes, he wanted to be whole—male pride dictated that it was his job to care for his woman—but more than providing, he wanted to be whole so he could embrace his new path in life. It was time to start asking questions and finding answers. Time to let answers come to him and figure out the questions to ask. Time, most of all, to discover the new world he was now part of.

He drew in a deep breath, taking his time to identify the different scents. His gaze pierced the darkness, saw much of what had previously been hidden to him.

"You're very quiet," Kangee said, coming to him.

He pulled her close. "Exploring a world I've lived in all my life and finding so much more than I ever thought possible."

She smiled. "You are a SpiritWalker."

Grinning, Night Warrior nodded. "Yes. Not so frightening now. I'd still like to know how it happened.

The healer saved my life. How did she make me a SpiritWalker? No one else she saved became a SpiritWalker."

"It is in your blood," a voice said from the doorway of the lodge.

Night Warrior shifted and even in the darkness, clearly saw his aunt. "Explain."

Wise Owl joined them. "It is something your uncle never talked about, yet it is why he knew why Blaze was different."

Kangee tipped her head to one side. "He was a SpiritWalker?"

"He carried the blood of a SpiritWalker, yet did not have the outward signs of being one."

"But our blood runs though the females. I do not share blood with my uncle."

Wise Owl grinned. "Do you forget that your father was cousin to my husband?"

"My father was not a SpiritWalker." Night Warrior glanced at Kangee, who smiled.

"But he carried within him the blood of our People and weak as it was, he passed that blood to you. When the healer saved your life, she awakened those traits."

Night Warrior looked stunned.

"You were always powerful," Wise Owl added. "The ability was there. My husband saw that and tried to teach you."

A soft hoot above drew Night Warrior's gaze. "He still is teaching me," he said, feeling a bit overwhelmed as he stared into the gaze of the owl, the gaze of his uncle.

Wise Owl sighed. "You have made him proud, *thoska*."

The owl fly out of the trees and past them, with a loud screech.

Night Warrior scented the air and grinned at Kangee. "I think your family has arrived.

Kangee whirled around and scanned the trees and the dark sky. Several large birds flew out of the trees at the same time wolves darted from the shadows. In moments, chatter broke the quiet of the night as wolves and birds shifted.

Running to her family, she searched for her father and mother. "Where are they?"

One of her uncles pointed. "There."

With Night Warrior's hands on her shoulders, she spotted a lone owl soaring much slower overhead. As he dropped lower, Kangee noticed the tiny, white owl on his back.

"*Ina!*"

The owl land on the arm of her uncle. She gently scooped the slumped owl off her father's back.

"*Ina.*" Tears blinded her. She felt the beating heart of the bird, but the bird was unresponsive.

"Here, daughter. Let me." Conrad held the bird tenderly. "Now, my love."

With help from Conrad, the white owl shimmered and blurred, then Eagle Woman appeared in her father's arms.

"Is she all right?" Kangee ran her fingers down the side of her mother's face.

"I am fine, *chunksi*. Thanks to you." Eagle Woman turned her head. She tried to lift her hand, but it fell weakly.

Kangee took her mother's hand in her own and pressed it to the side of her face. She couldn't speak past the lump in her throat and could barely see through the curtain of tears.

Blaze and her grandmother came forward.

"Take her inside," Grandmother ordered.

Blaze took Conrad by the arm and led him to the longhouse. Grandmother, leaning on her walking stick, looked from Kangee to Night Warrior. "You returned my daughter to me," she said to Kangee, squeezing her hand. Then she turned to Night Warrior and nodded. "You'll do."

The old woman hobbled back to the lodge.

"She's safe. She's alive," Kangee whispered, overcome. "It's over. It's really over."

Night Warrior glanced down at her. "No, it's just beginning." He scooped her up into his arms and strode through the growing crowd of people.

Kangee wrapped her arms around his neck. "Yes. A new beginning. For us."

Epilogue

The feasting and celebration in the lodges of the Turtle Clan lasted through the night. It was well past dawn, and Night Warrior sat with Kangee cradled close to him. Across from them, Conrad held his wife. Eagle Woman was pale and weak, but alive, as were her unborn sons.

Night Warrior studied Skye as she slept in in her mother's lap. He'd never forget how the little girl had shifted into a rat. He sensed great power in the child.

"What are you thinking?

"I've said it before, *thehila*. Your family scares me." He pointed across to where her uncle had shifted into a beast Kangee called a horse and was giving the children rides. He shook his head. "Think I'll ever be able to do that?"

She giggled. "These are your people now, my husband." Chief Two Arrows had married them just as the sun streaked the sky with rosy ribbons of color.

A loud, bellowing voice broke through the celebrating village. "Conrad, tell these young fools that I am welcome here!"

Kangee jumped to her feet. "It's Uncle Albert."

Night Warrior followed her to where a mountain-sized trapper was trying to get past the warriors guarding the village. He smiled as the big man greeted his family.

Off to one side, he noted that Tatonga, her brother, and their warriors were preparing to leave. He still worried about the possibility of war. Torn between wanting to go to her, to try one last time to make their parting peaceful, he frowned.

Tatonga was staring at Kangee's family with what looked like shock and disbelief on her face. Her jaw hung open, and she grinned widely, looking happier than he'd ever seen her.

As sudden as it came, the smile faded, replaced by anger, accented by her stomping steps as she stormed toward the family. Afraid she planned to cause more trouble with Kangee, he hurried after his wife.

Tatonga shoved her way through Kangee's family, past Kangee, not stopping until she reached the newly arrived Albert.

Albert stepped back from greeting Conrad and saw the woman. He looked stunned, then happy, then worried when Tatonga began lashing out at him.

"You promised to return," she shouted. Everyone around her fell into a hushed silence. "No more leaving. You stay. With me. With your family!" Tatonga shoved her hands onto her hips and switched to speaking halted French.

Night Warrior leaned close to Kangee. "What is going on?" It was clear that the two knew each other.

Kangee hugged his arm to her and chuckled. "I think my uncle just met his match. We should go find your chief and warn him that he will have another wedding to perform."

"A wedding? I don't understand." Glancing at everyone, he saw amusement and laughter. Except for Albert who looked as though he'd been knocked flat by a giant bear.

Conrad was now doing the talking. Then it was back to Tatonga, who, by her gestures, wasn't taking no for an answer.

"I guess I need to learn French as well as how to shift shape," he muttered.

Kangee took pity on him. "It appears the girl and my uncle have long been lovers. For years." She shook her head. "The woman you were to marry carries my uncle's child. That is why she was desperate to marry. She wanted a father for her child." She giggled. "Looks like she's going to get her wish."

Night Warrior could only nod as Albert swung Tatonga up into his arms and whirled around as he shouted out that he was going to become a father. Night Warrior grinned and knew he'd react just like that. "Your uncle is a happy and lucky man."

Kangee pulled him back toward the village. "Family is very important to Uncle Albert," she said sadly.

"Why so sad?"

"He'll have to be told about Uncle William and how he tried to kill my father and my brother. It is because of Uncle William that we nearly lost my mother."

Night Warrior pulled her close. "Your uncle will accept the truth. He has you and the rest of his family, and it looks like he now has a strong woman to share his grief. And a new life."

Kangee stepped in front of him and put her arms around his neck. "And Tatonga gets her mate. Just as I have mine. My SpiritMate." She rose up onto her toes and kissed him, long and hard, then pulled back when he sighed. "What's wrong?"

"There is one thing I must do. Will you come with me?"

Seeing the sorrow and pain in his eyes, Kangee understood. She leaned into him and closed her eyes. She felt his light touch in her mind and, with an ease that surprised her, fell into his dream world.

Opening her eyes, she stood once more on a soft, grassy mat still covered with pink flowers. Birds flew and sang. Water flowed and splashed into the pond. It was every bit as beautiful as the previous times.

She is here?

Yes. Night Warrior turned her in his arms.

Kangee spotted the young woman, barely past girlhood. She looked real, as real as her and Night Warrior, and Kangee wondered if she'd come near.

The girl took a few steps, then stopped and held out her arm.

An owl flew into their dream world and landed on the girls arm, then hopped up onto her shoulder. She smiled, looking happy and at peace. She lifted her hands and waved. The rosy petals at their feet shifted and whirled gently as though a gust of wind twirled around them.

Surrounded by the petals, Night Warrior and Kangee watched the girl walk away with the owl on her shoulder.

Night Warrior sighed. *She is happy and at peace.*

What about you?

I am as well. Now I'm taking you somewhere far from here, where we can be alone. There are too many people in my lodge.

I would like that, my Dream Warrior. I love you."

Night Warrior pulled her close, nuzzled his check against hers, wrapped his arms over hers, and held her tight, her back to his chest. *As I love you. You came to me in my darkest hour. You are the Light of my Life. You saved me.*

Kangee tipped her head back until she could see him. *We saved each other.* She reached up with one hand. *Dreams do come true.*

He groaned. *Yes, they do, but can we not talk or think about dreams for a while?*

She laughed. *Take us home, Warrior of my heart.*

In the space of a heartbeat, Kangee returned to awareness. The celebration went on around her and her mate as though they'd never left.

He scooped her into his arms. "We are going to find a place to be alone." He quirked a brow. "Unless you'd rather stay?"

Giggling, she shook her head. "I want to be with you and only you."

Leaning her head on his shoulder as he strode into the forest, she noted that her warrior was standing straighter, walking stronger. One day he'd be not just the warrior he used to be but much, much more than he ever imagined.

And her? She fingered her amulet. She'd never again be ashamed of dreaming, for dreams had given her the best gifts of all. She snuggled close and teased her husband with her own image of the perfect dreamscape and all the loving things she wanted to do to him. His indrawn breath and the tightening of his arms made her laugh, but when he sent his own image back, full of promised pleasure, she groaned.

"Better get us where you want us, warrior of the

night. I want you."

Night Warrior stopped. "Not as much as I want you. This will do. For now." Then he lowered Kangee to the ground. "Show me what you want, and I'll show you how I'll do it."

Soft laughter turned to groans of pleasure.

High above their heads, the old shaman took flight, leaving the couple to their autumn dreams.

About the Author

Susan Edwards is the author of fourteen Historical Native American/Western/Paranormal romance. She also writes erotic romance under the pen name Sydney St. Claire.

Susan resides in California. When not writing, she enjoys crafts of all sorts including quilting, sewing, cross-stitch, and knitting. She and her husband of thirty-plus years are avid gardeners. Camping, fishing, biking, and hiking are other outdoor pursuits she and her husband enjoy. She is, of course, an avid reader and hates cooking and housework.

Connect with Susan on the web.

Email: Susan@susanedwards.com
Website: http://susanedwards.com
Twitter: https://twitter.com/susan_edwards
Facebook: https://www.facebook.com/susanedwards1
Blog: http://susanedwards.com/blog
Goodreads: https://www.goodreads.com/susanedwards
Pinterest: https://www.pinterest.com/susanedwards2u/

To chat with Susan Edwards and other Wild Rose Press authors of erotic romance, join us at www.groups.yahoo.com/group/thewildrosepress